LYRICS OF A SMALL TOWN

#1 *NEW YORK TIMES* BESTSELLING AUTHOR

ABBI GLINES

Printed in the United States of America
First Printing, 2021

Abbi Glines Publishing
P.O. Box 3130
Peterborough, NH 03458
www.abbiglinesbooks.com

Editing by Fairest Reviews Editing Services
Cover designed by Damonza
Interior Design by The Illustrated Author Design Services

To Ava – thank you for all the recipes and ideas. You were my inspiration behind Henley's creations. I will miss next year when you're away at college and not making a mess in my kitchen with your healthy treats. After college, I'm thinking you and I need to open a *Signed Sips* of our own.

ACKNOWLEDGMENTS

When I started writing books, back in 2011, I would write 10K words a day easy. Over the years that has proven more difficult. This book however put me back in 2011 when the story consumed me and I couldn't stop writing. I love these characters so much. Expect more of them in the future.

Those who I couldn't have done this without:

Britt always is the first I mention because he makes it possible for me to close myself away and write for endless hours a day. Without him I wouldn't get any sleep.

Ava and Emerson for dealing with the fact I can't always be there when they want something. They're troopers.

My older children who live in other states were great about me not being able to answer their calls most of the time and they had to wait until I could get back to them. They still love me and understand this part of mom's world.

My editor Becky Barney at Fairest Reviews Proofreading Services. She worked with me to make the story something I can be proud of and I am so thankful for her help. This time around she had a lot going on in her life yet she made time for this book. She is more appreciated than she knows.

My formatter Melissa Stevens at The Illustrated Author. Her work always blows me away. It's hands down the best formatting I've ever had in my books.

Damonza for my book cover. I am as in love with this cover as I am with this story. They are always a pleasure to work with.

Natasha Tomic for doing my cover reveal and sharing the first exclusive excerpt for me!

Danielle Lagasse, Vicci Kaighan, Jerilyn Martinez, and Becky Potts (my mom) for reading the story for me and giving me feedback. They were great beta/proof readers. I owe them big!

Abbi's Army for being my support and cheering me on. I love y'all!

My readers for allowing me to write books. Without you this wouldn't be possible.

This was the place my mother ran away from at seventeen-years-old, yet it was the place I was now running to at twenty-one. Life is ironic that way. I would have told her as much, but she wouldn't have found the humor in it. Her dreams for me weren't here on the coastal shore of southern Alabama. As for my dreams, I didn't know what they were anymore. Too much had changed. Death has a way of doing that. It takes from you what you took for granted without any remorse.

Finding your way after losing someone wasn't easy and I was hoping coming here would give me some direction. My mother had informed me in her loud, exasperated way of speaking to me that there was nothing in this town that would ease my pain. I agreed with her because I knew a place itself couldn't replace a soul that was gone. She had never understood me. I learned to accept at a young age that I was nothing like my mother. Perhaps if I had known my father I would find the similarities. He had wanted nothing to do with being a father at eighteen-years-old and when he was twenty he had been killed in a motorcycle accident in some remote town in Georgia. My mother never spoke of him and I decided long ago to stop asking about the man that aided in my creation.

I inhaled deeply and enjoyed the smell of the salty sea air. The swing on my grandmother's front porch had once been a peaceful place or so Gran had said. The main road that went through The Shores was noisy and packed with people on their summer vacation. Her porch faced the road but her house was the first one on Sunset Street and Sunset Street was directly off the main strip. Over the years, as the town grew in popularity, her summers had changed yet she had remained in the house she and my grandfather had bought in nineteen-eighty, three years before my mother was born.

Larger houses had been built around them as the older homes were torn down and replaced. I could see the massive condominiums across the main street facing the beach. Gran had told me when they bought the house they could see the water crashing onto shore from this porch. Now it was blocked with high rise condos and parking decks.

My phone lit up beside me and I glanced down to see a text from my mother. I would respond tomorrow. She knew I'd made it safely and that was all she needed to know. The peace of being disconnected from my life back in Chattanooga was why I had come. My mother wanted to remind me of all I had left, but I knew I'd left nothing worth keeping.

Yelling and laughter rang out from farther down Sunset Street. The largest house sat three houses down on the right side of the road. My grandmother's house sat on the left. I glanced over my shoulder toward the three-story elaborate home and saw the activity on the very top of the house. It had a flat roof with a railing around it so that their view of the gulf was unobstructed. It sat so that it was directly between the two condo complexes that sat across the main strip.

If it was a vacation rental, it was for the wealthy. I couldn't imagine how much that would cost for just a night. Yet, the group of people on the roof appeared younger than expected and although there weren't many of them, they were obviously having themselves a party and did not care if their neighbors might be sleeping.

Just as I started to turn around, I saw someone emerge from the shadows below. The street light illuminated a guy with a bottle in his hand and the orange glow from a cigarette in his mouth. I couldn't see much else except that he was wearing jeans and a white tank. I thought about going inside but houses this close to the beach were all on stilts and the height gave me a sense of security from the activity down below. This town wasn't known for danger. He was probably coming from the house party and too drunk to drive. Either that or a tourist out for an evening walk.

"SAAUULL!" a female voice called out loudly from the darkness behind him and he paused for a moment as if he wasn't sure he wanted to turn around. When he did, he turned slowly then took a long pull from the bottle.

The sounds of summer drowned out anything else that was said between the two of them. The girl was tall, blonde and willowy. She leaned against him and they walked on toward the main street up ahead.

Once my life had seemed as content as theirs appeared to be. My chest ached with that loss. I had not been prepared for either loss but then are people ever ready to lose those they love?

Glancing back at the house so full of my Gran's things but empty because she was no longer here. Her gentle calming voice would never again be here as my source of comfort. I would never awake to the smell of her cooking.

Without her here, this place wasn't the same, yet it was where I hoped to find myself once again.

Henley,

I know this letter is going to upset you and that is not why I am sending it. Life happens and if we go through life pretending like it's all roses then when we end up in a pile of shit, we can't dig our way out. I do not live my life expecting roses. I live it tending to the gardens that could possibly produce those roses.

Now, if this Covid gets me, I need you to finish all my business for me. The list I've sent you is in order. When I'm gone please carry out my wishes in the order I wrote them. If I beat this virus, then I expect to see you in June just like we talked about. Except this time, you're making me breakfast. I want to try these new muffins you've come up with and that granola you told me about.

I love you, my sweet girl and know that you brought joy into my life from the moment you entered this world and every second after. I may have made some mistakes but I did what I thought was best at the time. Your mother never made it all easy but she loves you too and means well.

Love always and forever,
Gran

ONE

The gulf breeze was the only relief from the relentless heat. I reached up and adjusted my sun hat before picking up the last box of Gran's clothing to load in my car. This was number one on her list- take all the clothing in her closet to the church donation center.

When Gran had tested positive for Covid she sat down and made a list. It was the things she wanted me to do for her if she didn't survive. The list had come in the mail the day after she had been admitted into the hospital. I had been mad about that list. Mad because she had even considered she wouldn't survive. Mad because I could not lose her too. Mad because this list was another reminder of how precious and fleeting life could be.

Walking down the stairs, I took the box to pack it into my silver Mini Cooper she had given me when I graduated high school. Gran had wanted all her clothing to be taken to her church. They had a program for those in need and it ran solely on the donations of the community. It had been the first thing on Gran's list. Which did not surprise me in the least. Gran had spent her life volunteering in homeless shelters, nursing homes, and food banks. It had been at one of these volunteer efforts that Gran had contracted Covid. She had been wearing her mask and keeping the proper six-feet distance. I had spoken to her just that morning; she'd called to tell me she had her first vaccine scheduled for that Monday. When Monday came, so had Gran's fever.

I sat the box down on the sandy grass and opened the car door. I managed to shove the box into the back seat but getting the door to close was another thing. Just as I was leaning on the door about to try using all my body weight to get it closed, an old blue Ford truck slowed and then stopped right in the middle of the road, blocking Gran's driveway. I paused and stared at the truck, but I was unable to see much with the sun in my eyes. My sun hat had once again been blown back too far on my head with the strong gulf breeze and it was doing little to block the glare.

While squinting, I could make out a tall male, young, dark curly hair, and a nice deep tan that I was envious of standing a few feet away from me.

"Need some help?" he asked and I noticed he lacked a drawl. The kind you expect in the south, a thick accent unlike any other. Even in Chattanooga, it was something that was common place in our accent. This guy didn't have one. I glanced up at his truck again and thought how odd that seemed. He was a prime candidate for a thick southern drawl.

"Uh," I finally managed to say because he had caught me off guard. "Sure, thanks," I added. Still unable to see him clearly due to the brightness of the relentless sun. He came toward me and when he was close enough I stepped away and let him wrestle with the last box.

I took the moment to adjust my hat and get a better look at the good Samaritan while he lifted the box, shifted it in farther then closed the door as if it were the easiest thing in the world. I hated it when men made things look easy after I had struggled with it. I was thankful for his help though.

"Thank you," I said as he turned back around. I had forgotten how nice people were in small towns like this. If someone had stopped to help me back home, I would have been armed with my pepper spray. Things like this just didn't happen at home very often.

"You're welcome," he said and it was then I got my first real look at him. Not at all what I had expected. To go with his tan and dark hair, he had the bluest eyes I'd ever seen. The only imperfection on his face was a cut on his lower lip that appeared fresh, as if he had been in a recent fight. He looked like a model for some tropical vacation commercial and was currently pretending to be a regular guy. The only thing remotely regular about him was his truck and possibly the cut on his lip but then that would be healed soon.

"You're blocking traffic!" a female voice called out. We both turned our heads to see a red convertible pulled up behind him on the road and a blonde girl in the passenger seat standing up looking over the top at him.

"I'm coming," he replied then turned back to me. "You got anymore boxes to fit in the car?"

I shook my head no.

"Alright then," he replied then turned and walked over to the convertible and said something to the blonde who leaned over and threw her arms around his neck and laughed. She moved so fluidly and gracefully, her blonde hair blowing in the breeze in just the right direction so it didn't cover her face, it was as if she was part of his tropical vacation commercial.

I stood there in my large white sun hat that I'd found in Gran's closet and my khaki shorts, yellow polo top and pale skin feeling awkward. I was twenty-one years old and I had thought I was beyond seeing people that were beautiful by the world's standards and feeling less than.

Not appreciating how easily the guy and the gorgeous blonde with her designer sunglasses and bare golden skin hanging out of the convertible had made me feel plain, I straightened my shoulders and went back to the house to lock up before going to do the first task on Gran's list. I realized this was a part of life that Will had been my shelter from. When I had been with Will, I hadn't noticed the rest of the world. He never looked at other girls and I never felt insecure. Will had thought I was beautiful and his love had made me feel beautiful.

This was just another part of life without Will. I had thought I'd outgrown my insecurities, when in reality, I had only used Will as my buffer. Having a boyfriend who loved me since I was sixteen had made my teen years easy. I stopped at the glass door and stared at my reflection. Appearance should not be so important, yet when one has a mother such as mine, it is. I had been raised to believe beauty was the most important thing and I had never felt beautiful until Will. He had changed the way I looked at myself.

Since living in a world with no Will, all those insecurities from my past had slowly crept back in and they were one of the reasons I had to get away. Fate was a fickle thing. Just when you think it gives you a break, it decides to rip it all away. My pale skin would never be a golden brown, just as my brown hair would never be a glamorous red or stunning blonde and I would never have the confidence of the beautiful people. They lived in a world I wasn't a part of and I was okay with that. I didn't need their world. I had lived in a world with Will. It had been the very best world.

I locked the door and headed back to the car. I had come here to focus on finding a world I could live in again. Will had been my world for three wonderful years and since his death twenty months ago, I hadn't been able to find me. It was as if he had taken me with him and at times I wish he had. This summer I had Gran's list and time away from my mother, my job, and my life. It was time I focused on the future and found a way to let go of the past.

Driving to the church and unloading the boxes was easier than the loading had been. Several members of the church and volunteers came out to help and told me how much they loved and missed Honey, that was what everyone called my Gran. Her real name was Gertrude, but my grandfather had nicknamed her Honey because he said there was nothing sweeter in this world than my Gran. The name had stuck. There were few people who knew her real name and she told me once it was one of the reasons she loved my grandfather so much, because she had never liked the name Gertrude.

I accepted the chocolate chip cookies and lemonade a lady named Betty offered me because, first of all, I was positive she would follow me to my car and put them in it if I turned them down and secondly, my Gran would have wanted me to take them, even if I couldn't eat the cookies. I seriously doubted they were gluten and dairy-free. However, the lemonade came in handy because a man named Roger, who had fought in Vietnam with my grandfather, wanted to tell me about the time Honey and his wife Hazel ran out of gas on the causeway in a thunderstorm. The story was longer than anticipated and the lemonade was nice to have while I listened.

Two more stories about Gran from ladies she played Bridge with on Friday afternoons and I was back in my car mentally exhausted from smiling and nodding. I had thought the first item on the list would be the easiest. I now realized I was wrong. Unless I was right and the list was deceiving. Perhaps I was supposed to learn something along the way. I glanced in my rearview mirror. I had learned that those over the age of seventy really like to tell stories and hear themselves talk. At one point, I was worried Roger was going to get tackled by Henry when he began talking over him. I couldn't blame Henry. Roger's story did go on and on and on.

The second thing on the list was taking a box Gran had left on her dresser to the penthouse at the Hendrix IV Condominiums. She didn't explain anything about why or who it was to, which made it all the more strange. There was a silver and black key card on the box and it would get me into the private elevator that went to the penthouse. I was to take the box and inform whoever opened the door that it was from Honey. That was it. I could then leave.

I had no other plans for the day, and until this list was completed, I wasn't going to look for a summer job. Part of finding me again was closure. I needed closure after Gran's death. She had been taken so quickly and I hadn't even been able to say goodbye. This list was the last thing she had asked of me, so I would complete it for her no matter how odd the seven requests on the list may be.

TWO

Although I had never stayed at the Hendrix IV, I knew where it was. The Hendrix Condominiums were the most luxurious condominiums on the gulf coast. Just like the Hendrix Hotel chain was a five-star hotel found in very exclusive locations around the world. When the condominiums had come to Alabama's coast, it had made major headlines. Even my mother had talked about it. That being said, the issue I had with this item on Gran's list was that it was intimidating. Pulling up to the guarded gate around the place did not help my anxiety.

A bald man wearing a black suit walked up to my window and my first thought was he had to be burning up, my second thought was what the heck was I supposed to tell him. Gran had left me this key. She had said nothing about a man at the gate. I rolled down the driver's side window and took off my sunglasses. He was large enough that he was blocking any glare from the sun.

"Name," he said.

"Uh, well, see," I started and realized I sounded nervous and guilty but of what I had no idea. Trying to pull it together and successfully pull off Gran's second request on the list, I cleared my throat.

"Name," he repeated louder as if I hadn't heard him the first time.

"Yes, my name is Henley Warren, and you see my grandmother, she passed away and she left me this list." I stopped then and swallowed nervously. I could see my reflection in his sunglasses and I looked as nervous as I felt.

"Do you have a reservation, ma'am?" he asked me then.

I wasn't sure how I was supposed to explain the list and what I was to do for my deceased grandmother to this man and successfully get away with it. He appeared ready to have me turn my car around and leave. I wasn't good with words or coming up with things on the spur of the moment. I often forgot how to speak altogether when put in a corner such as this. Will had been the one who was good at this. Will would have known what to say. He would have charmed his way right inside that gate.

"She's with me," a deep voice said from somewhere outside the car.

The bald man looked from me to the vehicle behind me then he nodded once and walked back into his fancy brick headquarters, that I hoped was air-conditioned for his sake, while the gate opened up. I looked into the rearview mirror, confused by the sudden rescue, and the familiar old blue Ford truck was there. Was this guy everywhere?

Not waiting for fear the bald man would realize neither me nor the blue truck belonged here, I pulled forward and turned right following the arrow for the parking deck. I kept glancing back to see where the guy in the truck was going, but he turned the opposite way and I realized he was probably headed to staff parking. Twice in one day he had shown up when I needed some help. It was as if Gran had sent him as my helping hand to get this list done.

Wishing I had been able to thank him and at least get his name, I found a parking spot then grabbed the box Gran had left for whoever was in the penthouse. There was a letter taped to the outside, but I hadn't opened it and it wasn't addressed to anyone. Thankfully there were six elevators. One had a gold-plated sign over it that read *Penthouse.* I took out the black and silver card and swiped it. The doors opened.

Stepping inside the plush expensive interior of the elevator, I began to worry I might be arrested for this. Gran had a key, but she wasn't here anymore. Just because she was allowed up this fancy entrance did not mean I was. I glanced around, looking for a camera and then preparing myself for the doors to open and security guards to attack me. Mr. Blue truck could not help me out of this one.

My heart was racing and my palms were starting to sweat by the time the door opened and I exhaled in relief at the empty white and gold hallway in front of me. White marble floors with white walls and gold-framed mirrors lined the walls leading to double doors with a large gold lion head knocker on one side. I walked slowly so that if anyone was watching they could see I was of no threat. I considered leaving the box in the hallway, but Gran had asked specifically for me to give it to whoever opened the door.

"I feel you owe me big for this one," I whispered, just in case she was hanging around to make sure I did all she had asked of me. "I thought the stories from old people were bad," I added. "This is much worse."

When I reached the door, I noticed it had a fancy flat silver doorbell. Perhaps the gaudy lion was just for looks. I pressed the doorbell and took a deep steadying breath while I waited. This wasn't so bad. Whoever opened the door would know Gran. She had a key after all. I had made it this far.

A couple minutes passed and I studied the doorbell, trying to decide if I should press it again or if I should give up and just leave the box. Gran could see, if she was watching, that

I had done my best. Besides, if I left with this box, I quite possibly would never get back in this place again.

The door swung open before I had time to think much further on the matter. A woman dressed in a red satin robe, long dark hair piled atop her head in a messy bun, what I would guess were real diamond earrings in her ears, gold bracelets on her wrists, several flashy rings on her fingers and a cigarette between two of her fingers that showcased sharp red fingernails stood in front of me. This was not at all what I expected and I was, once again, at a loss for words.

"Can I help you?" she asked then put the cigarette to her lips.

"I need to give this to you," I said, holding the box out.

She glanced down at it but didn't reach for it. "I don't accept deliveries. The front desk knows that," she replied and started to close the door. I had to stop her or I was going to be forced to ring the doorbell again.

"No, wait, I am Honey Warren's granddaughter. She left me a list of things she wanted me to do. This is on the list. She wanted me to bring you this box and," I paused and reached for the key to the elevator in my pocket, "the key too."

The lady's face changed then. Her annoyed expression became one of sorrow. She stared at the box as if it held something more valuable than the jewels she was wearing and I was sure that it did not. My gran did not own anything that valuable. I waited as the woman stood there and took her time looking at the box. Her eyes began to fill with unshed tears then she sniffled and lifted her eyes to meet mine once again.

"Henley," she said my name.

I nodded, surprised she knew me.

"Please, come inside. I've heard so much about you from Honey," she told me and the emotion was thick in her voice.

I stepped inside and if I had thought the elevator and hallway were elegant, they were only a small preview of the inside. There were no windows looking out over the gulf, the walls themselves were the windows. It was a complete wide open view as if you were sitting there on the beach while lounging on the sofa or standing in the kitchen. I found myself caught up in amazement and forgot for a moment where I was.

"Honey loved this view too," the lady said as she came up beside me.

"She loved the water," I said, remembering how she said it was the only thing that could heal the soul.

"Yes, she did. God, how I miss her," the woman said then and I turned to look at her just as she wiped a tear from her face. She smiled at me sadly. "I'm sorry. Haven't introduced myself. I'm Lily. Your gran was the truest friend I have ever had. When I was at my lowest, and let me assure you I have had many low times, Honey was here by my side."

"That sounds like my gran," I said.

Lily laughed softly and held out her hands for the box. I gave it to her and watched as she held it as if it were precious. "I'll leave so you can be alone to read the letter and open it," I told her.

She nodded her head but didn't look at me. She was still looking at the box. "Thank you," she whispered.

I turned to leave and saw a child's drawing in a frame on the wall. It seemed so out of place here. Just as I reached the door, Lily called out my name. Looking back at her, she held out the key I had given her. "Take the key. Come visit anytime. The view is always here," she said.

I wasn't sure how I felt about having a key to the penthouse elevator or how I would ever get through the gate again, but at this moment with tears on Lily's cheeks, I didn't have the heart to mention it. I took the key and I would figure out the rest later.

"It was nice to meet you," I said not sure what else I should say.

She smiled through her tears.

Once I was back in the elevator and headed down to the parking garage, I slid the key back into my pocket. Perhaps I could find her phone number at Gran's and call her in a week or so to explain about the guard at the gate. She had been Gran's friend and as odd as it was with all her wealth, she seemed lonely to me. Maybe I had read it wrong, but there had been a brokenness deep in her eyes. One I recognized.

When the elevator door opened, I started to step out but instead came face-to-face with Mr. Blue truck once again.

THREE

"Hey," I blurted out, surprised to see him.

He smirked as if he was amused and stepped back so I could exit the elevator. "You leaving already?" he asked.

"Yes, I just had to drop something off," I explained then added, "thank you for earlier, at the gate." My cheeks heated and I knew I was red. Thanks to my pale skin, any and all embarrassment was clearly broadcasted on my face.

"No problem," he replied.

"Saul, you ready? I'm fucking starving," a guy called out, and Mr. Blue truck turned his head toward the voice.

He had a name. His name was Saul.

"In a minute," he replied then looked back at me.

"I swear I'm gonna take your truck and leave your ass if you don't, well hell-ooo. Who is this?" the other guy drawled as he walked around the corner into view. His hair was as light as Saul's was dark and his eyes were a hazel color that could be considered pretty because his eyelashes were so thick and long.

"I said I was coming," Saul repeated.

The blond was wearing a pair of jeans that hung low on his hips, no shirt and no shoes. "I'm not in a hurry," the guy said smiling at me. "What's your name, sugar?"

I didn't particularly like being called sugar, but I was in Alabama so I let it slide. "Henley," I replied, glancing from the blond to Saul then back to the blond.

He held out his hand toward me. "Drake," he said and I slipped my hand in his and instead of shaking mine, he lifted it to his mouth and kissed the inside of my palm.

"Jesus," Saul muttered.

Drake grinned and winked at me. "He's just jealous because I'm the pretty one."

I would greatly disagree with this statement, but I would do it silently. While Drake was, in fact, nice to look at and his lashes were things Maybelline would give billions for, he was not the better looking one. However, this was neither here nor there. It did not matter. I was leaving.

"It was nice to meet you," I said then looked at Saul. "Both of you. Thanks again." I started to take a step to move around Drake when he moved with me.

"Wait, we were just headed to a friend's house. There will be free food, beer, cocktails, whatever. She'll have it. Come with us," Drake asked.

"Drake," Saul said his name as if it were a warning. He didn't want me there. That stung and my deep bedded insecurities came bursting forth yet again.

"What? She's going with me. My friend. Not yours. Fleur can't bitch about it," Drake replied, sounding annoyed then shot me a flirty grin.

I stood there, wanting nothing more than to get to my car and go back to Gran's. I did not fit in with people like this and Saul knew it. Drake might possibly be drunk and not realize it just yet.

Saul was not pleased with any of this and I was taking it personally. He had been so nice up until now. "If she wants to go with you that's her call," he said, not sounding like it was fine at all then walked off leaving us there.

Drake turned back to me and gave me what I was sure he considered his most charming smile. "Saul can be a moody son of a bitch and when I say that I am being very literal. You have no fucking idea how literal. Ignore him. He will get a few beers in him, Fleur will lick on him some and he will be fine. Not that he is ever what one would call fucking happy. We love him anyway."

I glanced toward the parking deck and my car. "I would need to change," I said, thinking that might get me out of this.

"That's fine. Are you staying here?" he asked.

"No. I had to drop something off. I'm staying in my Gran's house on Sunset Street," I explained.

His grin only got bigger. "No shit. That's where Calli's house is. We can stop by on the way."

"My car," I began.

"I'll ride with you." He glanced out at the parking deck. "I'm fairly certain Saul left me anyway."

I was stuck.

And it sounded like I was going to the loud party house down the street. Who had parties every night? It was Wednesday for goodness grief. It was possibly the very last thing I ever wanted to do though, my good manners were making it difficult to just be rude.

"Now that we're friends, how do you feel about blow jobs?" Drake asked me so casually, he could have been asking me if I enjoyed sweet tea.

I opened my mouth to say something, but nothing came out. Had he really just asked me how I felt about blow jobs? Who does that?

The Ford truck pulled up in front of us. "Get in. We got to go bail Rio out of jail," Saul called out the window to Drake.

"Shit, again?" Drake asked as if this was an annoyance and a regular occurrence.

Saul nodded his head once.

'What the fuck he do this time?" Drake asked.

"Are you comin' or not?" was Saul's response.

Drake glanced back down at me. "Another time, sugar," he said, then walked away, leaving me there, which had been what I wanted in the first place. I waited until he climbed into the truck. Just as it began to pull off, Drake turned his head back in my direction and winked.

The Alabama license plate told me what I had already assumed: Saul was a local. Once they were gone, I headed toward my Mini, ready to go back to Gran's and take a shower, eat some dinner, and read a book. My typical evening. It was free of beautiful yet strange boys one who inquired about my feelings on oral sex and one with obvious mood swings. Those two were trouble and I wasn't here for that.

Walking back into Gran's house, the smell of vanilla and cinnamon always welcomed me. Even after the house had been closed up the three months since Gran's death, the house still smelled the same. Years of baking had made its mark on the place and it made it feel like she was still here. My love for baking had come from Gran.

Tomorrow I would need to make a stop at the health food store and pick up some things. Then I could begin my own baking this summer. It was my form of therapy. Gran had once told me it had been hers too.

One long hot shower later, I was eating a turkey and provolone sandwich with pretzels and watching *Jane the Virgin* on Netflix when I heard the faint music coming from down the street. I didn't have to look to know the party had started up. Rio must have been freed from jail and I was curious how those two were able to bail him out.

I reached for the remote and turned the volume up on the television, until I could no longer hear the sounds from down the street. Taking another bite of my sandwich, I leaned back on the sofa with my feet crossed in front of me and didn't give Saul or Drake one more thought. At least I tried my best not to give them one more thought.

FOUR

The third request on Gran's list was my goal for the day, then I thought I might find the library and spend a few hours there. I was procrastinating and I realized that but there were only seven things on Gran's list and yesterday I had completed two of them. This process made me feel as if I had Gran here with me. I needed to slow it down. Once I finished it, I was afraid it would feel as if she had truly left.

Standing outside Signed Sips, I held the letter in my hand that I was supposed to bring to a Mrs. Hillya Garry. Gran had said I was to tell Hillya Garry it was from Honey and that I was to wait on her to read the letter. Again, another awkward request. Thanks a lot, Gran.

Signed Sips however was interesting. From outside you could see the walls lined in books. There were thousands of books inside. In front of all the books was what looked like a coffee shop with bakery items. The place was unique as was the name. Luckily it didn't appear to be too terribly busy at the moment.

I opened the door and instead of the smell of coffee hitting me in the face, it was the books and I decided this was the best coffee place I had ever been. Don't get me wrong, I love the smell of coffee but nothing beats the smell of a physical book that you can hold in your hands.

An older lady was placing muffins into the bakery display and looked up at me as the door bells chimed.

"Welcome to Signed Sips. How can I help you?" she asked smiling brightly. Her hair was the purest color white I had ever seen. She had it styled in a short bob that made her face look as if it were heart-shaped.

"I'm looking for a Mrs. Hillya Garry," I said, returning her smile, glad to have found a friendly face since I was about to be annoying for a few moments.

The lady continued to smile. "You found her," she replied.

This was even better. The nice lady was Hillya. She looked to be my gran's age. This made sense. Another one of her friends. The kind I could picture my gran being friends with, unlike Lily who I visited yesterday at the penthouse.

I stepped up to the counter. "Hello, I am Henley Warren. My grandmother was Honey. She left me a list of things she'd like me to do after she passed away. I am to give you this letter," I said and held out my hand to Hillya. When she reached out to take it, there was an odd expression on her face. She wasn't close to tears or emotional. She seemed concerned almost. As if my gran had left her words she wasn't sure she wanted to read. Knowing I had to follow this through I continued, "I'm also supposed to stand here while you read it. I'm sorry." I added the last part because Hillya truly looked like she did not want to read the letter from my gran. Let alone have an audience.

Everyone loved Honey Warren or so I thought. Perhaps I was visiting the one person in this town who didn't love my gran. Was this Gran's way of making amends for something she had done. Hillya looked at the letter in her hand several moments then slowly opened it. I had expected her to ask me some questions first or tell me she didn't have time to open it now.

Not wanting to stare at Hillya while she read the letter, I focused on the options in her bakery display. She had blueberry, banana, and praline pecan muffins. The cake donuts came in chocolate glaze, strawberry, and maple cream. Her cupcakes were works of art with pieces of candy bars, cookies and even tiny cupcakes as toppings. I glanced up as a girl came from the back carrying a tray of cookies and sat them down before helping the customer who had just walked in the door.

Hillya cleared her throat and I turned my attention back to her, hoping this wasn't going to be something Gran had walked me into that was unsalvageable. If they had a grudge between them, I did hope Hillya could forgive Gran. She was gone now. There was no reason to hold a grudge. However, Gran doing anything to someone that would make them hold a grudge seemed unlikely.

"You bake gluten-free, dairy-free items?" Hillya asked me then.

I wish I had read that letter now. I had no idea what this was about and I had obviously been way off with my assumptions. "Uh, yes, I mean, not professionally. I just enjoy baking and I can't have dairy or gluten... so..."

"You good with the low-calorie granola mixes and those bowl things that are all the craze?" she then asked.

I nodded. "Acai bowls? I make them for me," I said.

Hillya folded the letter slowly and studied it before looking back at me again. "I've owned this place for thirty years. I've had to change it many times to keep up with the trends. Seems the trends have changed on me once again. Young people want healthier options. Nut-free options I have managed, but the gluten and dairy, I have not. I do not know how to make the granola bowls the way they want them or the best way to make them low-calorie. I will pay you twenty dollars an hour. Thirty hours a week. If you have any savory evening appetizers ideas, I am looking for those too. We add a full bar after four every day and stay open until ten. There are two different book clubs that are held here each month and we have a monthly author signing."

I stood there, unsure what to say. I had never made any of my recipes for anyone other than me. my family, and some friends. My mother had tried and liked them and Gran had enjoyed my experiments in the kitchen but that didn't mean others would. This woman was offering me twenty dollars an hour without even trying any of my creations. What had Gran said to her?

"Would you like me to make some of them for you to try first? Before you hire me?" I asked. I hadn't wanted to get a job so soon, but I also hadn't expected to get a job doing something I enjoyed. Something I thought I was good at, but I wasn't sure other people would agree. At least not sure enough for twenty dollars an hour.

"Honey's opinion is all I need," she replied and tucked the letter into the pocket of her white capri pants. "I believe baking runs in your blood, even deeper than you realize," she said with a smile that didn't quite meet her eyes. "Can you start tomorrow morning? Fridays are busy and I could use the extra help. I get here at four, but if you could be here by five that would give me plenty time to show you things and you can tell me what all you need in order to make your creations."

All I could manage was a nod. How could I say no to this? Well played, Gran. Well, played.

"Thank you," I said.

The expression on Hillya's face was sad, but there was something else there. Possibly hopefulness? Was her shop struggling that much? If it was on me to save the place that was a lot of pressure. "I believe we both have Honey to thank," she replied. "I'll see you tomorrow morning, Henley."

When I was seated back in my car, I thought perhaps I should start reading all the letters Gran left before I delivered them.

"What have you gotten me into this time, Gran?" I asked, but of course she didn't answer.

Starting the car, I pulled out onto the road and drove. I didn't drive toward Gran's house or the library. Instead I headed for the health food store in town. I needed to be sure they had what I needed before tomorrow morning. I didn't want to show up empty-handed. I would feel better about things if I could walk in and bake some items right away for Hillya to try. I might also feel more confident at five in the morning if I spent my day today baking what I planned to do tomorrow.

Will had loved my banana bread and it was not only dairy and gluten-free but organic. Mom always asked me to make the dark chocolate granola bars and I could do those organic as well if I could find the right ingredients.

My mind began turning over all the different ideas and I grew excited about the possibilities. I was going to get to bake things that I created for people to buy. I would be lying if I hadn't thought about it before but then I would push the idea away because I had no real training. I played around in the kitchen. I would have never had the confidence to apply for a job to do something like this, and yet, here I was with a job doing just that and it was all thanks to my gran.

FIVE

Two banana loaves, two dozen caramel oatmeal cookies, one batch of dark chocolate granola and one batch of brown sugar granola later along with a new idea in the oven I didn't have a name for yet.

It was well past six in the evening and I was covered in oat flour, batter of many different kinds, and happier than I had been in a long time. While humming a tune my gran used to sing in the kitchen, there was a knock at the door.

I wiped my hands off on Gran's yellow gingham apron and used my wrist to push the hair that had worked its way free from my bun out of my face then headed for the door. It wasn't until I rounded the corner that I saw who was on the other side of the glass door. Pausing, I thought of several things at once. First of all, my appearance. It was very likely I had flour amongst other ingredients on my face and in my hair. Then of course the most important thing, why was Saul here and was I going to open the door?

I didn't even know his last name. His eyes met mine and I knew I wasn't going to be able to turn and walk away now.

Not that I was so drawn to him but because I had better manners than that. I wasn't rude. Besides, whoever Saul was he had helped me not once but twice. I doubted he was here to be rude.

When I reached the door, I opened it and forced a smile I hoped was polite. "Hello," I said as if he hadn't just watched me contemplating not coming to the door.

The corner of his mouth curled as if this amused him. "Did I interrupt something?" he asked.

I shook my head no. "Not at all. How can I help you?"

He continued to appear as if he may laugh at any moment. "You got some flour on your nose and forehead," he said, nodding his chin in my direction as he said it.

"I am baking," I explained, refusing to reach up and wipe it off. With my luck, I would only make it worse.

"Then I am interrupting something," he replied.

Was there a point to this visit? My smile was pointless. I was sure it looked as fake as it felt. I dropped it. "Currently it's in the oven. I have a few minutes," I told him, emphasizing the word *few* so he would get to the point.

He didn't seem to care. Instead he looked around me and inside the house. "Smells good."

"I hope so," I replied.

His eyes shifted back to me. Then he reached into the pocket of his jeans, drawing my attention to the outline of his well-chiseled stomach under the thin fabric of his white tee shirt. I shouldn't be looking at that but it was hard to miss.

"I was asked to drop this off to you," he said, snapping my attention back to him and not his abs. He was holding out a small plastic card the size of a credit card.

Confused, I reached for it and immediately read what it said.

Hendricks was written at the top in the familiar gold letters of the hotel and condominiums' emblem. Underneath it was my name Henley Warren. Then lastly, there was a long number and a barcode.

I lifted my gaze back to meet his. "What is this?"

"Entry card. Lily sent it. When the guard on duty comes to your car, you just show him this."

Lily had sent me a card through Saul? I wondered how she knew Saul. Was he not just some employee? Did he find out who I had visited and alerted her to my having difficulty getting in the gate? I started to ask, but he spoke first.

"I overheard Lily asking a guard to have a card sent to you. I told them I knew where you lived and I'd drop it off," he explained, as if he had read my mind.

"Oh, well, thanks," I said. He didn't ask how I knew the resident in the penthouse and I didn't offer an explanation. We weren't to be friends. He had made that clear.

"It was on my way," he said. If he was concerned I was going to read too much into his gesture, he need not be.

"Of course," I replied, realizing he was once again headed to the house party. "Well, have a good night and thanks again," I said and started to close the door.

"One more thing," he said, stopping me, and I paused to look back at him. "If Drake comes around, don't take him seriously. He isn't for you," he said then turned and walked back down the stairs.

Had he just warned me off his friend? Had that been the reason he offered to bring the card here? I stood there staring at his back for a moment longer than necessary trying to process what he had just said and the way he had said it. There had been a definite smirk on his face. It had been slight but I had seen it.

Closing the door with more force than necessary, I growled in frustration. Saul might have been helpful, but apparently, he was also an elitist ass. An elitist ass who drove a beat-up old truck and worked at a condominium complex. Did his ridiculously good looks get him accepted by the trust fund brats down the street? Did I even care how he fit into their world? No. None of it mattered. He nor his friends were a part of my life and I did not have some hope that they would be. If he thought I was sitting around waiting on Drake to show up and flirt with me again he was sorely mistaken. It annoyed me more than it should that he thought I needed to be told not to take his friend's flirting seriously. Those two had taken up the last of my time. I would be sure to stay clear of them. Both of them.

I had what I believed I was going to call a dark chocolate roll in the oven that I needed to get out and let cool then add the icing. I wasn't going to dwell on Saul or Drake. They were not part of my plan this summer. After today, it was very unlikely I would see either of them again, unless it was them driving by to go party down the street.

The smell of books was not what wafted up to meet me when Hillya opened the back door to the café. The kitchen smelled of cinnamon, vanilla, caramel, and coffee. I held two paper bags in my hands that were filled with all I needed to make the items I had worked to create yesterday. I had one of the banana loaves with me as well as a plate with one of each of the other items I had made for Hillya to try. I had awakened at three unable to sleep any longer and made a fresh batch of the dark chocolate granola, deciding to try some goji berries this time, and I had been happy with the way they turned out.

"Good morning," Hillya said, closing the door behind me, "I see you came prepared."

"Yes, I hope it's okay, but I wanted to try a few things yesterday and went to buy supplies. I brought some samples for you, if you'd like to taste them and see what you think." I was still not sure of my baking abilities, at least not at this level. If she tried my samples and sent me packing, I would understand. I would possibly cry and eat my weight in oat milk ice cream, but I would still understand.

"You don't do anything halfway. A go-getter. I shouldn't be surprised," Hillya said with a smile. "Let's see what you got."

We spent the next half hour on stools as Hillya enjoyed some of all my baked goods while she drank a cup of coffee.

When we stood back up, I had my work schedule, and she had a list of the things I would need for her to order. This morning, I was to make all I could with the supplies I bought then put them out front to sell.

It was almost ten when the last of my banana bread sold. It had been what I had the most of so it had lasted the longest. The granola had been gone by nine and the dark chocolate rolls had been gone in the first hour. I was amazed. If only Gran could have seen this.

The bell chimed on the door, and I stood up from taking the empty tray that had been holding the banana bread out of the display case to greet the customer. Hillya was in the back working on lunch items and Jill had left after the morning crowd. She was a cashier that worked mornings, but I heard her say this was her last week so I wouldn't be getting to know her.

Drake's face lit up in a grin when his eyes met mine. He had his arm thrown around the shoulders of a petite brunette with dark brown eyes in a hot pink bikini top with a pair of tiny white shorts. "Good morning," I said, returning Drake's smile. The brunette didn't smile or acknowledge my greeting. She was looking up at the chalkboard menu behind me with a bored expression.

"Henley," Drake drawled out my name. "Are you gonna be making my morning cup of joe?" he asked.

"I'll just get a water. I can't get a cappuccino here. This place doesn't have low-fat oat milk. I don't do soy," the girl said, glancing up at Drake obviously annoyed.

"I have low-fat oat milk," I replied and went to put her order into the computer. The only reason we had low-fat oat milk was because I had brought some with me today. It was not something Hillya typically had. I wasn't sure how to ring it up, so I just put it under special.

"It's not on the menu," the girl told me.

"No, it's not, but I brought some in this morning to use for the dairy-free, low-fat banana bread I made," I explained to her, keeping my smile in place. Her eyes widened some when I said that and her demeanor changed.

"You have dairy-free, low-fat banana bread?" she asked.

"We did. Just sold the last of it. We will have more in the morning. It is also gluten and nut-free," I added.

The girl looked up at Drake. "Oh my god. Why didn't you tell me they had things like that here? I thought it was just a regular coffee shop. I have to text Amy," the girl said then walked off with her phone in hand.

"Well, damn, girl," he said impressed. "I've not seen her that excited about anything since I met her, but I just met her yesterday or was it the day before. I'm not real sure. Anyway, get her that drink shit she's so pumped for and I just want an Americano."

I added his order into the computer when he said, "Give me one of those strawberry donuts too."

I put it in then went to the espresso machine to start on the cappuccino.

"Amy and I are coming in the morning at eight," I heard the girl tell Drake.

"That's great. Now, which one is Amy?" he replied.

"The redhead," she answered him. "Want to come with us?"

"Will it end in a threesome or a blow job?" he asked hopefully.

The girl laughed. "Uh, no. Absolutely not."

"Then no thanks. I'll be in bed," he replied.

It sounded like Drake asking girls about their feelings on blow jobs was common. I wanted to think it was just him being funny and making a joke… but I didn't think it was. I was fairly certain if a girl replied that she liked giving blow jobs, he would take her up on it that very moment.

I finished her cappuccino and Drake's Americano then placed them on the counter. She picked hers up and headed for the door. I put Drake's donut in a bag and he gave me a lazy smile as he took it from me. "Now I know where to find you," he said.

"I guess you do," I replied. However, his buddy would not be happy about his looking for me. I also was not Drake's type and he wasn't mine.

"When do you get off work?" he asked me.

I glanced over his shoulder at the brunette talking on her phone just outside the door. "It appears you have enough company today," I told him.

He shrugged. "She's getting boring."

"Don't be a jerk," I replied.

He placed a hand over his chest. "Ouch. You wound me."

"I doubt that. Have a nice day, Drake."

He shook his head grinning. "Don't play hard to get, Henley. I like that game." Then he turned and walked out of the door. I watched as he, once again, put his arm around the girl and they walked away.

With a sigh, I picked up the low-fat oat milk and put it back in the mini fridge under the counter. I needed to find the chalk and add the oat milk to the menu. Then I needed to add it to the list of things for Hillya to order.

Tomorrow I needed to plan on making an extra loaf of banana bread and two more batches of the dark chocolate rolls. If the brunette helped spread the word, we may just need them. Smiling, I headed back to the kitchen to find my list. Gran must be sitting back and smiling right now as she watched this unfold. I liked to think she was always watching.

SIX

Doubting my gran had always been a waste of time. My new job was just more proof of her wisdom. She was right; I was good at this and my new boss was very happy with my first week. We already had new regulars who came in just for my items.

Drake had returned alone twice this week, but we had been so busy I didn't speak to him much. Saul had come in once with the blonde; I hadn't been the one to take their order, but the blonde had ordered an acai bowl and I had to make those. I had only made eye contact with Saul once when I handed the blonde the bowl. He had been watching me or it appeared like it and I managed a smile then went back to working on a drink order for someone else.

Falling into a routine had been easy enough and I was enjoying working with Hillya. She was possibly my only friend in town or the closest thing I had to one. I saw her more than I saw anyone else. The only issue with my working so much was that I hadn't made it to the fourth request on Gran's list.

After I worked eight days straight, Hillya had decided we needed to schedule my days off. She had given me Sunday,

Monday and Wednesday off, but I would still deliver items in the morning before they opened for them to sell. She said once she hired someone that I could teach to make the items, I could have real days off. I didn't mind how things were now though. I also wasn't sure how I was going to teach someone to make something when I had never written down an actual recipe for anything. I didn't even know the exact measurements of my ingredients. I just guessed, and it always turned out good.

The two large tool boxes full of my grandfather's tools were in my back seat as I pulled into the parking lot of Deep South Farmer's Market. Again, I was confused by Gran's request. It seemed odd that I was taking Granddad's tools that she had kept this long to a man who owned a farmer's market. Not just any farmer's market either, the largest one in Alabama. It was famous around here and even held a Watermelon Festival every year that brought in thousands of people from all around the southeast.

Perhaps Lloyd March liked tools as well as produce. I didn't know the man, but I had been here plenty as a child with my grandparents to get their weekly fruits and vegetables as well as homemade ice cream. It had been a while since I'd been there, but the place brought back memories. I wondered how likely it was Lloyd would be here. Gran seemed to think he would be easy enough to find in the letter. It had simply said:

Take Granddad's tools that I have in storage room to Deep South Farmer's Market. The man who owns it is Lloyd March. Ask for him and personally give the tools to him. Tell him that your granddad would have wanted him to have them.

Not once in all the years we had come to this farmer's market had I met this man, yet my granddad was close enough to him that he'd want him to have his tools. It seemed odd but then all Gran's requests had been strange. Except the first one. It had made enough sense.

The tool boxes had been heavy and a struggle to get in the car. I decided I would leave them there and go find this

Lloyd March before fetching the tools. Stepping out of the car, the humid heat hit me in the face followed by a gulf breeze. I wished I'd brought Gran's white hat. The sunscreen I had applied this morning would have to do its job.

Glancing around the parking lot, where I had found it difficult to find a parking spot, I tried to decide the best way to find Lloyd in this mad house. The tourists were everywhere with their bags of fresh homegrown items and ice cream cones. Every other person I walked past had a watermelon tucked under their arm. The employees had Deep South tee shirts on, but they were all different shades of summer colors. It was hard to decipher who worked here and who didn't with so many bodies moving about.

I headed for the shade of the covered building before my white skin turned a bright pink and then pushed my sun glasses up on top of my head so I could see better. It took a few minutes but a girl wearing a cotton candy pink tank top that said DEEP SOUTH FARMER'S MARKET walked in front of me carrying a basket of apples.

"Excuse me," I said before she could escape into the crowd.

She glanced over her shoulder and smiled brightly. "How can I help ya?" she asked with an accent so thick it had to be fake. Either that or this girl was from Mississippi.

"'I'm looking for Lloyd March," I told her.

"Alrighty then, jus' let me put this here basket uh apples down and I'll show you to 'em," she replied.

Yeah, she had to be from Mississippi. I returned her smile, grateful this wasn't going to be difficult. "Thank you."

"Yer welcome!" she exclaimed loudly.

She put the apples down beside the others, told a lady where she could find the restroom, picked up a dirty napkin, and helped a kid find the ripest plum before she made her way back to me. I was so impressed with her work ethic I didn't mind the wait. When she made it to me she nodded her head to the left. "Sorry 'bout that. Right this way," she told me then began to walk or possibly bounce a little as she led me past the rest of the fruit and toward a closed-off area. The bright blue door read "Employees Only" painted in a sunny yellow.

She pushed the swinging door open and I followed her inside the cool interior of a storage area. A couple of guys unloading some boxes glanced at us with curiosity.

"Y'all see Lloyd?" the girl asked them.

The taller boy, who was covered in freckles, wiped at his brow and then pointed behind him. "He's with Rio."

The girl sighed heavily. "Good Lord on high, what did he do this time?" she asked, sounding exasperated.

The guy shrugged and she glanced over her shoulder at me. "Might be a situation," she said then continued on her way.

I wasn't sure if I was supposed to follow her or not but I did. Mostly because I needed to find Lloyd and she was taking me to him. There was this small part of me who remembered hearing the name Rio before and I was curious. This was a small town. I doubted there were that many Rios walking around.

"If you don't want to find yer ass right here fer the rest of yer life then keep on doin' just what yer doin'," a deep voice boomed as we turned the corner. The girl in front of me paused and sighed again. When she looked back at me, I wondered if this was where she told me now wasn't a good time.

"Sorry 'bout this," she said then turned back around. "Daddy, someone is lookin' fer ya. I brought her back here. Y'all might need to finish this later."

Daddy? Lloyd March was her dad? She couldn't be out of high school yet. How old was her dad? Before the questions could keep piling up in my nosey head, she turned back to me and waved for me to come forward.

I rounded the corner of the wooden crates of corn to find a man, who was, indeed, old enough to have fought in Vietnam with my grandad, standing there his gaze locked on me immediately. He appeared bothered by the interruption.

"I'm sorry. Did we have an appointment?" he asked.

I swallowed, once again nervous and hating being put on the spot. Especially in the middle of what appeared to be a family situation. If this was the Rio who often got arrested, I could understand Mr. March's frustration.

"Uh, no, sir, I'm Honey Warren's granddaughter," I began and didn't wait for a response before continuing, "She left me a list of things she wanted me to handle for her. One of those things is to take my grandad's tools to a Mr. Lloyd March at the Deep South Farmer's Market. I, uh, should have called first. I'm sorry."

Lloyd March shook his head. "No, I'm glad you're here. Thank you for taking time to come. I am sorry you had to walk in on this." He shot a warning glare in Rio's direction.

I too shifted my gaze to Rio for a brief moment. He wasn't as tall as his friends, but he was muscular, tanned and his dark hair was almost shaved it was cut so short. He met my gaze and smirked. I quickly looked back toward Lloyd.

"I have the tools in my car. They're just heavy and I wanted to find you before I got them out," I told him.

He smiled then but it was a sad smile. His eyes seemed to tell a story with that smile and I wondered how he had known my grandad. I doubted very much Lloyd March was going to keep me here telling me stories like the people at the church had. He may be in his seventies, but he was a busy man and still raising kids. His wife must be young.

"Honey wanted you to bring these here to me?" he asked.

"Yes, sir," I replied.

He shook his head and he stared at me a moment. His thoughts were either lost on memories of my grandparents or he was trying to decide if I was making a mistake.

"Alright then, Honey," he muttered under his breath as if he were talking to my Gran. Then he looked back at Rio. "Go help Henley with the tools," he said.

I hadn't told him my name yet he knew. Did this whole town know everything about my gran? It was odd being known by so many and not knowing anything about them. Lloyd March was a strange one too. What had he meant by "Alright then, Honey?"

"Are we done?" Rio shot back at Lloyd.

Lloyd shook his head and sighed. "For now." He looked back to me then. "It was nice to finally meet you. I've heard a lot about you over the years. Your grandparents were awfully proud." He looked like he wanted to say more, but he didn't. Instead, he walked off leaving me there with… Rio. I realized then that his daughter had already left and I hadn't realized she'd walked away.

"How heavy are we talking? Do I need to get a trolley or some shit?" Rio asked me.

"I carried each tool box to the car by myself. I think you can manage," I replied.

"Then lead the way."

I did as instructed, and Rio fell into step beside me. We walked back out into the open air and I slid my sunglasses back down over my eyes when we left the shade of the building. I was just about convinced this would be a silent endeavor when he cleared his throat.

"Pop called you Henley. That your name?" he asked.

I nodded.

"Heard about you," he said then.

"From who?" I asked, already sure I knew this answer.

"Some friends. They mentioned you the other night." He was grinning as if he knew I wanted more details and he wasn't going to give them to me.

"Must be the same friends that bailed you out of jail," I replied in my most casual tone.

His head turned toward me then and he chuckled. "Heard about that, did you?"

I shrugged. Two could play this game. He didn't want to give details then neither would I.

We reached my car then and I opened the back door and stepped back. "There they are," I stated the obvious.

Rio didn't make a move to get them. Instead, he leaned up against the passenger side door and crossed his arms over his chest then turned his head to study me. "So, tell me Henley, how would you like to go to a party with me tonight?" he asked.

I laughed. "Sorry, I think I'll pass. I've already been invited to one of those parties and I can assure you I am not wanted there." I think he already knew that too. Which was why he was asking.

His grin showcased dimples on each cheek. "I mighta heard about that," he replied.

I didn't respond. This conversation was pointless.

"Look, I tell you what. You come to the party with me tonight and I swear it will be a friends' only thing. I'm not looking to hook up. You're safe with me."

So he was looking to annoy the guy who bailed him out of jail. The guy who couldn't have as much access to money as he did. I shook my head no.

"I much prefer Netflix or a book over going to one of those parties," I told him.

"You've never been, how would you know?"

"I hear them. Y'all have them nightly. Or almost nightly. Last night was surprisingly quiet for a Saturday. Do you people not have anything better to do?"

He laughed this time. "We aren't going to Callie's. Her step-mommy showed up for the next few weeks so Callie left for Nantucket."

Nantucket? Seriously? "How unfortunate for her," I replied.

"You've not met her newest stepmother," he said and waggled his eyebrows.

I didn't want to meet her either. I didn't want to be a part of that life. It wasn't a life I was looking for. Their world wasn't why I had come to this town.

"Thanks for the invite but my answer remains the same," I told him.

He shook his head while looking as if I was missing out on something truly remarkable. "That's a shame. Might have wanted to get to know me. You never know what we might have in common." He said this smiling, but it wasn't a dimple-flashing smile. This one was forced.

"I'm not looking to date," I said then, wondering if I had hurt his ego.

"I think I already mentioned this would be just as friends. I'm not looking to date you either. That is not why I invited you. Trust me."

He was being sincere. That much I was sure about. I just didn't trust his reasons for inviting me. "Listen, I need to be somewhere. This conversation is going nowhere. Can you just take the tool boxes for your dad?" I asked as politely as I could.

He laughed. "Pops ain't my dad. He's my grandfather," Rio said then and straightened up from his relaxed position on my car.

"Oh. Well, the girl who brought me back there, she called him dad," I was trying to work this out in my head. The girl had to be younger than him. She looked several years younger.

"Yep. My aunt is five years younger than me," he said with an amused smirk on his face.

"Oh," I heard myself say again.

Rio leaned into the back of the car and pulled out both of the tool boxes. When he looked at me again, he said, "Welcome to Alabama," as if that explained everything.

I nodded, slightly unsure what to say to that.

He chuckled then closed the car door. I thought he was about to walk off and finally leave me alone when his gaze turned serious. "I didn't know your gran personally but I'm thinking her reason for sending you here with these tool boxes had little to do with my Pop," he said and for a moment I thought he was going to say more. He didn't. Instead he just started walking away.

Confused by his last comment I stood there, wondering if I should just let him go or ask what he meant. Knowing my curiosity would drive me crazy, I gave in.

"What do you mean by that?" I called out to him before he got too far.

He stopped walking and it took a moment before he turned back around to face me. I wasn't sure he had any clue what he was talking about but if he knew something about my gran then I wanted to know. Although I didn't know what some reprobate who kept getting thrown in a small-town jail could possibly know about my grandmother.

"Why don't we start with tonight, the party," he replied.

I felt as if I had just been set-up, but the small little nagging in my gut told me that there was possibly something I didn't know . I battled with myself for a few moments then decided one elitist party wouldn't kill me.

"Fine," I said, knowing I would regret this.

A slow smile spread across his face. "I'll be by your gran's house at eight to pick you up," he replied then walked away without another word.

What had I gotten myself into?

Better yet what had Gran gotten me into?

SEVEN

The rest of my day I had played over every second of my visit to Deep South Farmer's Market and every word out of Lloyd and Rio's mouths. By the time Rio arrived in his black Jeep to pick me up, I had convinced myself this had all been a ploy to get me to this party. But why? What was the purpose?

When I climbed into Rio's Jeep, I didn't wait for small talk, getting straight to the point.

"You are aware that Drake invited me to one of these parties and Saul made it very clear I was not welcome," I said the moment the door closed firmly behind me.

Rio glanced at me just for a second. He didn't even do a once over on my outfit that I had spent more time than I cared to admit picking out. I did feel more comfortable with him because of it. He hadn't been lying when he said this was a friends-only invite. There was no other interest behind his gaze.

"That was a different kind of party," Rio said and didn't elaborate. This of course left me to ask more questions.

"How is this party different? Don't y'all just spend your days being rich then partying all night?" I asked with obvious disgust in my tone. I couldn't even try to mask it.

Rio let out a bark of laughter. "Oh yeah. That's definitely what I do all day. In between sweating my ass off for Pops unloading produce, that is. It's a tough schedule to keep."

Okay fine. So, he had a job. I should have realized that since he was at the market today in the back. "Maybe not all of you," I replied.

"Maybe not," he agreed, grinning as he kept his eyes on the road. "Tell me, are you always this judgmental or is this just a special case?"

That stung, perhaps because it was true. I was judging people I did not know simply by the way they looked and the noise they managed to create down the street nightly. "I think this is a special case," I said.

He laughed again. "Good to know. I'd hate to think you were always so damn uptight. Kind of reminds me of the ladies at my gramma's church."

I had wondered where his grandmother was today, since it was obvious Lloyd was married to a younger woman since his daughter was in high school. I didn't know the details or anything but that was my assumption. "Are your grandparents still married?" I asked then and instantly wished I hadn't. That was rude and nosey.

He shot a glance my way then but he didn't appear offended. Simply amused. "Yep," he replied then waited a moment before adding. "You're wondering about Hazel, aren't you?

If Hazel was the girl from today then yes, I was in fact wondering about Hazel. I felt bad for admitting it though. However, his family tree was rather complicated.

"Hazel was the product of a bad situation that happened at the market. One of the field hands that Pop hired ended up raping one of the younger girls that worked as a cashier at the market. She was only fifteen and she got pregnant. The girl's parents went to Gram's church and they don't believe in abortion. They decided to let her have the baby but put it up for adoption. A lot of shit happened. The family moved because the girl needed special care for the trauma she had been through. This town and all brought back too much. Anyway, long story short, my gram and Pop adopted Hazel. She's been theirs since the day she was born."

Wow. That was not at all what I'd been expecting.

"We're here," he announced then, snapping my thoughts from his story to the present. Rio had pulled the Jeep into a sandy gravel driveway that belonged to a two-story white beach house. There were several vehicles parked outside. I recognized two of them. The blue Ford truck and the red Mercedes convertible.

"Whose house is this?" I asked, not opening the door to get out.

"Mine," Rio replied and I jerked my gaze from the house that sat directly on the beach with a wraparound porch and balcony in front of me to look at him.

"Yours?" I asked not sure if he was joking or not.

He smirked. "You look like you don't believe me," he replied.

"Well, if your pop pays you enough at the farmer's market to afford a one-point-five-million-dollar house then I might need to come apply for a job."

He opened his door then and started to move to get out. "I live here with two other friends."

"So y'all rent this place?" I asked, still doing the math in my head and not seeing how three people in their early twenties could afford this place.

"Two of us rent, one of us owns it. That isn't important. Just get out of the Jeep," he replied then did as he told me to do.

I reached for the handle and got down out of the vehicle. The noise level here was much different from their friend's house down the street from Gran's. All I heard was the ocean waves breaking against the shore. At least this was where Rio lived so there wasn't a chance of Saul asking me to leave.

Rio walked around the Jeep and glanced up at the balcony and the open double doors. "it's too damn hot to leave the doors open. I don't want to pay my half of that electricity bill," he grumbled then looked back at me. "Why are you so nervous?" he asked me then.

I had just met this guy today, but I felt oddly comfortable around him. "I'm not good with people. At least new people. I prefer to keep to myself," I told him honestly.

"Stepping out of your comfort zone," he said. "Impressive."

I stopped walking then and stared up at him. "No, it isn't. I'm doing this because you said you would tell me what you meant by my gran not sending those tool boxes to Lloyd for the reasons I thought." I didn't want him to forget there was a reason I was here.

He smiled just as he looked away from me. "I know," was his only response. "Still fucking impressive." Then he continued toward the steps leading up to the door.

He had shared something personal with me in the Jeep about his aunt, but he hadn't even hinted about what he had been referring to earlier today. I didn't know how my coming to this party did anything for him. He was clearly not using me to make anyone jealous. He wasn't attracted to me. This entire thing made no sense but yet here I was walking in the door of his house and into his world of wealthy friends who may or may not want me here.

The inside was even nicer than the outside. I may have guesstimated how much this place cost incorrectly. There was a possibility this was closer to two-million and who in the heck owned it?

"Rio!" a female voice called out in greeting. "I made your favorite Long Island mix but you're late. It's already gone."

I looked to the left where a wide-curved staircase came from the second floor. The girl was standing near the top of the stairs, leaning over the railing with a tall glass of what I would assume was a Long Island iced tea. Her dark blonde hair was pulled up into a messy bun and she was wearing a black bikini. The suntan oil was still on her skin and she looked as if she'd just come inside from tanning.

"Thanks, Kay Kay but you have to hide that shit from Drake. Whoever has the double doors open on the balcony up there tell them to close the damn things or they can pay the fucking electric bill," he replied and then glanced at me not waiting on her response. "Come on," he said.

I followed him through the open entrance, straight down a wide hallway that led into a large open living room. It had two levels. I could see on the lower level there was a massive white U–shaped sectional sofa that set in the middle of the room with a couple I didn't recognize sitting closely on the far-right side talking. There was no one else down there but them. I lifted my gaze to the vaulted ceilings and exposed wooden beams. Ceiling fans that hung down from the top seemed to be on high speed but I wasn't sure they did much good in a room this size. The entire back wall was floor-to-ceiling windows. I could see a few people out on the back deck. The sun would be setting soon and the view outside was going to be beautiful. I understood why everyone would want to be outside.

A well-stocked bar set off to the right of the first level of the room, once you were completely inside and could see it. In front of the bar itself sat three stools. The brunette that Drake had brought to Signed Sips was sitting on the middle stool, wearing a black zebra print bikini. I was overdressed in my blue sundress.

The guy behind the bar making a drink was not Drake, but it was clear she was flirting with him. The guy noticed us and grinned.

"Rio, where've you been?" he asked, then ran his hand through his shaggy dark blond hair.

"Work," he replied. "When did you get in town?" Rio asked, and I followed him as he walked over to the bar.

"This morning. Packed up the rest of my shit from Baylor Friday and headed this way, but I had a stop to make yesterday," he said.

"You're the girl from the coffee shop," the brunette said and I nodded. She then turned back to the guy behind the bar and said, "she makes a fab cappuccino."

"I'll remember that," he replied, his brown eyes now focused on me.

"Benji, this is Henley, Henley this is Benji," Rio said by way of introduction. "He's Drake's older brother by one whole year and the academic of the family."

I could see the resemblance now. They had the same facial features minus the eye color. Benji's were brown.

"Where are you from, Henley?" Benji asked.

"Chattanooga," I replied simply. I seriously doubted he wanted a full rundown.

"Here for the summer?" he asked me.

"I think," I replied because I wasn't sure when I would leave.

"Summer girl," he replied with a chuckle.

"Not what you're thinking," Rio said then and Benji raised his eyebrows and shifted his gaze back to me.

"I wish I could stay for the summer," the girl pouted and leaned forward just enough for her cleavage to be on display.

"You want a drink?" Rio asked me then and I almost said no when I decided having something to hold in my hand may make me feel less awkward.

"Sure."

Benji held his arms out wide. "We've got it all. What's your poison?" he asked dramatically.

"Uh, club soda?" I asked and his face fell.

"Please tell me you want Titos with that," Benji replied.

I shook my head no.

"I'll get it," Rio said and went around the bar to start making my drink.

"So, she's your DD. I get it," Benji said as if it made sense. "Pops making you ride with a DD after the last DUI? Or does he know? Saul said he handled it. Did someone leak it to the old man?"

Rio shook his head but said nothing. Benji shrugged and turned his attention back to the brunette. "You need another?" he asked her. "I'm about to head out to the deck. I need some salty air."

The girl jumped down off her stool. "I'm good," she said, ready to go with him it would seem. "I want to see the sunset."

His gaze shifted back to me and he smirked then picked up his drink. "See y'all outside," he said before walking around the bar.

Once they were gone, Rio slid the club soda across the bar. "Guess you know why I had to be bailed out of jail now," he said with a crooked grin. "Not my best moment."

It didn't sound like it was his only moment either but I didn't point that out. I took a drink of the soda and he reached into the ice bucket and pulled out a bottle of beer.

We walked down the three steps to the second level of the large room and Rio didn't even glance over at the couple on the sofa. He kept walking toward the doors leading outside to the deck. I wished I had taken one shot of vodka in my soda now. It would have relaxed me enough for this. There were at least ten people from what I could see out there and I was going to have to meet several of them and face the one who wouldn't be happy I was here.

The door hadn't even closed behind us when my eyes found Saul, leaning against the railing with his gaze locked on me. I quickly looked away from him, now more nervous than ever. Rio, however, walked directly to the one person I was trying to avoid. I wanted to grab his arm and pull him back then beg him to go talk to anyone else out here. Anyone. I did not care.

Now that we were outside I could see that the railing Saul was leaning against had an opening that went down to a second deck with a swimming pool. The pool had an unobstructed view of the beach. I was surprised the majority of the people weren't enjoying the pool.

"Henley!" Drake's voice called out and I found him sitting on a lounge chair with a different brunette in his lap. I wondered if he had asked her about blow jobs yet.

I lifted my hand in a wave, wishing we had walked in his direction instead. Unfortunately, we had already arrived just a few feet in front of Saul. Forcing myself, I shifted my gaze back to Saul and took a drink of my club soda, hoping I appeared calm.

"Didn't know you two knew each other," Saul said then took a drink from the bottle in his hand.

"We met today," Rio explained.

"Hmmm," was his response as he glanced over toward the far right of the deck. "Shelby came with some girl Drake invited. You two done?"

Rio shrugged. "It wasn't serious."

Saul turned his attention back to me and studied me a moment. I stared directly back at him, not about to let him know how uncomfortable this was for me. Whatever it was Rio had to tell me about my gran better be worth this. I had told myself I would stay clear of Saul and Drake, yet here I was.

"Here," Rio said and held out his hand toward Saul. Saul looked down at what Rio was holding then back up at Rio. "Take it. Pops is already mad enough."

Saul reached out and took a roll of bills from Rio's hand. "Why'd you tell him?" Saul asked.

Rio shrugged. "Just did."

Saul scowled and shook his head then took another drink.

"He would have found out anyway," Rio said.

"Yeah and maybe next time you'll fucking walk," Saul replied.

"I guess I will," Rio agreed.

Saul looked at me as if he were going to say something then shifted his gaze to the waves and took another drink. He didn't seem angry that I was here and I wondered if I had misunderstood his warning. "She's not wearing a swimsuit. You two not gonna swim?" he asked.

Rio hadn't mentioned swimming and I was very thankful for that.

"I'll be back later when it thins out," Rio said, surprising me. We were leaving? That's all I had to do? Why did I have to come with him for that?

"How's the job?" Saul asked then and I realized he was talking to me. His clear blue eyes were again locked on me and I wished they weren't.

"Uh, it's good," I replied.

"Haven't seen you at the Hendrix. Job must be keeping you busy," he said, still watching me too intensely.

The way he said it made me feel guilty for not going to visit Lily again, but I didn't know the woman. Gran had not asked me to befriend her. I had no reason to feel guilty. Yet with his clear blue eyes staring at me, I felt as if I had failed the lady somehow.

"Yeah, it has," I said finally.

He said nothing but then he didn't take those eyes off me either. In the light from the setting sun, they stood out even more and drew you in.

"Let's go for a walk," Rio said and I tore my gaze from Saul's to look up at him. I managed a nod and he gave Saul one last look before walking past him and toward the stairs that led down to the beach below.

"Where are you taking her, Rio? She was my friend first!" Drake called out.

"We will be back later," Rio replied then shook his head. He leaned closer to me. "Be careful with that one. Don't take him seriously," he whispered.

Almost the same words Saul had said to me. I glanced back at Saul then but the girl who I knew now was named Fleur was standing in front of him with her arms around his neck. I quickly looked away and headed down the stairs.

We said nothing while we took off our shoes and left them there at the bottom of the stairs. I fell into step beside Rio and wondered how long we were going to walk and if this was where I got my answers about Gran and the tool boxes.

"Saul and I moved here about the same time. Neither of us had grown up here and we were outsiders together."

I waited silently for him to say more. When a few moments passed and he said nothing, I thought about just asking him about the tool boxes.

"When I was sixteen, my mom decided she had lived enough life. I found her, but she knew I would. No one else lived there with us. All she left behind was a note apologizing for my life and a lot of bills she couldn't pay. My pops came to get me that day. We lived about five hours from here in a town called Sumiton. Before that we had lived in Atmore and before that it was Pelham. Mom would meet a man then things would go badly and we would pack up and move without a warning. This town, it's the longest I've ever lived in one place. And Saul, he's the longest friendship I've ever had."

My heart hurt as I listened to Rio's story. I didn't understand why he had chosen to tell me all of this, but I was going to listen. He needed someone to, it seemed, and he had chosen me.

"I never knew my dad. My mom got pregnant when she was eighteen and he wasn't interested in being a father," he said.

"I didn't know mine either," I told him. Although my life with my mother may have been hard, it was not as awful as what he had suffered.

"I know," he replied.

I stopped walking and stared at him confused by his response. "You know?" I asked.

He stopped a few feet in front of me and turned around to face me. "Yeah. I do."

EIGHT

It was one of those moments when so many thoughts hit you at once and you had to wade through them to decide which one was the most important or made the most sense. I stared at Rio with the setting sun behind him and the waves crashing on the shore and tried to figure out a link between tool boxes, his pop, him, his mother, and me. Things that I knew were not possible crossed my mind, but in the end, I simply asked, "How did you know that?"

He sighed then and his shoulders rose and fell with the action. He looked out over the waves instead of at me, as if he needed to gather his thoughts. I waited patiently, but it also gave my mind more time to make up possibilities that I didn't want to believe.

"I found a box of letters about a year ago in the attic. They were mixed in with other things like concert tickets, a dried rose, a silver ring with a small stone in it, and a piece of torn fabric. The box had been my mother's. She had several shoe boxes stuck in the attic at my grandparents' house. They were full of her memories. I read the letters. All of them. It told me more than I had ever known about my mom and my father." He shifted his gaze back to me.

"Majority of the letters were ones written to my mom from my father their senior year of high school. They weren't lengthy or very informative. Mostly just the guy responding to whatever letter my mom had left him. It was their method of texting it seemed. Anyway, the last three letters were from someone else. A girl, younger than my parents. She was a sophomore from what I read and the letters were not meant for my mom. She was writing them to a guy. I am assuming was my father, but she never addresses him by name in the letters. How my mom has them I don't know. What I do know is the girl was scared and she was pregnant and it was this guy's kid. The girl signed the letters *Lyra.* I found my mom's senior yearbook and looked up a Lyra in the tenth grade. There was one. Lyra Warren." He stopped talking then.

I said nothing. I wasn't sure what all this meant or if I was connecting the dots correctly. It was more complicated than I had first assumed. When a moment passed and he said no more, I knew he was waiting on me.

"You think your mom had the letters my mom wrote because my mom had written the letters to your mom's boyfriend?" I asked to clarify things.

Rio nodded.

"I don't even know my dad's name. My mother wouldn't even talk about him."

"My mom wouldn't either. However, in the letters she calls him, Rebel. There is no Rebel in the senior class that year. I can only assume it was a nickname," Rio explained.

"How did your father die?" I asked then, wondering if this would link up our stories.

"Drug overdose," Rio replied.

"Mine was a motorcycle accident," I told him.

Rio didn't look convinced. He gave me a sardonic smile. "And you believe that?"

"Do you believe yours died of a drug overdose?" I shot back.

"Nope. My mom lied to me all my life about my father and that was if I could get her to answer my questions."

We stood there silent for a few moments. I didn't know what to think about this or the letters. I wanted to see the ones my mother had written. I wanted to show them to her. Make her explain them. Both Rio and I needed some honest answers.

"I spent a year researching. I found very little. My grandparents shut down whenever I ask them anything. The photos I found of my mom when she was in high school all have the guy that would have been in the photo cut out. There is nothing in the yearbook or my grandparents' attic that tells me the name of my father. The only thing I managed to do was find out who your mother was, that her mother still lived in town, and that your mother did have a daughter my age. When Drake mentioned you living in your grandmother's house, I had started thinking up ways I could meet you. Then you come walking into the market with tools for my pop. I just, I don't think it was a coincidence. I think it was orchestrated," he said.

I stared at him a moment and wondered if he was right. Had Gran done this? Had she known? Was this a secret my mother had kept from me and if she had kept this from me then that meant... I had a brother.

"I don't." I shook my head. "I don't think Gran would have kept the fact I had a half brother from me my entire life"

Rio shrugged. "Maybe not but if she had and she'd done it at the request of your mother then wouldn't it make sense for her at her death to make sure you found out?"

There was one simple answer to that. "Yes." Because Gran would want me to know. This could very well have been her way of putting me in the right place to make connections in hopes that the truth came out. A truth she wanted me to know. A truth I deserved to know.

"How do we find out who this Rebel is?" I asked.

Rio shrugged. "I don't know. I was thinking there might be answers hidden away somewhere at your grandmother's. I've exhausted my grandparents' house."

I inhaled deeply and exhaled before running my hand over my face. This was a lot. So much of it made sense, yet so much of it seemed unlikely.

"Can I see the letters? Just the ones my mom wrote?" I asked him then.

He nodded. "Yeah. We can start there."

We. There was a *we* to this. We both wanted answers we had never gotten from our mothers. Yet, what if the secrets were there for a reason? To protect us? Should we dig into something we might not want the answers to?

Gran had sent me there. Rio was right about that. She had sent me to take tool boxes to Lloyd. Had she been hoping a connection like this one would happen? If she wanted me to know the truth then it couldn't be that bad. Right?

"Okay, yeah. That's where we will start," I finally said.

"Sun has almost set. It'll get dark soon and the crabs will be out. Want to walk back to the house. The crowd will either have thinned or moved inside. Depends on Saul's mood," he said as he started walking back that way before I could even answer.

I fell into step beside him and even though my mind should be turning with all this new information, instead I was thinking of someone else. "Why does it depend on Saul's mood?" I asked.

Rio chuckled. "Because it is Saul's house. Drake and I pay rent. Everyone will gauge Saul's mood before deciding to stay or not. Typically he's the first to leave a party."

I had no reason to be so intrigued by Saul but hearing he owned that house only made me more curious. If he could afford a house like that then why did he drive an old beat-up truck? "How does he afford that house?" I asked bluntly.

Rio shrugged and for a moment I thought he was going to say nothing. I was being nosey and I understood if his shrug was the only response I would get. "That's Saul's story to tell," he said finally.

I said nothing more and we walked back in silence. My thoughts finally moved from Saul back to the letters that could possibly lead to information about my dad… and Rio's. Was it possible he was my brother? The idea seemed so insane I didn't even take it seriously. But what if? How would that feel? And did my mother know?

If Rio was my brother and my mom knew about him, I wasn't sure I could forgive her for not telling me.

The pool and deck appeared empty from down on the sand. Rio glanced up and then back at me. "Saul must have been done," he said with a smirk then headed for the stairs.

I slipped back on my sandals, after dusting the sand from my feet, and followed him up the stairs. Rio had reached the top step when he said, "Run them off already?"

Saul was sitting in one of the teak double lounge chairs with a bottle in his hand. His gaze was on the crashing waves, but he turned his head in our direction at Rio's question.

The moonlight cast shadows, making it hard to see his face clearly. "Drake called a poker night. Most are inside around the table," he said.

"Ah, should have expected that with Benji back in town," Rio replied. Then he glanced down at me. "You any good at Texas Hold 'Em?"

"I've never played," I replied, hoping he didn't want me to go learn.

"Mind if I go sit in a few hands?" he asked.

I didn't mind at all, but I also wanted a ride home. The reason I had agreed to come tonight was done. Staying here in a house that belonged to a guy that did not want me around didn't sound like a good time. Telling him all of this with Saul watching us, however, was difficult.

"Uh," I replied, trying to decide how to word this.

"You can keep me company," Saul said and then put a cigarette I didn't know he had to his lips.

I stood there unsure what to say.

"Great, I'll be back after I take some of Drake's money," Rio said and gently patted my upper back before walking toward the door. He was just going to leave me out here. Alone. With Saul.

NINE

"I'll put it out if you don't like the smoke," Saul said when I made no move.

I shook my head. "No, it's okay. I don't mind," I replied and unable to help myself added, "But those things can kill you."

I wasn't sure if that was a smile or a smirk on his face from where I stood. The shadows made it hard to see.

"I've heard something about that," he replied then waved the hand holding his beer at the padded lounge chair connected to his. "I don't bite. For the most part."

I couldn't continue to stand here and be awkward. Walking over to sit beside him, however, was difficult. I managed to appear as if he didn't make me nervous or at least I hoped I did. Taking the seat beside him, I stretched out my legs in front of me and crossed them at the ankles. All the while giving myself an internal pep talk.

"How long are you staying in town?" he asked me.

I didn't want to explain the list Gran had left me to him. "For the summer, I think."

He didn't respond to that for a few moments, so we sat in silence. He might have been waiting on me to say something more but what did one say to a guy who you were aware didn't want you at his house?

"You're nervous around me," he said finally. He didn't sound amused when he said it. He didn't sound anything. It was a simple statement.

"It's your house and you've made it clear you don't want me around your friends," I replied honestly. If he was going to bring it up, then I was going to put it out there.

"Yet you're here," he said then turned his head to look at me, as if challenging me to respond to that as quickly as I had the last.

"Rio invited me," I replied.

"And you came."

I nodded. "Yeah, I did." Because what else could I say?

"Drake ask you for a blow job yet?"

The way he so casually said the word *blow job* caught me off guard. I let out a short laugh. "Yeah, he mentioned it."

Saul took another pull from his cigarette. "Figures," he replied.

"Does he ask all females that?"

"Just the ones that are breathing," Saul said and cut his gaze back to me with a half-smile on his lips.

"Glad I made the exclusive list then," I replied.

Then he laughed. It was a low, deep laugh, but it made me feel all tingly inside. I'd made him laugh. I wish it didn't feel so nice but it did. He wasn't just unattainable; I didn't want to attain him either. He was nothing like Will. Saul was not the security I longed for and missed so terribly.

A door opened and I turned my head to see the blonde from the red convertible. Her hair was piled in a messy bun on top of her head with tendrils hanging down, yet she still looked stunning. I looked nothing like that with my hair in a bun. The short white dress she was wearing hung off one shoulder and highlighted her golden tan.

She didn't say anything at first, just stared at me as if she were measuring me up. Did she think I was some sort of threat to her? Her eyes finally shifted from me to Saul. In the darkness, I couldn't read her expression and I wished I could. I needed to know if I should exit the situation swiftly or not.

"I'm lonely," she said and moved from the doorway to saunter toward us or just him.

"I thought you left," he replied and I glanced over at him to see he was taking another drag from his cigarette.

"Just to take a shower and change," she replied as she reached the end of his lounge chair then moved to crawl on top of him. It was seductive and I felt in the way.

Saul appeared amused, but he said nothing as she straddled him. He seemed to welcome her body and closeness. There was a small tug inside I knew was jealousy, but it couldn't be over Saul. It was just I missed having someone. I missed touching and being touched. I watched as he put his cigarette out before placing his hand on her thigh. I decided it was time for me to go now.

"I think I'll go see how Rio is doing with the uh… game," I said as I stood up.

Neither of them said anything and I didn't look back at them again for fear of what I might see. If they were going into full on make-out mode I didn't want that image in my head. I feared that something deep inside me might defy my belief that I wasn't jealous of the blonde because she had Saul. I was too smart to want someone like Saul. I had the best once. I would never want less. I made my way to the door and just as I was about to walk through, his voice made me pause.

"Nice talking to you, Henley," Saul called out and I managed a nod but didn't look back at him before hurrying inside. Finding Rio wouldn't be too hard because I could hear voices and I followed the sound. There was an arched door to the left of the bar and on the other side, there was a large round table with several guys around it. I took in the scene and wondered what I needed to do to get back to Gran's.

Rio didn't even notice I had walked into the room as he studied the cards in his hand. I hated to ask him to leave for me, but I was done with this evening. It was Drake that looked up and locked his gaze on me, his mouth slowly spreading into a smile.

"I didn't know you were still here. Hell, I'd have stopped playing cards if I'd known," he said in his thick southern accent. Then he winked at me and put his cards down on the table. "I think I'm gonna call, fellas," he said.

I watched as he stood up and stretched then picked up his beer. Not sure what to do with this I glanced at Rio who raised both his eyebrows. I wasn't sure if that was a warning, reminder of what he'd told me about Drake, or a question. I didn't have time to think it through before Drake was at my side.

"Where've you been hiding, sugar?" he asked me.

"Uh, I was outside," I replied then glanced back at Rio who was now focused on his cards again.

"Drake, you promised me you'd go swimming with me when you were done!" the brunette from the coffee shop said in a pouty voice.

He ignored her and leaned closer to me. "Come with me," he whispered and then I felt his hand touch the lower part of my back as he moved me toward the door with him. I went, but I wasn't completely sure if it was a bad idea or not.

"Where are we going?" I asked him.

He shrugged and led me into the living area. "I have no fucking idea. I just wanted to get out of there. Too many folks."

I glanced out at the deck to see Saul and the blonde were still there and it appeared that they were busy doing something other than talking. That was exactly what I didn't want to witness. Drake noticed it too.

"Looks like the deck is taken," he said then took a drink of his beer. "Damn Fleur is a parasite."

Frowning, I glanced back out at the deck. It seemed to me that Saul was enjoying himself although it bothered me, just a little. It shouldn't and I knew it. I barely knew Saul and sure, I was attracted to him or to his physical appearance. Like in a way one would be attracted to a movie star. That made me feel slightly better about the knot in my stomach at seeing him and Fleur kissing among other things.

What bothered me more than my reaction to Saul was the way Drake spoke about females. It was harsh. I'd heard him do it at the coffee shop with the brunette and now calling Fleur a parasite was just cruel. His charismatic smile and the confident way he carried himself was tarnished with the offensiveness of his words. I didn't know Fleur, but she wasn't doing anything Saul didn't want her to do. There was no need for Drake to get nasty.

"You should work on how you talk about females. Especially to other females. Because any girl worth her salt won't give a guy the time of day if he's trashing another girl," I said the words before I could think it through. I didn't regret them though.

Drake smirked. "Trust me, sugar. They give me the time of day."

"Did you miss the part where I said worth her salt? Because a girl worth spending time with doesn't like hearing other females brought down," I replied and stopped walking, pulled away from his hand on my back then put my hand on my hip. The attitude had been ignited and I was ready to give him a lesson.

Drake looked at me, his eyes wide with surprise or amusement. I wasn't sure which one. I was, however, positive I did not care.

"I like it," he said then grinned and shook his head. "You're different."

I started to say something more when Rio walked into the room. My eyes met his and he looked from me to Drake. "Ready to go?"

I nodded. He had no idea just how ready.

TEN

Waking up at four in the morning to bake the items for the shop, then dropping them off after a late night hadn't been easy. I had slept very little when I finally got in bed last night. One would think I had lain awake thinking about all Rio had told me and I did at first. However, my thoughts had ended up on Saul and our brief conversation.

Which was why I had gone back to bed and fallen asleep quickly after taking the baked goods to Hillya this morning. When the roar of a lawn mower right outside my window woke me up only thirty minutes later, I was not happy. I was far from it. One could say I was furious. Lack of sleep is not something I handle well.

Covering my head with the extra pillow on the bed didn't help muffle the sound and I finally growled in frustration and got up. Stalking to the door, I slipped on my fuzzy pink house shoes and swung open the door with more force than necessary. Whoever was outside cutting grass at this hour should be shot. This was ridiculous. People were sleeping.

It wasn't until I was down the stairs and on the sidewalk headed toward the grassy part of Gran's yard that I saw the truck. The blue Ford truck that seemed to taunt me with its presence. Was this a joke? Turning, I looked at the cause of my interrupted sleep.

Saul was wearing a cowboy hat and pushing a red lawn mower in my gran's yard. He lifted his hand and saluted me but did not stop his noise-making machine. The white tank he was wearing should be as illegal as his cutting grass this early in the morning. It clung to his skin from the humidity and sweat, making his muscular chest even more pronounced. I forgot my anger for a moment while I took in the sight of his arms and the way they flexed as he worked.

The sound cut off and my eyes snapped back up to his face. Saul had pushed the hat back on his head and was wiping his face with a towel. I hoped that meant he hadn't noticed me staring at him. Although I was sure he was used to it. You didn't look like that and not get ogled daily. It was part of his penance for being beautiful.

I remembered why I was out here and tried to get my anger ramped up again before he made his way over to me, if that was what he was going to do. I was already getting a damp sheen of sweat on my body from just standing outside in this humidity and heat. Why was it so hot so early here?

Saul stepped around the mower and began walking in my direction. The jeans he was wearing were ripped and hung on his hips just enough to be sexy. Although I was positive he could be wearing a pair of khaki pants and a polo and still appear sexy. It wasn't the good ole boy way he dressed that made him visually appealing. That was all genetics.

I tried to remember how good the bed had felt when he'd so rudely woke me up.

"You need something?" he asked me and squinted from the sun shining in his eyes. He reached up and pulled the hat forward until it shaded his face.

"It's eight in the morning and you're cutting Gran's grass," I stated the obvious.

He nodded. "Yeah," he agreed.

"Why are you cutting Gran's grass?" I asked him since he wasn't going to elaborate.

"I always cut her grass," he replied.

Frustrated I sighed and put a hand on my hip. "I'm not Gran. I didn't ask you to cut the grass."

He studied me a minute. "Were you going to cut it?" he asked.

I hadn't thought about it. The grass was fine when I got here and cutting grass had never been something I gave much thought. "I don't know," I shot back. "But I do know I was asleep and now I am not."

Saul ran a hand through his curls. I tried very hard not to get distracted by that. "Don't you have a job?" he asked me.

"YES, I have a job and I was up at four this morning baking for that job. This is my day off, so when I finished delivering the items to the shop I came back home to sleep!"

He didn't say anything for a minute and I wondered if he was going to apologize or if he even should. Did he expect me to pay him for cutting the grass? That was another issue if he did. I hadn't hired him to do it.

"Did you take it all to the café?" he asked me.

Confused, I frowned. "What?"

He glanced up at the front door. "Is there some of your baked goods inside?"

I followed his gaze then looked back at him. "Uh, yes," I replied because there was an entire banana loaf I hadn't been pleased with its appearance.

"I'll stop mowing if you'll feed me."

Again I stood there confused. "What?" I repeated.

"I'm hungry. You give me food and I'll finish mowing later today when it's fucking hot as the surface of hell out here," he said.

I did not want him in the house and I did not want to feed him, but I was southern. I couldn't be rude. It was in my blood to feed a man when he asked. How annoying.

"I didn't hire you," I told him because that was something I could be rude about.

"I know. I wasn't doing it for you," he replied.

He was doing it for my gran? He hadn't said it but neither of us needed him to clarify. There were several things I did not like about Saul, but this wasn't one of them. Whatever the reason he felt he needed to keep mowing my gran's yard after she was gone, said more about him than his faults did.

"Fine. Come on up to the porch and I'll give you an entire loaf of banana bread," I told him and began walking back to the stairs.

He smirked. "You're not going to invite me in?"

I didn't stop and look back at him. I simply said, "Nope." Just because he was good to my gran and even after her death he was mowing her lawn did not mean I felt charitable enough to ask him to come inside. We weren't friends and I wanted to go back to bed.

When I reached the front door, I glanced back over my shoulder. "Milk or coffee?" I asked.

"Whole milk?"

"I have low-fat oat milk," I replied with a smile.

"Coffee," he said then and for some weird reason, I enjoyed the fact I didn't have the kind of milk he would prefer. Lack of sleep made me testy. I was going to blame it on that. Besides my less than eight hours of sleep was now completely his fault. Last night he'd been in my head and wouldn't get out, and this morning, he'd been cutting the grass in a freaking white tank.

Opening the door, I walked inside and when I turned to close it, I saw him walk over and sit down on the swing. I hoped he wasn't going to sit out there and eat. I was making this meal to go because he needed to go. I needed for him to go. If he didn't, I would end up doing something stupid like bringing him a plate and asking if he needed creamer for his coffee.

I started a pot of coffee then I wrapped up the banana bread in foil and placed it in a paper bag I had from the shop. Only twice did I glance out the window while doing this. Both times Saul had been sitting in the swing looking toward main street. I was glad he hadn't lit a cigarette while on Gran's porch. I didn't want the smell of cigarette smoke on her patio furniture.

Once the coffee was done, I poured it into a thermos and then put two napkins in the paper bag before picking it up and heading for the door. I hadn't tasted the bread, but I was sure it was good. The uneven way it had risen was why I hadn't taken it to Hillya. I wanted it to look appealing not warped when she put it in the bakery display case.

Saul shifted his gaze to me when I stepped outside and then stood up as I held out the bag and thermos to him. "Here you go," I said, not moving in his direction. He needed to walk to me to get it then he could keep walking until he was in his truck.

The amused grin on his face said he knew exactly what I was doing. He stopped in front of me and took the bag and thermos. "Thanks," he said.

"You're welcome," I replied, wishing I had said nothing at all.

"Sorry I woke you," he then said.

He was still damp with sweat and I felt a pang of guilt at having acted the way I did. He'd been mowing the lawn. He was right; I wasn't going to mow the lawn. For starters, I didn't know how to mow a lawn or how to start the lawn mower up and did it use gas? I should be thanking him. My pride wouldn't allow that though.

"I'll be back later today to finish up," he said then turned and left with the bag and thermos.

As he walked away, I could hear Gran's voice in my head saying, "It don't fix a thing if you treat others the way they treat you, Henley. Only kindness can fix bullshit."

I went back inside and closed the door before replying to the voice in my head.

"Some bullshit is better left alone, Gran."

ELEVEN

It was time I did the next item on the list. I wouldn't get another chance until next Sunday. Besides, Saul would be back and I didn't want to be here for that. That being the case, it also meant Saul would not be at the Hendrix working and if I stopped by to visit Lily then there would be no chance I would run into him.

The photo album filled with trips Gran had taken with a group of ladies called the Southern Mamas was in my back seat and after I finished visiting Lily, I was to take it to a woman named Wanda. I assumed Wanda was one of the Southern Mamas and Gran wanted her to have the photos. It seemed like an easy enough request.

Getting the visit with Lily done first would ease my guilt of not stopping by sooner, so I chose to get that done. The elevator and hallway leading to her door was as impressive as it had been on my last visit. How my gran had become friends with this lady still baffled me. She was definitely not one of the Southern Mamas. I could not imagine this woman on a bus traveling cross country with women twenty plus years older than her, singing church hymns to pass the time.

I rang the doorbell and waited. At least two minutes passed and I decided to try one more time. After another minute passed, I was ready to leave when the door opened.

"Fuck," Saul cursed when he saw me standing there. "You're not her." He then left the door standing open and turned to walk away, leaving me there.

First of all, I should have been the one cursing. Secondly, what the heck was he doing here? I had come here to avoid him, yet here he was once again. I wasn't sure if I should leave or wait to see if Lily was here. I didn't have much more time to figure it out when he stopped and looked at me.

"Do you have a phone on you?" he asked me.

I nodded.

He walked back to me and held out his hand. "Let me see it," he demanded.

I wouldn't normally hand over my cell phone, especially to someone demanding I hand it over, but there was a panicked look in his eyes that had me reaching into my pocket, unlocking it and handing it over to him without question.

He dialed a number then put it to his ear while walking away from me again.

"Where are you?"

"Fuck that, Mom! Tell me where you are. I found the empty vodka bottles hidden in the closet."

"Mom, listen to me. Tell me where you are and I'll come get you."

"Okay."

He hung up the phone and turned back to me. "Thanks," he said and held the phone back out to me. I walked toward him and took it while so many thoughts were going through my head at one time.

The only thing I could manage to say was "Who is your mom?" Although I was pretty sure I had that one figured out.

He sighed and looked around the room as if he were looking for something. "Lily," he said then his gaze came back to me. "I gotta go," he then added. "You need to go too. Today's not a good day to visit her. Probably need to wait a couple weeks before you try again."

"What's wrong?" I asked although I had an idea since I heard him say something about empty vodka bottles in the closet.

"I have to go get her. It'll be tomorrow before I'm back to finish the lawn," he said and started walking toward the door.

I followed behind him as I put pieces together the best that I could. "Do you need help?" I asked and he stopped at the door.

He didn't turn around. "Not from you," he replied and then walked out into the hallway, leaving me to close the door.

His response stung but getting angry at him for, once again, being rude seemed wrong right now. Lily wasn't okay and he seemed to expect that. If Lily was an alcoholic and her son had to take care of her, my gran being friends with this woman seemed even more unrealistic than when I thought she was just some rich woman living in a penthouse.

"You had to use my phone for a reason," I said as the elevator door opened and I followed him inside.

He said nothing.

"She wasn't answering your calls," I continued. I wasn't sure this was the case. Maybe his phone was dead. I was guessing here.

He remained silent and kept his gaze fixed on the now closed elevator doors.

"She may be easier to handle if I am there," I said. I wasn't sure of this, but she seemed very fond of my gran and I was thinking like a woman here.

His shoulders rose and fell with another heavy sigh. He hung his head forward and for a moment, he didn't look like the guy from a coastal vacation commercial. He looked like a guy with the weight of the world on his shoulders.

"Fuck," he muttered. "Okay, you're right." When he lifted his head, he finally looked at me. There was no gleam in his eyes or smile on his lips. Only fear and weariness. My chest ached and emotion began to stir inside me. This wasn't new for him and I didn't know how long he had lived this over and over again. From the look on his face though, I would guess more times than he could count.

I didn't say anything more. He may not want me to help but he needed me. This wasn't about his hot and cold behavior toward me. At this moment, I didn't care about that. He needed help and I was possibly the only person he had that could be of use in this situation.

The elevator doors opened and he held out his hand for me to exit first. I did so then waited for him to join me in the parking deck. "Let's take my car. There's more room for all of us," I said, thinking about his truck.

"I have her keys," he said and pulled out a key fob. A sleek black Tesla's headlights came on that was parked in the reserved spot directly to our left. "I can't trust her with the keys," he said simply then headed for the car.

I followed him then had to pause when I couldn't figure out how to open the passenger door. Saul looked at me over his door as it slid up slowly. He said nothing but walked over and opened the door for me. "Get in," he said and I did as I was told. He closed my door behind me before going back to the driver's side.

We drove out of the parking deck and out the gate onto the main road. He didn't say anything and I didn't ask questions. When he turned right at the light and headed out of town and toward the Florida state line, I wondered exactly how far we were going. Lily didn't have access to her car so how far could she have gone? Did she have friends that would have come to get her? I wanted to ask, but Saul probably didn't want to answer my questions at the moment or ever.

"Lily loved Honey," he said.

I looked at him, waiting to see if he said more but he didn't.

"How did Gran know Lily?" I asked him since he brought the topic up.

"Honey brought snacks to the local AA meetings. Every other day, she was there with cookies, cupcakes, chips, and lemonade. About five years ago, Lily went on a bender and missed two meetings. Honey showed up at the gate of the Hendrix and I found her trying to talk security into letting her inside. She was there to check on Lily. She went with me to find her." He stopped and glanced at me a moment. "Like you."

Of course, my gran would take snacks and drinks to an AA meeting when she had never once needed to go to one herself. That was just like Gran. Always helping others. Always looking for ways to better the world. Always trying to "fix the bullshit."

My tears stung thinking of Gran, but I blinked them away. Crying was not what Saul needed right now. He needed me to be Gran. I would never be the woman Gran was, but I would do everything in my power to help him and Lily.

"I miss her," I said.

"Yeah, so do I," Saul replied.

We may never be friends and tomorrow he could go right back to disliking me and being rude, but right now, none of that mattered. Gran was still here fixing things it seemed. Even from the grave.

Saul crossed the state line and immediately turned left down a narrow street then pulled into the parking lot of a run-down bar. It was built from cement blocks with three flashing beer lights in the windows. The open sign blinked off several seconds then back on as if it wasn't sure it wanted to work or not. Only three cars were in the parking lot.

Saul glanced over at me. "If you don't want to go in there I understand," he said.

"I'm going, I just need you to open my door," I replied because there was no way I wasn't going to go inside and help him with Lily. That was why I was here. I just wasn't going in if he didn't get me out of this futuristic fancy vehicle.

His smile was grim and didn't meet his eyes. I waited until my door slid up and opened then climbed out to join him in the heat of the relentless summer sun. I fell in step beside him as we made our way to the solid red door that had Vern's painted on it in black.

Saul went to open the door then looked at me. "I'll go in first. Just stay right behind me."

I nodded, although I didn't see what kind of danger could come from a bar with only three vehicles outside. The dim lighting made it hard to see after coming from the bright sunlight. I squinted and hoped I didn't run into Saul or someone else while my eyes adjusted.

"My boy!" Lily's voice called out loudly over the country music playing on the speakers.

I followed the shadow of Saul's body as he moved toward the sound of his mother's voice. Even though I was struggling to see clearly, it was obvious Saul was tense, as if he was preparing for a battle. I did a quick glance around the room, but there was nothing threatening as the place was almost empty.

"Is that Henley?" She asked with a high-pitched slur. "You brought Henley!"

Finally able to see clearly, we came to a stop at the bar and Lily. Her glamorous appearance was gone and her cheeks appeared sunken in. The dark circles under her eyes were joined with bags, making her appear much older. The stench of stale cigarettes and whiskey wafted from her or maybe that was just the bar itself.

"Yeah, she's here to come bring you home. She came to visit and you weren't there," Saul told his mother in a gentle tone.

Lily sat her glass down and looked at me. "I wasn't there and you came," she said. "I'm so sorry." Tears began to well in her eyes and she shifted her gaze to Saul. "I should have been there. Honey would be so disappointed in me."

Saul put several large bills down on the bar and slid an arm around his mother's back. "Yeah, she would," he agreed.

That response caused Lily to break down sobbing and then she started repeating the words, "I'm sorry," over and over again. I wanted to assure her it was okay, but Saul ignored her and looked at me. "Lead the way," he said.

I did as he instructed and opened the door so he could walk her out.

"I just wanted a cocktail," she said to him and leaned heavy against him.

"That's all you ever want," he replied, "but you can't have one. You can't stop at just one."

"I didn't take anything," she said with a hopeful voice. "I didn't go looking for any."

"Good. One less thing to deal with," he replied.

When we got to the car, I studied the door, wishing I had paid closer attention when he opened it for me.

"Stand back," he said to me and then he reached forward to open it. He put Lily in the back seat then stepped back, so I could get in the front. Lily lay over in the seat until she was curled up on her side. She closed her eyes and didn't say anything more.

When Saul was in the driver's seat and driving back on to the main road, Lily began to lightly snore. "That was easy thanks to you," he said.

"I didn't do anything," I replied, not sure how my opening a few doors helped make it easy.

"You have no idea how ugly that can get. She saw you and she didn't turn on me. She didn't want to let you down. You aren't Honey, but she sees you and remembers."

I felt tears sting my eyes again. When Gran died, it had hurt. I'd felt completely alone in the world. She had been my rock in this life. What I hadn't realized was she had been other people's rock too. Her death had not only been hard on me, but it had been just as hard on others. Especially Lily… and Saul.

"How often does she do this?" I asked him.

"Longest she has gone clean and sober is ten months, three weeks, and a day," he said. "When I let my guard down and don't check on her daily, things can get bad. If left without someone to watch over her, she can end up on things worse than liquor. It takes three months or more in rehab when she starts with the pills or worse."

My chest was tight again with emotion I couldn't express. I sat there silently until Saul pulled into the parking deck at the Hendrix. After he parked her car, he turned to look at me. "I've got it from here. Thanks for your help," he said, before opening his door and getting out.

I waited until he had mine open and I got out wanting to do something more. Help him get her to the penthouse at least. It felt wrong just leaving him here like this.

When I didn't walk away, he ran a hand through his messy curls. "I need to do the rest alone," he said, understanding why I hadn't moved.

"Why?" I asked him because I disagreed. He needed help.

"Because, Henley. This is what I fucking do. Just go." It wasn't the cold pitch in his voice that sent me away; it was the warning glare in his eyes. He did not want me here.

By the time I reached my car, the tears were freely streaming down my face. Not because Saul sent me away but because it was all he knew. He didn't trust people enough to rely on them. He did it himself. Except when Gran came along. He hadn't been able to send Gran away.

TWELVE

I never made it to Wanda with the photo album. The rest of the day I had spent trying new recipes in hopes baking would make things better. It hadn't, but in the end, I had been distracted. Being back at work today was a relief. Hillya's great-niece, Emily, was visiting for the summer, and I had spent the morning training her to work the register. She was a year younger than me and just finished up her second year at Florida State.

Her hair was a deep shade of auburn and it made her pale skin appear porcelain. I would have hated her for that alone if I hadn't immediately liked her. She worked hard and had a good sense of humor. Something about her felt familiar but I couldn't place it. By lunchtime, we had bonded and by three when she got off work, we had planned a beach day the next time we both were free.

Hillya had sent me home after four because she was closing early today. I would be off again tomorrow, but then on Thursday, the store was hosting a book signing and would be open late. I was needed to work the bar that night. Hillya served red and white wine along with a signature cocktail at signings. This would be my first one and I was looking forward to it. I'd never been to a book signing before.

I texted Rio that I would be home and available after six tonight if he wanted to bring the letters over. When he texted that he would be there at seven thirty, I decided to head to the address Gran had left me for Wanda and get the album delivered. I smelled of baked goods and coffee, but I doubted Wanda would mind that.

The address led me to a nursing home and I sat in my car for several minutes after parking, staring at the building. I was vaccinated, but I wasn't sure what the protocol for visitors would be at a nursing home. I reached over and opened my glove compartment to takeout a mask. Although the world had slowly begun to become normal again, especially in the southeast, I kept a stash of masks for the places still requiring them.

I grabbed the album and headed for the entrance. There was a nurse at the door and the sign on the door clearly stated masks were required. I slipped it on and took my vaccination card from my purse to show her.

"I need to get this album to a Wanda Sellers. My gran passed away and she left instructions to bring Mrs. Sellers this album," I explained.

The nurse smiled. "Oh, Mrs. Wanda will love this. A visitor and a gift. Come right on in," she said as she pointed down the hallway. "You can find her right down there. Third door on the left. Room number fourteen."

"Thank you," I replied and headed down the hallway toward door fourteen. The resident of room eleven was sitting at her door holding a doll with brown curls and wearing a large wide smile. She was running her hand over the dolls curls and whispering something to it when she noticed me. Her head snapped up as if I was there to take her doll from her and she looked ready to defend the baby.

I smiled at her. "You have a beautiful baby," I said.

The lady's fearful expression vanished and she beamed up at me from her wheelchair. "Thank you. She looks just like her daddy," the lady replied.

"He must be very handsome," I told her.

She nodded her head vigorously. "Oh, he is! He'll be here to get us soon."

I held my smile and then waved at her before continuing on to door fourteen. It was across the hall and one door down from eleven. There was an older lady with pearls around her neck, white hair in a neat bob, and a yellow dress trimmed in white standing there observing me. I didn't know if this was Wanda Sellers or not. Although she was dressed as if she were about to go to church, she was much older than I expected. This lady had to be ten years older than my gran had been.

I stopped at her door with the album tucked under my arm. "Hello, I am looking for a Mrs. Wanda Sellers."

The lady looked me up and down. I suddenly felt as if I should have changed into something nicer than my work clothes. When her gaze met mine, she smiled. "You're Honey's granddaughter."

Relieved, I nodded. "Yes, I am." I wasn't sure how she could tell that, but I was glad I wasn't going to have to explain.

"He will be here soon! Keep a look out and you'll see him. The best-looking man in Alabama," the lady from eleven called from across the hall.

I glanced back to see her still beaming at me.

"Come on in my room. Gladys will continue to yell out crazy things if you don't. The rest of the place has learned to ignore her. Bless her she's been insane for a couple years now," the lady I was assuming was Wanda told me as she turned and walked into room fourteen.

I took a quick survey of the place and it reminded me of a bedroom from the fifties A chenille bedspread with blue and yellow flowers covered the bed. At the foot of it, there was a white lace shawl. Old photos in elaborate frames as well as newer photos sat everywhere. The lamp on the bedside table was made of white hobnail glass. It was similar to those I had seen only in antique stores. A wooden rocker with a crocheted blanket the same blue as was on the bed in the corner.

"It's not home, but I did my best to make it feel like I had some home here with me," the lady said.

I turned to look at her and she stood over by the door. "It's lovely," I told her and I meant it. This was nothing like the boring white bare walls I had imagined a room here to look like. I wondered then what room eleven looked like inside. If Gladys had decorated it.

"You are the spitting image of Honey when she was your age."

"You knew Gran when she was my age?" I asked her, suddenly very interested in what she had to say.

She let out an amused laugh and nodded. "Indeed, I did." She then took a step toward me ad held out her hand. "I see you have no idea who I am. I'm Wanda Sellers. I was Honey's eleventh grade literature teacher then years later, I became her friend."

I placed my hand in hers and the soft skin of her palm was cold as we shook hands. "It's nice to meet you, Mrs. Sellers. I'm Henley Warren."

Wanda released my hand and nodded her head. "Yes, I remember the day you were born. Your momma had left town and your grandmother was beside herself with worry. But Lord she was so proud of you. The pictures were always in her purse and she wouldn't let a soul pass her by without showing off her granddaughter to them."

I hadn't known that about Gran. My memories of her were sparse until I was about six years old. My mom started leaving me with her some during the summers.

"I often wished my mom had raised me here," I told Wanda.

Wanda gave me a sad smile. "Perhaps your life would have been different. The path you were given is yours to walk.

Wishing for a different path only hinders your success on the path you are on."

She even spoke like a literature teacher. "Yes, I guess it does." I took the album from under my arm. "Gran left me a list of some things she wanted me to do for her around the time she got sick. She thought, well, she wanted to be sure if she didn't survive Covid that I would handle things for her. This is on the list," I said as I held the album out to her. "She wanted me to give this to you."

Wanda took the album from me and held it in her hands for a moment before walking over to the rocking chair and sitting down. I stood there and watched as she opened it so very slowly, as if she already knew what was inside and thought it was something to be cherished.

She studied each page carefully before turning it. I wasn't sure if I should stay or go, but then I decided I would stay until she looked up and acknowledged me again. I wanted to tell her goodbye. After the fourth or fifth page, she sighed and smiled then lifted her gaze from the photos to meet mine.

Her smile was teary and I wondered what it was that made her so sad about the album. The ladies in it were younger than she was and she couldn't have been on the trips with them. Which made this all the more interesting.

"Thank you for making sure I got this. I didn't know she had these photos," she told me, but it still didn't explain why she cared about pictures from a trip my gran had taken with other people.

"You're welcome. I'm glad they mean something to you," I said, not willing to ask her questions and invade her privacy. If she had wanted me to know she would have shared it.

"Oh yes," she said, smiling fondly at the photos in her lap again. "Honey always knew of my love for Nancy. She never judged me or condemned me for my ways. Even when she was a young girl in school, I think she knew about my secret affair," she chuckled softly.

To keep my jaw from falling open in shock was a feat I deserved an award for. I stared at Wanda as she looked on at the pictures. I wasn't sure what to say or if I had understood her correctly. She was in her mid-eighties. She had to be. Her room looked like something decorated by every southern grandmother at the Baptist church.

"Nancy wasn't as young as your mother. Don't go judging me there. She was in her second year of college when I met her. I was fresh out of college and had my first real job teaching school. She had the most beautiful blonde hair and those dimples when she smiled. I think I fell in love with her the moment I met her. She loved me too, just not enough," she said sadly and glanced up at me.

"I too often wonder about the road I wished I had been given. The road that doesn't judge so harshly and allows you to love whomever you choose. I didn't have that road and neither did Nancy. She could never openly love me. She cared too much about what others would do and say. She was fragile. Although she never married either. I believe it was because her heart was taken and always would be." She paused then and I swallowed past the lump forming in my throat.

The world had been cruel to so many in the past. It still was at times, but things were changing. They had to... so people like Wanda could love freely.

"Nancy passed away five years ago. She had cancer. Although she had no children, she had a multitude of friends and family who loved her. She had her church and I believe that was what was most important to her. I understood and accepted it, but I loved her dearly." Wanda held up the album. "And now I have pictures. I had none but that one," she pointed to a faded polaroid photo of a girl that looked to be about my age smiling at the camera. It was in the most elaborate frame in the room, making it the most cherished photo in the room.

I quickly glanced at the other pictures and wondered who the children and the couples were if she had no husband or children of her own. The photos showed a life fully lived. It appeared as if she had led one of happiness.

"I may not have had a husband or children, but I taught school for over fifty years. I have more children than any one person could want. There were many I grew close to and I have ten godchildren and one great-godchild. Your mother is one of the ten. The day she was born, I gave her a silver spoon with her name and birthday carved in the handle. Then when you were born, I knitted you a pink blanket-"

"With white flowers," I finished for her. I still had that blanket. I had loved it dearly.

Wanda smiled at me and nodded her head. "That's the one," she confirmed. "I made my path the best that I could. That's what matters in the end. You don't get another path. Never forget that."

I moved then. I walked over to Wanda and bent down and hugged her. I felt robbed that I hadn't known her until now. "Thank you," I whispered and her hand came around and patted me on the back.

"Thank you, Henley Warren."

I let her go and stood back up. "I wish I had gotten to meet you before now."

She smiled. "Oh, child, you have met me before. I made you cheese and marshmallow sandwiches while you played in the sprinkler in my yard."

The memory of the redheaded lady with her polka dotted dress serving my gran ice tea on her back porch while I played in her yard came back to me. "That was you?" I asked then, wondering how many years it had been.

She nodded her head. "Yes. That was me."

"But we didn't come back again," I said.

She sighed. "When you were eight years old, I moved to Louisiana. I got a position as a professor at LSU. I needed to get away from the town and the life it had forced upon me."

"Oh," I replied, understanding full well her need to leave.

She looked down at her album again. "But when I retired there was no place I wanted to be but here. This is home."

I realized something standing in that lavender scented room filled with things from times gone by. My gran could have given this album to Wanda after Nancy's passing, but she held onto it. I wasn't sure why she did but I did know why she wanted me to be the one to bring it to her. This was Gran's way of making sure I met Wanda. She was teaching me things even after she had passed on. I thought of the rest of the list and wondered if more lessons were to come or even possibly a few revelations.

THIRTEEN

Rio had been sitting on the front porch swing when I pulled into my driveway. I had texted him when I left the nursing home. My visit had taken longer than anticipated. Wanda Sellers had ended up being more than an old lady I was to drop a book off to. I promised to come back and bring proper ice tea because the stuff they serve at the nursing home has no sugar in it, according to Wanda.

I headed to go up the stairs and stopped when I reached the top. "Sorry," I said although I wasn't sorry I had gone.

He shrugged. "You're just thirty minutes late," he held up a bag from the burger place in town. "Gave me time to eat dinner."

"Okay, well, want to go inside to do this?" I asked him and went to unlock the door.

He picked up a large 11 x 14 envelope and his burger bag. "Yep. Especially if you have some muffins or cookies."

"I have cupcakes I made yesterday as a trial. They are gluten, dairy and nut-free, but I think they turned out good.

The icing needs some work before I make them for the café," I said.

"I'll eat 'em," he replied, and I closed the door behind him.

"Make yourself at home. I will get the cupcakes and a couple bottles of water unless you like oat milk and want that instead."

He scrunched his nose. "I'll stick with the water."

"Thought so," I replied and went to make up a tray with the cupcakes and a few slices of blueberry loaf I had left.

"Can we go search the attic after you read these?" he asked, as I walked back into the room with the food and drinks.

"Sure. I've not been up there yet because I hate ladders, but I will toughen up."

He handed me the envelope then reached for a strawberry cupcake. "These look like a professional made them."

I shrugged. "Well they don't taste like it, yet."

Rio took a bite as I pulled the letters from the envelope. I wasn't sure what I was going to find out or if Rio was right in his way of thinking. What I did know was he was right about something. Gran's list wasn't a simple list of things she wanted done after she passed away. It was more than that.

As I was unfolding the first letter on the stack, yelling from outside caught my attention and my head snapped up to look toward the window.

"What the fuck?" Rio muttered, standing up and walking over to see what was going on.

I put the letter on the coffee table and followed him as another shout rang out.

"Dammit, psycho bitch," Rio said and started for the door.

"What is it?" I asked, hurrying after him and out onto the porch.

"Fleur," he said, heading down the stairs, and I realized then the red convertible was in the middle of the street two houses down and she was standing on the hood of it spinning in circles.

On the street in front of her stood Saul. He was the one who had been shouting. "Get DOWN, Fleur!" he yelled and she stopped spinning then threw her head back and laughed.

Rio was running down the street with his cupcake in hand toward Saul when I reached the bottom step. I couldn't figure out what she was doing or why they were yelling or why the car was parked in the middle of the street. But what concerned me most was where Lily was and if she was alone.

Rio reached Saul and he glanced at him then turned his head to look back in my direction. The sun was starting to set, but there was still plenty of light left to see his scowling face clearly. It was as if our day yesterday hadn't happened and we still didn't like each other.

"You don't love me!" Fleur called out then spun around again. I was starting to wonder why he didn't just get her off the car and that was when it moved. Both Rio and Saul jumped out of the way and I covered my mouth in horror. No one was driving the car, but Fleur was on the hood of it. Had she left the engine on and the car in neutral or in drive? Why would she do this?

"FUCK!" Rio shouted and his cupcake fell out of his hand onto the ground as he went to grab the driver's side door as Saul did the same with the passenger's side. I continued to stand there with my hand over my mouth. If Fleur fell off the car, it could roll over her, or she could bash her head on the asphalt, or she could break her neck…

And it was at that thought the first siren roared to life and turned down my street.

Fleur lay over the front window of her convertible then flipped head first inside the car, causing it to roll backward, even as the guys were holding onto it. The cop came to a stop and jumped out of his patrol car. I couldn't hear everything, but I did manage to get that Fleur was drunk and high.

With the officer's help, Saul was able to climb inside and put the car in park. Then Fleur was cuffed and taken to the cop's vehicle while she laughed about it. Saul talked to the officer and I saw him shake his head no. Two more cops arrived and the neighbors all seemed to be coming out onto their porches or front yards.

Long after Fleur was put into the back of the police car, Saul stood there talking to all three cops. Rio remained by his side and a few nosey neighbors made their way out to ask questions. When the first cop drove away, Rio and Saul began walking back toward Gran's house. Saul looked furious and Rio looked annoyed.

It was Rio who reached me first and then Saul turned toward Rio's Jeep and climbed in the passenger side. I said nothing, waiting for Rio to speak. A few neighbors were still outside looking our way. I felt like we were on display.

"I've gotta go," he said. "Saul needs a ride to the station to get Fleur bailed out."

"Oh," I replied, thinking maybe she needed to stay behind bars a little bit until she sobered up.

"Tomorrow?" he asked me.

I nodded. "Yeah, that's fine."

Rio glanced back at Saul who was sitting in the passenger seat with his head back and his eyes closed. "What is wrong with her?" I asked Rio, looking back at him.

"She's a fucking spoiled bitch who uses Daddy's money to get herself high when things don't go her way. Blames it on some shit that happened to her when she was younger. Saul won't talk about it. Anyway, he saves her ass when she does this shit. It's a damn cycle that's been going on for years. He's never loved her, they're more old friends than anything."

He was saving Fleur, just like he saved his mother.

Why would he want to be with a girl that had the same issues his mother did? Hadn't he learned from his mom that this may never end? His mom needed him right now and he was having to deal with Fleur.

"Don't judge him. He sends her away. She comes back after he's had time to get over it. Then this all over again. Remember he saved my ass twice when I did something stupid. I gotta give him a ride. You read the letters tonight. Tomorrow, we will go on our search."

I nodded and watched as he walked to his Jeep. When they pulled out of the drive, I headed back up the stairs and inside. I had letters to read and hopefully it would distract me from everything else.

FOURTEEN

I put the last letter down around midnight and stared at the pile on the coffee table. Rio was right about the Lyra who wrote the letters being my mom. I would know that handwriting anywhere. It was my mother's alright. Albeit a bit neater back then.

Whoever Rebel was that was the man who aided in my creation. I didn't doubt that. The way Rio's mom had written him, I was pretty sure Rebel was the only guy in her life too. There was a ninety-nine percent chance in my estimation that Rio was in fact my half brother. He had been sure of it when he took me out on the beach and told me, and now I could see why.

Proving this was going to be another issue. Although we could easily take a DNA test. Did those tell you who your father was? Or would it just tell us we were siblings? I had never had to think about this before and DNA tests weren't something I knew much about.

Gran's grandfather clock began to chime twelve and I knew I had to get in bed. Four in the morning would be here too soon. Yawning, I stood up and started toward the kitchen when a knock at the door caused me to yelp in surprise. Spinning around to see who had knocked, I froze when I saw Saul standing on the other side of the door. I stared at him a moment and he held my gaze.

Why was he here?

Slowly I moved to the door and battled with myself over if I should open it or tell him to leave through the glass. When I reached it, I already knew which side of me had won. It was the stupid side. I unlocked the bolt then the knob itself before turning it and opening it up.

"Can I help you?" I asked him, hoping to at least sound snippy since I had opened the dang thing.

"No," he replied and his short response was the reminder I needed to close the door back.

His hand flattened on the glass and stopped me before I could move. It was as if he had read my thoughts. Maybe he had that power too. He could look sexy in anything he wore, he could make girls do stupid things, he had the ability to sting you with one glance, why not read minds? Seemed feasible. If you were Edward Cullen at least. Yeah, I was getting delirious and needed to get some sleep.

"Can I come in?" he asked me.

"No," I replied.

He sighed. "Please," he added.

Damn, damn, damn, I was such a girl. I stepped back and opened the door wider but said nothing. I would let him say what he wanted then I would tell him to leave so I could go to bed.

Saul walked inside and stopped just a few inches from me. I closed the door behind him and waited. He had come here. I hadn't invited him. I did not have to make conversation or beg him to tell me why he was here. But he stayed silent.

"How is Lily?" I asked him. That was the only thing I cared about.

"Better, for now," he replied, but he didn't turn his head to look at me.

I wanted him to elaborate on that but decided I would go visit her myself and find out. He had brought me the gate key to get into his mother's penthouse but hadn't mentioned then Lily was his mom.

The longer he stood there not looking at me and not talking, my aggravation turned to anger. Why had he come here to act weird and say nothing? He didn't like me; he had made that clear. I knew now that the few times he had been nice to me was for my Gran's sake and not mine. I knew nothing about him but that he had an addict for a mom, but was also very wealthy, which was probably how he afforded a million-dollar home, and he had a girlfriend who seemed to be heading down that path as well.

"It's late, I have work in the morning, I don't know why you're here, but I need you to go," I told him.

He didn't move nor did he look at me.

Was he on something? Did he do drugs too? Was that another secret I didn't know about him?

"Saul, please leave," I said with more conviction and started to move to open the door back up.

His hand shot out so quickly I didn't see it until his fingers were wrapped around my wrist. It wasn't painful, but it was firm. "Don't. Please," was all he said.

Sighing in frustration, I tried to free my arm from his grasp, but he didn't loosen his hold. "Saul, if you're high, I can call Rio. He can come get you, but I am tired and I am done with this-"

"Rio," he said, interrupting me. "He was here. Two nights this week you were with him. You like him?" he asked, finally turning to look at me.

I stared at him completely baffled by this line of questioning. Was he here to warn me away from Rio too? Well tough luck because Rio may be his friend, but it was looking like he was my brother. I had greater dibs.

"Not your business," I said, pulling harder on my arm this time with no luck.

Saul groaned and muttered a curse word. "Just tell me. Do you like him?"

"Why does it matter?" I shot back. "Are you going to tell me to stay away from him too?"

"No," he said. "Rio isn't Drake."

His response surprised me enough to be still and stop pulling at my arm. Saul lifted his eyes and met mine. "Do you like him?"

I growled in frustration. Why did he care so much? "Again, not your business."

He turned then and he was facing me. Much too closely. He smelled of sunscreen and cigarettes. "Rio is my friend. My best friend," he said.

I waited for more and fought the urge to step back. He was too close.

"Then ask Rio," I replied.

"I want to know if *you* like Rio," he repeated.

"Why?" I shot back at him.

He took a step closer to me, his eyes hooded and hard to read. "Because, Henley, if you like Rio, it changes things."

"What things?" I asked confused.

"Fuck it," he muttered.

At that moment, it felt like slow motion, but it also happened so quickly I didn't have time to prepare. Saul's mouth was on mine and his hands were on my hips, pulling me against him. His hard chest pressed against my softer one and I was overwhelmed to the point my knees no longer felt very sturdy. I swayed slightly and one of his hands grabbed the back of my head to hold me there as his mouth opened over mine and I was tasting him. I was sure he could feel the pounding of my heart as I found myself holding onto his arms for support.

The warmth of his body and scent of sunshine on his skin was intoxicating.

The kiss was turning into something much more intense than two lips colliding. Everything inside me was humming with a pleasure I had never experienced. Clinging to Saul, wanting to get closer to him and not ever let go. All the anger, hurt and annoyance that had built up from his treatment of me vanished in the moment. I cared only about this.

Saul's hand slid down over my hip, and just as I thought he would touch more of me, he was gone.

I stumbled from the loss of his support as my eyes snapped open in confusion. My gaze met his and he looked to be in some sort of physical pain while I had been experiencing the exact opposite.

"I can't. This… we…. I can't." He said the words in a hoarse whisper before he turned and left the house. The firm click of the door closing behind him.

I stood there unable to move. My lips still tingling from the kiss, my head still reeling from all that had happened. My heart slightly damaged from a beautiful boy who was set on breaking me.

The next day I woke up at four, baked my items, delivered them, and tried to go back to sleep. When I couldn't sleep, I called my mom, listened to her complain about me wasting my summer, how I needed to move on with my life, how I was messing up my future, then I went for a walk on the beach. Rio didn't come over because he had to work an extra shift to pay off the bail money his pop had given him to repay Saul. I didn't feel like attacking another item on Gran's list. I wanted to believe it was my phone conversation with my mother that had gotten me in this funk, but I knew… it was because of Saul.

FIFTEEN

The line of women and a few men began forming outside Signed Sips around two in the afternoon. The book signing did not begin for another five hours. I hadn't known what was happening at first and thought the ladies outside were waiting to enter. When an hour had passed and the line had only gotten longer, I had asked Hillya what they were doing.

"They're here for the signing," she told me.

"But that's hours away," I replied confused.

"Yes, and the line will continue to grow. It's Colleen Hoover and she always brings a crowd. This will be our third summer to have her here. Last year, there were over three hundred in her line. We sold tickets this year. Each reader gets a drink of their choice, a slice of cake, and one of her new books to be signed for their ticket price. I had hoped it would lessen the number of people, but we sold three hundred and sixteen tickets."

My mouth dropped open in shock. This was going to be a long evening. "Do we have enough cake?" I asked.

Hillya laughed. "Yes. What do you think I've had Emily in the back doing all morning. She's slicing the cakes. I started making them yesterday morning. We have blueberry cream, cinnamon coffee cake, and lemon pound cake. There should be over four hundred slices when we are done. However, if you will go in the back and make up some of your banana loaf and chocolate cake, I will run the front. Having gluten and dairy-free options tonight will be good advertisement."

I glanced once more at the line of over twenty women and one man outside. "Do you think I should take them some water after I get the cakes in the oven?"

Hillya nodded. "That would be nice of you. Maybe take them some of the items in the bakery case that have been there since yesterday. We need to clear them out today anyway."

"Okay, I'll be back out in about thirty minutes," I told her and headed for the back. It had to be at least ninety degrees outside today and those people were out in the heat, waiting to meet an author and get books signed. I had never known there were readers that dedicated. I was looking forward to the evening more than ever now.

This was a distraction I desperately needed. I had barely gotten any sleep, woke up at four to bake, delivered the items, and stayed instead of going home like Hillya suggested to get some more sleep since it would be a late night. Saul was in my head and had been since he kissed me the other night.

I had compartmentalized him before. I didn't allow myself to think of him too much and I could shut it down. Until that kiss. It was as if my lips knew what I was thinking about and they would tingle from the memory. Saul had been an issue since day one, but now he had made it even worse. I was not here to develop feelings for a guy. Especially one who didn't feel the same.

My reasons for coming here had been deeper than that. I had to keep remembering why I came and stop thinking about Saul. His brooding was too much for me and his life was much darker than anything I'd ever experienced. I didn't need that kind of damage in my life. I was trying to fix me; Saul would do the opposite. I feared he could destroy me if I gave him the power.

"Oh thank God, please tell me you're back here to slice cake," Emily said as I walked into the kitchen.

"Afraid not. I have to make a couple banana loaves and a chocolate cake, but I promise I will slice them when they are ready," I told her.

Emily groaned. "Why would so many people come to get a stupid book signed? Just buy the damn thing on your phone and read it. Who needs to meet the author? Heck, I can't remember who wrote the last book I read."

Laughing, I began to get my ingredients and place them on the counter. Apparently Emily wasn't a big reader. I would guess her last book was one she had to read for a class. If she truly loved reading, she would remember the author's name. Now, the line forming outside was shocking to me, but I did find it cool. I just had never considered going to stand in line to meet someone before.

"Do you remember the last book you read and the author's name?" she shot back at me.

I grinned as I poured my ingredients into a bowl. "The Perfect Game by J. Sterling."

"Oh my God. Please don't tell me you go to book signings and wait in line for hours."

"No, I go to the library and pick out books, read them, return them, repeat," I told her.

Emily sighed. "I don't care much for reading."

"You haven't found the right book yet. When you do, it changes things. You're reading the wrong things," I explained.

"I'm reading what I have to read to pass my classes," she replied.

"Exactly. Why don't you get one of the books from the author coming tonight and try it out? Might be your thing," I suggested.

I glanced over at her while I stirred the batter. She did not look convinced, but she shrugged. "Maybe."

The rest of the afternoon, I ended up baking three of the banana loaves and two chocolate cakes, which came to fifty-eight slices. I took cups of water and baked goods to the thirty- seven people in line at four- thirty, and I made a dairy-free espresso martini for Hillya to try out. She had cases of red and white wine and her signature cocktail she was offering was an espresso martini. She just hadn't considered that those with dairy allergies couldn't have it. I gave her another option and she went and added it to the chalkboard menu.

By seven o'clock, the author was here and the line was almost at three hundred people. It wrapped around to the back of the building and then was separated into three sections. Hillya had hired some security to keep things safe and orderly out back. Per city ordinance, we could only have sixty people in the shop at a time. Mrs. Hoover was friendly but swift with each reader, making them feel special while they came up to the table but not letting them stay too long. She was obviously a pro at this.

I poured more white wine than anything, but occasionally, there was an espresso martini order. Three of those had been for the dairy-free martini. My banana loaf and chocolate cake had also been a surprise to those with allergies. I had heard several of the readers talking about the fact we had those options.

Twice Emily and I had been asked if we were sisters. I was surprised the first time, but after the second time a lady asked, I figured it had to be the pale skin. That and we did work well together.

Mrs. Hoover managed to get through four hundred readers in three hours. I was amazed. When she finally got to leave, we led her through the back and sent her off with a large bag of baked goods. She and her family were in town for a mini-vacation and we had enough slices of cake left to feed another hundred people.

Once the place was emptied out we began the clean-up. I was washing pans in the kitchen when Emily came running back there.

"HOLY HOTNESS, there is a sexy as hell guy asking for you out front. He came in and I told him we were closed and he said he was looking for you," she gushed.

I immediately thought of Saul, but why would he be here? He had kissed me and ran off. Coming to my work place this late seemed odd. Rio was waiting on me at Gran's to go through the attic. I was exhausted, but I didn't want to cancel either. I was curious about the man who could be the father of both of us.

Drying off my hands on the apron I had tied around my waist, I walked around Emily and headed for the front of the shop. When I saw Drake standing in front of the empty bakery display, I was both disappointed and relieved. Although why he would come looking for me I had no idea.

"Hey," I said.

He turned at the sound of my voice and flashed me the charismatic smile of his that made it okay for him to ask girls questions about blow jobs and get away with it. "Henley," he drawled out my name.

"Drake," I replied. "You wanted to see me?" I asked, thinking of the dishes I still needed to wash and Rio being at the house waiting on me.

"Yeah, when are you leaving?"

"Uh, hopefully I can get out of here in thirty minutes, but I-"

"Have Rio at your place. Yeah, I know," he said interrupting me.

I just nodded and waited for him to say more.

He cleared his throat and glanced at the front door. "Can you step outside a minute?"

"I guess," I replied frowning.

Hillya was sweeping the far side of the store where the signing had been held. She glanced up at me and I assumed whatever Drake came to say he wanted privacy.

"I'll be right back," I assured her and she nodded.

Following Drake outside, I was curious, but I hoped this was quick. When we were outside on the sidewalk, he turned to look at me. "It's about Rio," he said.

If he was here to warn me off Rio, I was going back inside. I raised both my eyebrows and waited. Drake cleared his throat and for the first time since I had met him, he looked like he was struggling for words.

"Saul is playing his guitar again. He is closed-off in his room, but he's playing it. Writing a song it sounds like," he paused and I took advantage of it.

"Saul plays the guitar?" I asked surprised by this.

Drake shifted his feet. "Yeah, he does but he hasn't in a long time. We've been friends since he moved here. Rio and Saul were friends first then me. Anyway, Saul plays the guitar when he's happy or maybe that's not the word. He's not really happy. He plays it when he's inspired. When life doesn't seem like shit. When he has hope," Drake shrugged. "He started playing it the night you came to the house or that's the first time I heard him play at least. I wasn't sure what had him playing again but then he said something about you and the way he looked when he said your name... I realized you're the reason he's playing again."

I held up my hand to stop him. "No, Drake. I can assure you one hundred percent that it is not me that has him playing again. He doesn't like me," I said the first part with conviction, but the last part I wasn't completely sure about. Last night had me questioning his dislike for me.

Drake ran his hand over his mouth as if trying to cover his grin. "You think so, huh?"

I nodded but said nothing.

"Then explain to me why he threw a glass against the wall and then just walked out of the kitchen without a word after he found out that Rio was at your house tonight?"

This had to be exaggerated or misconstrued. "I find it hard to believe it was because of me and why would he throw a glass against a wall? It was probably an accident."

Drake let out a short laugh. "No, Henley, it wasn't an accident. He asked where Rio was when I was getting a bag of chips. I casually said 'told me he was headed to Henley's' and then I turned around to face him. BAM! Glass shattered against the wall. Then he walked off."

As difficult as it was to believe Saul had smashed a glass over Rio being with me, last night's weird conversation and kiss did happen. He had kissed me like he wanted to kiss me. It had been almost desperate. I shook my head.

"He has Fleur," I reminded him.

Drake frowned. "Not anymore. Did you not hear about her insanity on the roof of her car?"

"I saw it," I told him.

"Right, well, do you know why she was on the damn roof of an unparked car in the middle of the street?"

"She was high or drunk," I replied.

"Wrong. Saul had broken things off with her, told her to leave again, and she flipped her batshit crazy switch."

"What?"

Drake shrugged. "Saul ended things with her. She was wailing about him not loving her and that he wanted someone else."

"He ran after her to bail her out of jail," I informed him.

"Of course he did. That's what Saul does. He rescues people. He got her ass out of jail, although I thought she could have used a couple days of reality check, and then he called her rich daddy in Mobile to come get her."

I glanced at the window to see Hillya now vacuuming. I had to get back inside.

"Listen, Drake. If you are here to tell me not to date Rio or whatever, I am not dating him. We are friends and will only ever be friends. I don't know why Saul broke the glass, or whatever. But this is a conversation that y'all need to have at your place. I don't think it has anything to do with me, but I am flattered that you believe I could draw Saul's attention."

Drake stared at me a moment then laughed. I wasn't amused and glared at him ready to just leave him out here and go back inside. Today had been too long and I didn't have nearly enough sleep for all this.

"Rio and Saul have been best friends for a long damn time. Don't be what comes between them," Drake said. "You're more dangerous than you realize." He winked then and turned to walk away.

I didn't respond and I only stood there a moment, looking at him walk out to the road before going inside and finishing up. My mind was turning over everything Drake had said, though and by the time I left for the night, I wasn't sure what I believed anymore.

SIXTEEN

Rio was asleep on the sofa when I walked in the door last night around eleven. I tossed a blanket over him before I went and got ready for bed. I barely remembered my head hitting the pillow. When my alarm went off, it felt as if I had just lain down.

I left the house and headed for work with Rio still on the sofa asleep.

Hillya was busy icing cupcakes when I arrived to start the new granola for the acai bowl I intended on calling the Summer Splash. She had Emily rolling out dough and the local country radio station was playing. Emily mumbled a good morning and looked as tired as I felt. Hillya had a travel mug full of coffee beside her and was wide awake and focused.

We spent the next hour baking; Emily did some dancing when a song she liked came on, and Hillya asked me questions about my new acai bowl recipes. She was intrigued by the bowls and I knew she wanted to be able to make them herself.

My mornings here were becoming something I looked forward to and enjoyed. I felt like I had found a place I fit in and people I liked being around. Gran had known this and thanks to her, here I was. The next item on the list would need to get done on Sunday. I was hoping to get two of the requests accomplished that day, but I was finding that Gran's list wasn't always cut and dry.

"What ingredients do you need for the Banana Rama acai bowl you were telling me about?" Hillya asked me.

"Several, do you have some paper? I can write it down," I replied.

"Emily, go to my office and find me a pen and paper please," Hillya told her niece.

Emily did a little shimmy to Little Big Town's newest song about beer and whiskey on her way out of the kitchen. Hillya just shook her head and smiled. I went back to mixing more granola and my thoughts drifted to the things Drake had said last night. I had been going to talk to Rio about it, but he hadn't been awake.

"I'm sorry," Emily said, coming back into the kitchen holding a picture frame.

Hillya looked at it and frowned.

"I might have done a hip kick and I knocked this picture of Rebel off the shelf. It broke, but I'll buy you a new frame," she said.

I don't know what else was said after that because my brain locked on the name Rebel. I stared down at the granola in the bowl, not wanting either of them to see the shock on my face. I had to work this through in my head before I asked any questions. How likely was it that there were two people named Rebel in this small town in the past forty years? I'm thinking that possibility is low.

Emily had said Rebel. I'd heard it very clearly. There wasn't another name I could think of that I could be confusing it with. I looked up and Hillya was gone from the kitchen. Emily appeared fine though and was pulling muffins from the oven. Where had the photo gone? Did Hillya take it back to her office? Why hadn't I listened?

"Where did Hillya go?" I asked as casually as I could.

Emily shrugged. "Uh, to the office I think," she replied.

"I needed to give her the ingredients." I also wanted a reason to go in her office and look at the broken photo.

"Oh yeah," Emily said scrunching her nose. "She left without getting those."

I tried to think of something to say that didn't make me look suspicious. "Uh, is she upset over the frame?" I asked.

Emily shook her head. "No the pic is okay. Just broke the frame."

I nodded and smiled, wishing she would say the name of the person in the picture again. "Good," I said. "Maybe I should go find her and remind her about the ingredients."

Emily was doing a hip sway dance with the music while she poured batter into a pan. She didn't respond. I could wait. I probably should wait. I picked up the bowl and poured the granola onto a baking sheet, glancing back toward the hallway leading to the office. The answer to so many questions could be in there, but if it was then…

Gran.

Gran had sent me here.

Just like she had sent me to the farmer's market.

I stared at the door, trying to put pieces together and make sense of it all. If Rio was right and the tool boxes had not been the point of that visit, then was my coming here to work because I liked baking not the point of this job?

"Emily?" I asked looking at her.

She lifted her head to meet my gaze. "Yeah?"

I took a deep breath then just asked. "Who is Rebel?"

Emily glanced back at the hallway then looked at me. "Hillya's son. His real name was Ryan but no one called him that. He died a long time ago though. Before I was born. He was my mom's only cousin. Hillya only had him," she said in a whisper.

I stood there staring at her. Hillya had a son. His name was Rebel. He died before Emily was born. Gran... was this it? Is this why you sent me here?

"How old was he?" I heard myself ask her, but it felt as if I was a spectator watching the scene instead of being a part of it.

"Twenty. Car accident or maybe a motorcycle, I can't remember what Mom said. Somewhere in Georgia, I believe. He was in college. I don't remember the details. It's been a long time since I asked Mom who he was," Emily told me still whispering.

I managed a nod and replied, "Poor Hillya."

She agreed and then I went back to making the granola because what else was I supposed to do. Gran knew and I now had no doubt why I was here, but did Hillya know... did she know about me?

The rest of the morning was a blur. I messed up two drink orders, forgot to give someone change, and dropped an entire tray of granola on the floor. I kept looking at Hillya, trying to find the resemblance. Then there was Emily. Our parents were first cousins. Did we truly look alike and just not see it? Others had mentioned it. Hillya never had.

By the time the lunch crowd was gone and the afternoon crowd began to slow some, I had almost talked myself into asking Hillya a few questions to see if she acted weird. She may be clueless but then she may be waiting for me to figure it out. Did she think I knew? What if she assumed my mom had told me or my gran? There was so many questions and my head felt like it was going to explode.

"You two can leave. I have an evening shift coming in and I'll stay until they get here," Hillya called to us as we wiped down the front while we had no customers.

"Want to go shopping?" Emily asked, looking hopeful.

"I need sleep," I told her because this morning that would have been true. Right now, I needed to be alone. I also needed to get in Gran's attic and see if I found anything.

Emily sighed. "Yeah, I probably do too. I think I drank too many espressos though."

I managed a smile and went to take off my apron, heading for the back. Hillya was pulling a lemon pound cake from the oven when I walked in. I wanted to study her closer but knew I couldn't just stand there and stare at her. If she knew I was her granddaughter, wouldn't she have told me? I also wanted desperately to go see the photo of Rebel in her office. She sat the pound cake on the island in the middle of the room and then looked at me.

"Are you sure there is nothing more I can do before I go?" I asked her, wanting to ask her things far more important but afraid to.

She smiled at me, but I could see she was exhausted. Her eyes looked tired and I was worried about her. She shook her head. "No, I'll be leaving soon too. Go on home and get some rest. You've had a busy two days."

It was then she tilted her head to the side and sighed with a smile that I saw it. Or should I say, I saw me. It's an odd thing. Looking at someone else and realizing you resemble them. I could see myself doing something just like that while looking at my reflection in the mirror. I had to shake myself out of this and stop gawking at the woman though.

"Uh, okay," I said heading for the back door. "See you tomorrow," I called out.

"Bye, Henley," she replied and I held up a hand to wave but didn't look back at her.

SEVENTEEN

Rio was gone and the blanket I had thrown over him last night was neatly folded on the end of the sofa. I was glad he wasn't here. I needed time to process first. I put my purse on the counter and went down the hallway toward the pull-down attic near the back bedroom. Stopping underneath it, I stared up at it. The fear of the ladder wasn't what made me pause. It was what else I may find up there.

When I went to work this morning, I hadn't known that I would find out that the answers to my father had been right under my nose for weeks. "You could have just told me, Gran," I said aloud. If she hadn't been preparing to die, would she have ever told me? I had spent so many summers here and not once had she taken me to meet my other grandmother, or mentioned I had a brother. Why couldn't she just have left me a letter telling me all this? The list she left lay in her bedroom on the dresser. I wondered if it held more secrets and just how deep this was going to get.

I brought a chair from the kitchen and stood on it to reach the pull string on the attic entrance. Once I had it down, I didn't think too long about it or the ladder would start to freak me out. Instead, I just went for it. At the top of the ladder, another string hung down and hit the side of my face. Reaching for it, I pulled and the light came on, illuminating the attic.

There were boxes stacked against the far-right wall, and Christmas decorations covered the entire left side of the space. My throat got a lump in it when I saw Gran's Santa in the back corner. It was life-size and when you pressed its hand, it would sing Jingle Bells. It was always beside Gran's tree in the living room.

I stepped up and stood on the floor and did a full circle. There was an old green trunk behind me and beside it was a coat rack with hats that I recognized as my granddad's hanging on it. What looked like prom dresses were hanging on hooks on the wall behind them, covered in clear bags to protect the fabric. They had to have been mom's.

There was a lifetime of memories up here. Were all attics this way? My fear of ladders may have caused me to miss out on a lot. I went to the boxes on the right and began searching through them. Some were labeled with Gran's handwriting and a permanent marker. Most were not.

It took only a few minutes and some searching to find the first box of things that had been Mom's when she was younger. Concert tickets to Hootie and the Blowfish, Boys 2 Men, and Garth Brooks, photos of Mom with friends, her first temporary driver's license, and a blue-ribbon award for a Science Project.

The box under it had mostly photos, so I sat it aside to take downstairs with me. It was the last box I came to that held letters. Folded-up lined paper that looked like something that was passed around in class in an old movie from like the eighties. I put it with the photo box and made sure there were no other boxes that might hold answers.

Once I was sure I had everything, I went back to the ladder and took a deep breath to calm myself, before having to climb back down it while holding two boxes. Turning off the light on my way down, I managed to make it to the ground without an issue.

In the living room, I placed both boxes on the coffee table then sat down on the sofa. Opening the one with the photos first, I went through them slowly. There was a photo of my mom at her Sweet Sixteen birthday party in Gran's back yard, standing with a younger Wanda Sellers smiling at the camera. I sat that aside. I would take it to Mrs. Wanda when I went to visit her.

Taking my time, I studied each photo for some clue or possibly a guy. It wasn't until I got to the last four pictures that I saw him. He was tall, had dark hair, and Mom was looking up at him with love. Was this Rebel? Or was it someone else? I looked at the next photo and this one was in someone else's house. Mom was sitting on the boy's lap and they were kissing. I couldn't see his face clearly, but it was the same boy.

Then there was a strip of images from a photo booth. They kissed again, they smiled at the camera, they looked at each other, and the last one, the guy made a funny face while Mom was laughing. She seemed happy. I wasn't sure I had ever seen my mom this happy. She was typically uptight and difficult to deal with. The girl in the photos didn't appear that way at all.

The last picture was just of the boy. He was on a motorcycle, no helmet, looking at the camera but not smiling. Mom had said he died in a motorcycle accident. Rio's mom said he overdosed. Emily had said he died in a car accident or motorcycle accident. Was "he" the same guy in these photos?

I set them all to the side and put the rest of the pictures back in Mom's box. The letters would hopefully tell me more. Just as I reached for the box of letters, there was a knock on my door. Looking up, I saw Rio and suddenly felt guilty for going to the attic without him.

I put the letter box back down and went to let him inside.

"I went to the attic," I said and waved a hand toward the boxes.

He nodded. "Good. Find anything?" he asked, but he seemed distracted.

"Yeah, I think so," I replied, not sure how to explain Hillya's son and if I should tell him until I had spoken to Hillya. I wasn't sure what the right thing to do was.

"Okay, uh, you can fill me in later. I don't have much time. Pop is expecting me to unload the strawberry truck that is coming in. The Strawberry Festival is this weekend and he's gearing up."

"Oh, alright. I didn't know there was a Strawberry Festival here," I said, surprised by the fact he didn't seem interested in what I had found out.

"This will be its fifth year. It's new. But have you seen Saul?"

I shook my head confused as to why he would come ask me if he couldn't find Saul.

Rio sighed and ran his hand over the top of his head. "Shit," he muttered.

"What's wrong?"

"It's his mom. She's," he paused and looked torn about saying any more.

"Is Lily on another binge?" I asked.

He nodded. "Yeah, he woke up late last night at her place and she was gone. He texted both me and Drake around one in the morning, but we were both asleep and missed it. Now we can't get him on the phone and he's not been back all day. She gets into some dark shit and I'm worried he's in trouble."

"As in drugs?" I asked, fear slowly crawling up my spine.

He nodded. "Yeah. Last time he had to pull her out of a drug house. We went with him. That shit ain't pretty."

"Drug house?" I repeated horrified. I thought she took pills and drank too much. Saul had said nothing about drug houses. I wasn't sure what drug houses were exactly. My sheltered life had made sure of it.

Rio nodded. "I've got to go unload the strawberries. If you hear from him, let me know. If no one hears from him by the time I'm off work, I'll have to call his dad."

"Dad?" I asked. I hadn't realized he had a dad around here. Not that I knew much about Saul. I didn't even know his last name.

"Yeah. Saul will be pissed. He was last time I had to call his dad, but dammit he needs to respond to my text or answer my calls." Rio sounded frustrated with the entire situation.

"I take it he and his dad aren't on good terms," I said.

Rio grunted. "You could say that."

"Does his dad live here?" I asked.

Rio laughed then shook his head. "No." He reached for the door knob. "I gotta go. I'll let you know if I hear from him."

I wanted to ask why he laughed when I asked if Saul's dad lived in town, but he was in a hurry. "Okay, bye," I said instead.

Rio left and I looked at the letters again. My mind was now on Saul and Lily. I wasn't sure I could focus on the letters right now. How could I help? How had Gran helped them?

"You could have left me a journal or something, Gran. If you were planning on bringing these people into my life, then a little direction would have helped."

EIGHTEEN

A shower, a change of clothes, and a batch of caramel oat cookies later, there was still no word from Saul. I had considered going to Lily's penthouse and seeing if they were there more than once, but I didn't. I kept waiting for Rio to text that Saul was okay.

After putting the cookies on the cooling rack, I topped them with oat-milk chocolate chips so that they would melt slowly and coat the tops then walked over and picked up my card to the Hendrix IV. They may not be there, but I could at least give it a try. Sticking it into the back pocket of my cut-off jean shorts, I headed for the door.

I didn't get far. Saul was coming up the stairs when I stepped outside. I wasn't sure if I should hug him, ask if he was okay, ask about Lily, or tell him to call Rio immediately. Instead of any of those things, I just said "Hey."

He stopped at the second step from the top and looked at me. There were dark circles under his eyes. "Hey," he replied.

We stood there like that, neither of us saying anything. He looked so defeated. We barely knew each other, but I realized

I cared for him. I had been worried about him. I liked him. More than I should. More than was smart.

"Where's Lily?" I finally asked.

He sighed and rubbed his temples. "Hospital," he said. "She'll be okay."

"I'm sorry, Saul," I told him, not sure what I should say. I had never known anyone who dealt with something like this. My mom no longer seemed difficult. I would call her tonight and see how she was. Her vanity and selfishness I could live with. There were much worse things that she could have done.

"Yeah," he replied. He dropped his hand back to his side. "I don't know why I came here."

I didn't say anything right away. I waited to see if he was going to say more. He didn't.

"Maybe coming here is a habit. Gran used to be here and I assume you used to come to her for help with Lily."

He glanced off into the yard then back at me. "That would make sense," he said. "But it's not why."

"Oh," I replied.

"She talked about you. Honey did," he said, his gaze coming back to mine. "She talked about how sweet you were and how sheltered your life had been. She spoke about how although you were born to a teenage mother that you both had made it work. You had a plan for life and were on the right path." He smiled then but it didn't meet his eyes.

"She left some shit out though that might have been helpful that first day when I saw you struggling to put boxes in your car and I stopped to help."

Knowing Gran had talked about me to Saul felt strange. I had never heard her speak of him or Lily, but he had known about me. He had stopped that day to help me because he knew who I was and what I was doing. It made sense now.

"What did she leave out?" I asked him.

He let out a hard laugh and shook his head then looked off into the yard again instead of at me. "She left out that your eyes express your every thought," he replied. "She left out that when I looked into your eyes the first time I would find it hard to fucking catch my breath."

He turned his gaze back to me again. "She left out that I could see just how damn sweet you were by looking into your eyes and she left out that it would be impossible for me not to want to be around you after I met you."

There were no words for this. I stood there staring at him, thinking possibly I may have fallen asleep and this was a dream. I knew what I looked like the first time we met and I was well aware that there wasn't anything about me that would make a guy like him want me.

"But if she loved you so much then why the hell did she ever tell me about you? If she hadn't told me about you, I wouldn't have stopped that day. I wouldn't have known who you were. I wouldn't have given a shit that you needed some help." He sounded angry.

"What does that have to do with her loving me?" I asked confused by his train of thought.

"Because, Henley, I am fucked up. She should have kept you from me. My life is a dark fucked-up mess. Everything about it. I'm not nice. I don't have a damn clue what my path is or where to get on it. All I know is I have an addict for a mother and if I don't keep her alive then no one else will. That's what I fucking know about my future. It's a dark, sad story and you don't fit into it. You're light and motherfucking rainbows. Me? I'm some level of Hell." He stopped ranting and ran a hand through his hair, causing the curls to fall in a messy disarray. There was so much pain in his eyes I wanted to cry. This beautiful boy who I thought had walked out of a tropical vacation commercial appeared to have it all, yet he was tortured.

I took a step toward him and reached out my hand to take his. He looked down at our hands as I threaded my fingers through his. I wasn't sure there was anything I could say that would make him see things differently but I wanted to try.

"You watch over your mom, you bail your friends out of jail, you stop and help a complete stranger because you liked her grandmother, and you risk your safety to save a girl who is acting out just to get your attention. That's not things a dark person does. I don't know what your life has been like, but I do know that through all the crap you have been dealt, you are still a nice person. You can say you're aren't but that's not true."

He closed his eyes tightly and let his head fall back as he let out a frustrated sigh. "God, Henley. You can't say shit like that," he said then looked at me again. "I came here to push you away so that you didn't let me get close enough to kiss you again. I came here to warn you."

Saul was nothing like Will. I had loved Will, knowing he would never hurt me. There had been a security with him that would never come with Saul. If I allowed myself to develop real feelings for Saul, if I spent time with him, if we kissed some more, I could be hurt. He could break my heart. It was a risk. I wasn't a risk taker.

"What do you want from me?" I asked him.

"What do I want?" he asked and I nodded. He ran his thumb over my hand as I continued to hold his in mine. "I want to know you. I want to see you smile, at me. I want to be around you," he paused. "And I want to kiss you again."

I pulled him toward me with the hand I held. He came up the last step and I had to tilt my head back now to look up at him. "Then do it," I said.

He grinned then. "Are you telling me to kiss you?"

"I'm telling you to do all of it. I'm not scared of you," I assured him.

A look of pain crossed his eyes. "You should be," he whispered.

"I think you're wrong. Gran thought you were wrong," I said.

He frowned. "Your gran would never be okay with this."

"Oh really? Do you think that her sending me to Lily's was innocent? Because I can tell you it was not. I am finding out more and more every day that the list she left me is a very well laid-out plan that Gran is conducting from her grave," I informed him.

He chuckled and shook his head. "No, your gran would have never wanted you with me and I owe her a lot. Problem is, I don't think I'm going to be able to stay away from you. I've fucking tried."

My mouth curled into a smile. There was so much I didn't know about my life and about Saul, but I liked being here with him. Talking to him like this. I was happy. That was all I needed to know for now.

"SAUL!" Drake yelled out.

Saul let go of my hand and turned to look back as Drake was getting out of the passenger side of Rio's Jeep and Rio out of the driver's side. Our moment was over.

"What the hell, man?" Drake called out, throwing his arms up in the air. "We were about to call Archer!"

Saul tensed at that name and I realized it must be his father. "I was about to call you back," he replied.

Rio was looking at me and I could see the questions in his eyes.

"Replying to a fucking text message would have been nice," Drake told him as he started toward the stairs. Rio came up behind him and put a hand on his shoulder, stopping him from coming up.

Drake looked back at Rio.

"He's okay. We don't need to stay," Rio said and Drake turned his head to look back up at us. It seemed to slowly dawn on him that they may have interrupted something.

"Ooooh, so you two." Drake waved a finger between the two of us. "You came here first. To her. I see… niiiice. She'll be a helluva lot better to have around than Fleur's crazy ass."

Saul was looking at Rio and ignoring Drake. There seemed to be some challenge in his gaze. Rio held up his hands and backed up. "I told you we were friends. That is it. That's all it ever was. You didn't believe me."

"I know you," Saul replied. "You don't have female friends."

"I do with this one," Rio said, nodding his head at me.

Drake hit Rio's arm with the back of his hand. "Dude, she's hot. He's not an idiot."

"Shut up," Rio said to him with a roll of his eyes.

I stepped around Saul so that I was standing beside him. "He's telling the truth," I said in his defense.

Drake let out a hoot of laughter. "Sure he is!"

Saul was silent. He didn't find any of this amusing. He was still watching Rio.

Rio looked at me then and I could see the question in his eyes. If he wanted to tell them we thought we could be siblings, I didn't mind. As long as he didn't know the details for Hillya's sake. I shrugged then nodded.

Saul turned to look at me and I smiled up at him. He didn't return the smile. He seemed to be trying to read something into the situation that wasn't there. As if he expected the worst and we were lying to him.

"Saul," Rio called his name as he walked closer to the bottom of the steps. When Saul didn't look at him but continued to study me, Rio further explained, "We are just friends and we are about ninety-nine percent sure we have the same dead father."

Saul swung his gaze back to Rio then back to me. His eyes wide in disbelief. I understood that because I had felt the same way when Rio had told me about this. Now, I knew better. More than Rio, as a matter of fact.

I heard Drake say "No shit!" but I didn't look at him. I kept my eyes on Saul.

"Seriously?" he asked me.

I nodded. "Yeah. It's one of those things Gran is orchestrating from her grave," I told him.

"Damn," Saul said under his breath.

"Yeah," I agreed.

"So Hendrix, you staying here because we are heading out. I got two sorority girls from Texas headed to the house in a few. Both like to give blow jobs." This time it wasn't Drake talking about blow jobs that stood out.

Hendrix?

NINETEEN

Saul closed the door behind him and I stared at the cookies that I had left cooling while I tried to put this together. Drake had called Saul, Hendrix. Lily lived in the Hendrix IV.

"You didn't know," Saul said behind me.

I turned to look at him. "What is it I should know?" I asked him.

There was a small turn at the corner of his mouth and he looked like he wanted to laugh. "I knew you didn't at first, but I thought you would have figured it out by now." He looked pleased as he said it. "Damn, Henley if that doesn't make me like you more. You gotta stop doing shit like this."

"Is your last name Hendrix?" I asked him.

He nodded.

"How? Are you related to the Hendrix people or whoever owns the Hendrix stuff?"

Then he began to laugh. I wasn't sure why this was funny. I was trying to figure this out.

"I am the Hendrix people, Henley. My father is Archer Hendrix, the CEO of Hendrix Corp."

What? Was he joking? I studied his face to see if he was serious. Wasn't the Hendrix Corp a massive chain worth billions of dollars? He drove a beat-up old truck and lived here. In this small town — the freaking Redneck Riviera.

"Your mom?" I asked, not sure what I was asking really. But wouldn't the wife of Archer Hendrix live somewhere in a fabulous mansion?

"My parents divorced when I was fifteen. Mom's addiction to drugs and alcohol was more than Dad wanted to deal with. He moved her here and I followed. Someone has to take care of her, but he didn't care about that or her life. He and I aren't close," Saul explained.

I leaned back against the counter and crossed my arms over my chest. Today had been a day for revelations. I wasn't sure how much more could be packed into one day.

"I stay out of the spotlight, but I have gotten into some things that the media or tabloids get a hold of… most girls recognize me from that."

I looked up at him. "I don't read or watch that kind of stuff. I prefer Netflix and books," I told him.

He started laughing again and reached out and put his hand on my waist. "You keep making me fucking laugh and I may never leave," he said.

When he was close to me like this and I could smell the sunshine on his skin, he was the scent of summer, it was hard to think of much else. Saul Hendrix was the best-looking man I had ever seen. Looking at him was very easy to do. But he was more than that and because of who he was, despite the messed-up life he had been dealt, I really, really liked him. Too much and far too quickly.

I would have to be careful about that. I'd only cared for one other boy and I had loved him. There had been no other boyfriends or dates. Just Will.

Until now… and I wasn't sure how to do this. Any of it. I just knew I wanted to.

Saul tugged my arms free from their crossed position over my chest and then with both hands took my hips and pulled me against him. When his lips touched mine, I was ready. This kiss was different. It was deeper and there was more emotion attached to it. I slid my hands into his hair and savored the taste of him. Everything about Saul was sexy and my body was reacting to that fact.

When his lips left mine and began to brush along my jawline, I shivered. He lifted me up then and sat me on the counter. His hands moved down to my bare thighs and he looked me in the eyes, but he didn't move any closer. I wanted him to. My entire body wanted him to.

"You're special. It's the main reason I tried to stay away from you," he whispered then pressed a kiss to my cheek. "But I'm a man and if we keep doing this, I'm gonna want more."

I didn't see a problem with that. Right now my entire being wanted more. "Okay," I replied.

He chuckled. "Don't look at me like that, Henley. I'm being good here. It's a rare thing. Let me succeed at it."

A lot happened today. He was beyond weary. I could see that in his eyes. He was also right. I had stuff to process and sleep would be nice. Sighing in defeat, I nodded. "We could both use some sleep."

"Yeah, we could," he agreed then stepped away from me and I felt instantly cold. I wanted him to come back and for us not to care what was right. For once I wanted to just act on how I felt.

He glanced at the door then back at me. "I'll see you tomorrow," he said.

I wanted him to stay but that was again too much, too soon. "Okay," I managed a small smile.

We stayed just like that for another moment, staring at each other. I wasn't sure if he was about to change his mind. A large part of me hoped he did. Finally, his shoulders dropped and he stuck his hands in the front pockets of his jeans. "I'm gonna go."

I nodded but said nothing.

He looked torn as he finally broke our locked gazes and walked toward the door. I jumped down off the counter, thinking I should follow him to the door and at least say goodnight. However, he was already walking out. He didn't glance back as he closed the door firmly behind him.

I stood there until his truck lights came on and he backed out onto the street. Then I went and locked the door, turned and looked at the letters from my mom's box before turning off the lights and walking past them on my way to the bedroom.

The next thing I knew I was reaching for my phone to shut the alarm off. Groaning I stretched and wished I could just go back to sleep. It felt as if I had just laid down. Getting up at four every morning was getting old. Maybe I would try and figure out my recipes in order to write them down for someone else.

My feet hit the pink fluffy shag rug by the bed and I stood up. Yesterday had been a lot. Now, that I faced going into work and seeing Hillya again, I was brought back to Rebel and who he was and who he could be to me and Rio. Thinking of how I would even bring up the subject of Rebel with her was an obstacle I wasn't ready for today. I didn't know when I would feel prepared for that and if I even should. It was very likely she already knew.

Saul had said he would see me today. I didn't know how or when that would happen but the thought of seeing him made me smile. It helped get the heavier things off my mind or at least push them back and not dwell on them so much.

TWENTY

It was right after the breakfast crowd and just before the lunch rush when Saul came walking into Signed Sips. I hadn't looked up when the bell signaled that the door had opened because I was busy writing the new lunch acai bowls on the daily specials' board.

"Hello! What can I get for you?" Emily asked in her flirty voice and that got my attention. I took a quick glance to see who had made her switch from her regular voice to the one she used for cute guys only. Saul's gaze was fixed on me and the bubble of excitement that came with seeing him there should have concerned me; it didn't.

"Hey," I said to him, putting the chalk down and walking over to the counter.

"Oh, you know each other?" Emily asked with curiosity.

I gave her a smile and replied, "Yes. I'll help him."

She simply nodded, but the twinkle in her eyes told me I was going to be questioned the moment he left. "Okay, I'll go to the back and get those… uh… things we need," she said, then backed away a few steps watching us before turning and hurrying through the kitchen door.

"Did I come at a bad time?" he asked me when I looked back at him from the swinging door Emily had just went through.

"Not at all. Perfect timing," I assured him. His eyes still looked weary and the dark circles weren't gone. "How's Lily?" I asked.

He sighed before answering, "Better, I think. I stopped by this morning to check on her. They're going to let her out later today, but the doctor strongly suggested I get her in a rehab facility again."

"How long has it been since she was in the last one?" I asked.

"A year," he replied, looking grim. "There are things that set her off. Honey passing was only a matter of time before this happened." He said that part slowly, as if he were unsure if bringing up Gran's death was a good idea.

I dealt with Gran's death daily living in her house. It didn't sting to be reminded. Waking up here every morning was making it easier.

"Are you going to send her to rehab?" I asked.

He shrugged. "Fuck if I know. She's adamant she doesn't want or need to go. She cried on me this morning, promising she wouldn't run off again. I just, don't know."

My chest ached for him. I wanted to help, but I didn't know how. I wasn't my gran. She knew how to handle everything. I felt clueless. Glancing at the bakery shelf, I saw the fresh praline cake donuts that Hillya had brought out just ten minutes ago.

"Want a donut?" I asked him. "They're fresh."

He grinned then. "Did you make them?"

"Nope. They are full of dairy and gluten. They even have pecans. Completely delicious."

He looked as if he were going to say yes, but he did a quick survey of the display case then replied, "I think I'll have the gluten and dairy-free chocolate chip muffin."

It was the only item I had in the case. Everything else had sold out. "Are you sure? You don't have to order something I made. It won't hurt my feelings if you want a donut," I told him.

"I've been wanting a chocolate chip muffin all morning," he replied with a serious face that made me laugh.

"Sure you have," I said, knowing that was a lie. I went over and took out the muffin then put it and a donut in a paper bag. "Just in case the muffin isn't enough."

"An Americano too please," he added.

I went to make his drink and wished I could go sit with him while he ate. The lunch crowd would be in soon enough and I knew that wasn't possible. But everything had changed so quickly with Saul. Getting to spend more time with him was something I was anxious to do. In the middle of my life being flipped open like a book because of Gran's list, I found thoughts of Saul made me happy.

When I handed him the items, his hand brushed mine longer than necessary. "Thanks."

"You're welcome," I replied.

We stood there silently for a few moments then he placed a twenty on the counter. "I'll see you after you get off work."

I picked up the money. "This is too much."

He smirked. "The rest is the tip."

I started to argue when he opened the door and walked outside.

A twelve-dollar tip was ridiculous, but we split the tip jar daily, and Emily would be thrilled with this extra bonus. I rang up his items and put the change in the jar all the while smiling.

I got off work a little after two and headed home. I didn't know when I would be seeing Saul, but I wanted to shower and get ready so when he showed up, I didn't smell of coffee and baked goods. It didn't take long to get myself cleaned up and when I was finished, I found myself back at the coffee table with the letters.

Not every letter was informative. Unless I wanted to know what color dress my mom had been planning on wearing to prom or if she had skipped study hall. But there had been three letters in the box that I read several times, each of them mentioning Rebel.

One had mentioned Rio's mother. I was certain now that my mother and Rebel had been secretly seeing each other behind Rio's mom's back. They were cheaters. It made me view my existence in a whole new light and it wasn't pretty. Mom had claimed she loved Rebel in one of the letters, but there were no letters from Rebel to her, confirming how he had felt about her. It was clear with his abandonment of both my mom and Rio's mom that he hadn't been in love with either girl.

I put the letters and photos together that I had found proof in that my mother and Rebel were together. The rest I tucked away back in the attic where they belonged. I sent Rio a text to let him know I found some information and when he had time I would tell him. I didn't say anything about Hillya though. I would but just not yet. I wasn't sure if I should talk to her or tell him first.

Saul hadn't texted or called since I got home. He could be dealing with Lily getting released from the hospital and I didn't want to bother him. This was all very new and kissing and attraction didn't clarify how to handle things with him. I would wait until he contacted me. Sitting here doing nothing was pointless though.

I had the next item on Gran's list and it seemed simple enough. That of course didn't mean it was. I wasn't sure I wanted anymore revelations right now. Taking a hat box filled with my gran's scarfs, some costume jewelry, and a beaded purse that I had never seen her carry to a Miss Keerly Evans didn't seem like it could lead to anything. Unless I was going to find out that Keerly Evans was my long-lost cousin or sister or even that I was adopted and this was my real mother.

I seriously doubted all those things and put the address Gran had left into my GPS then took the hat box to my car. The house was only ten miles away. I could get this done and marked off the list. That would leave me with only two more things to do before it was complete.

The address was located in a nice subdivision just out of town. The homes were newer and all large. The driveways had bikes, basketball goals, and other items that said kids lived there. The back yards had tall privacy fences and I imagined pools. When I pulled into the driveway of Miss Keerly Evans' home, there was a three-car garage tucked off to the back left of the house and one of the garage doors was up. I could see a new Mercedes SUV parked inside.

This looked harmless enough, but thanks to Gran's previous request, I was still a little nervous as I walked up the sidewalk with the hat box in my hands. "Please, Gran, just let this be simple. No relations I didn't know about or life-changing events," I whispered before I reached the front porch.

The two large wooden doors looked like elaborate barn doors. I pressed the doorbell and waited. This was one of the larger homes in the subdivision and I wondered why someone who lived here would want Gran's old scarves and fake jewelry.

When the door on the right opened, a lady with long pale blonde hair draped over one bare tanned shoulder stood there smiling at me. She wore a pair of white shorts and a hot pink tank top. Her feet were bare and her toenails were painted the same color as her shirt.

"Hello," she said then looked from me to the hat box. It took only a moment for her to recognize the box. I could see her eyes widen before they shifted back up to meet mine. "You're Honey's granddaughter."

I nodded. "Yes. Are you Keerly Evans?" I asked.

Her bright smile widened and her perfect white teeth made you wonder if there was any flaw on this woman. "Oh no, I'm Isla Evans. Please come inside," she said, stepping back. "It's blazing out there today."

I came inside the house and it smelled of coconut. It was as if the house had been bathed in suntan oil. Isla closed the door behind me and walked over to the wide curved staircase and called out, "Keerly!" Then she turned back to me. "She's going to be so excited."

"Great," I replied unsure what else to say.

"Would you like something to drink? I just made a pitcher of fresh lemonade. Keerly likes to help me squeeze the lemons. It takes entirely too long, but it entertains her so that's how we do it," Isla said, just as small footsteps caught her attention. We both turned to look up the stairs at the railing and a little girl with dark brown curls and big brown eyes stared down at us.

"What Momma?" she asked and I understood then. They must go to Gran's church. Gran loved to keep the nursery and preschool at church. Keerly must have been one of her little friends.

"Honey sent you something." Isla glanced back at me. "Her granddaughter brought it to you."

The little girl's small chubby hands grabbed the rails as she peeked through them down at me. She looked to be about three maybe. "But you said Honey went to live with Jesus." Her voice sounded sad and unsure.

"She did, but Honey wanted you to have something of hers," Isla explained.

Keerly studied me a moment then she noticed the hat box. Her eyes lit up. "Oh! It's Honey's scarves and jewelry!" she exclaimed and turned to run down the stairs.

"Careful! Hold onto the rail!" Isla told her, walking over to meet her daughter as she reached the bottom.

Keerly ran right past her mother and came to me with her hands held up anxious for the box. I placed it in her little hands and she sat it down immediately and took the top off. "It's all of them, Momma!" she said and began to pull out the scarves and drape them over herself.

Isla looked up at me. "Honey babysat for us when my husband and I had a business dinner or just needed a night out. She always brought this box and she would dress herself and Keerly up in the scarves and jewelry. She made dresses with the scarves and-"

"The purse! She gave me the purse!" Keerly said with pure joy, jumping up with the beaded purse and clutching it to her chest as if it were the most precious thing on earth.

"She sure did," Isla replied and patted Keerly on the head affectionately.

Isla looked back at me. "Thank you for doing this. She's missed Honey and well, this is just really special."

"I'm glad Gran sent me," I told her honestly. Seeing how my Gran had impacted yet another life felt good.

"Come have some lemonade," Isla said again. When I hesitated, she said, "Or at least take some to go."

Keerly looked up at me then, her face suddenly very serious. "When is Honey coming back from staying with Jesus?"

Isla bent down then and took her hand. "Sweetheart, remember I told you she can't come back."

Keerly's little shoulders fell and with them, the lump in my throat rose. I understood all too well what it felt like to miss my gran. "I wish she had stayed here," Keerly said.

Isla hugged her and looked up at me apologetically. "I know," she soothed.

"When I start missing her, I talk to her. I think that even though I can't see her that she can hear me," I said then.

Keerly studied me a moment. "Does it make you not sad anymore?" she asked.

"Not completely. It's okay to be sad and miss her. But she would want to know you're happy and enjoying the things she left you. So, I try to think about the good times I had with her and smile."

The little girl sighed and then put a scarf covered in pink hydrangeas up to her chin and inhaled. "These smell like her," she said, then smiled up at me. "She made good cookies."

I nodded. "Yes, she did. The very best cookies."

"She smelled like cookies," Keerly added.

I laughed. "She did!"

Isla stood back up and I could see the unshed tears in her eyes. "Thank you," she said.

"Gran would love to see how happy these things made her. I'm glad she sent me, so I could witness it."

Isla nodded and sniffled. I could tell she was struggling with not crying. It was time I left.

"It was so nice to meet you both. I need to get going. I have some other things to get done," I told her and she nodded again, reaching up to wipe at a tear that had escaped.

I looked back down at Keerly. "Bye bye, Keerly. I am so glad my gran's scarves are safely with you now."

The little girl nodded then waved her small hand at me.

When I was back in the car, I let out a deep sigh of relief. There was no big revelation. Nothing new for me to figure out. It had been a simple task that Gran had wanted done. Nothing more. Thank Goodness.

TWENTY-ONE

When I pulled into the driveway, the grass was freshly cut and a sweaty, dirty Saul was sitting on the top of the front porch steps. I climbed out of the car and made my way up to him.

"You cut the rest of the grass," I stated the obvious.

He smirked. "Looks that way."

"You didn't have to do that," I told him.

He cocked one eyebrow. "Because you were going to?"

I bit my bottom lip to keep from smiling. How was he even more attractive all dirty and sweaty? I had never been a fan of guys in tanks, but when one had arms like Saul, they worked. Seriously worked.

Thank you," I said.

He grinned. "You're welcome."

"Do you want to come inside and get cooled off?" I asked.

He raised his eyebrows. "Why don't you come to my place? I have a pool," he reminded me. "We can watch the sunset."

The idea of wearing a bathing suit in front of him with all my pale skin on display made me panic for a moment. He was waiting for me to respond and I had no excuse to keep from going. I wanted to spend time with him, get to know him. If I had to put on a bathing suit then so be it. I could do this.

"Okay," I agreed

He stood up. "Where've you been?" he asked me.

"Another item on Gran's list checked off," I told him then went to unlock the door.

"I take it there was no major revelation in this one, you don't appear shaken."

I shook my head and went inside the house. "No, it was easy enough. Just dropped off some of her items to a friend." I turned to look at him then. "I'll just go get my bathing suit. If you want something to drink, there is bottled water in the fridge."

"Thanks," he replied and walked toward the kitchen.

I hurried back to my room and had the debate over one-piece or two-piece. My two-piece was nothing like the bikinis I had seen on the females at his house party, but I liked the color on me. The turquoise had made my pale color more attractive or so I had thought when I bought it. Picking it up, I put it in a bag then added a beach towel. Taking one last look at myself in the mirror, I took a deep breath an exhaled slowly.

When I made my way back to the kitchen, Saul was leaning against the bar drinking a bottle of water. His tank was sticking to his sweaty chest and I took a moment to admire the view. It had been awhile since I allowed myself to even look at a guy. After Will, I didn't notice guys at all. I didn't notice a lot of things. I hadn't been living life just going through the motions.

My life had become routine and since moving to Gran's, I realized just how boring I had been. Will would have never wanted that; Gran definitely hadn't wanted it.

Well, Gran, it's not boring now.

"I have some cookies if you want one," I offered.

He cut his eyes to the cake plate on the counter that the cookies were being kept. "I noticed. Wasn't sure if they were for the café or not."

Walking over to the cake plate, I took a napkin and put two of the cookies on it then handed it to him. "They were a trial run. When I get stressed or bored or just in the mood, I begin making up recipes. I tried one and I liked it, but I need a second opinion."

He took a bite of one of the cookies and I realized I was watching his neck muscles flex in the process. Snapping my eyes back to his face, I caught him grinning. I knew I was blushing, but there wasn't much I could do about it.

"These will sell. Fucking delicious," he said then put the rest of the cookie in his mouth.

"You can take the rest. I won't eat them and I'll have to make fresh ones for the shop," I told him.

After I bagged up the other cookies, I started to turn around and hand them to him, but he backed me up into the corner of the bar. Both of his hands lay flat on the marble counter top and he looked down at me with a small grin tugging at the corner of his perfect lips.

"Before we go," he said in a low voice then he lowered his head and his mouth found mine. I may have let out a small moan of pleasure because even sweaty having Saul Hendrix this close made me lightheaded. He tasted of my cookies and that made my heart do a silly little flip.

He growled then broke the kiss but ran his nose across my jawline before standing back up. "I'm nasty and if we don't stop, you're going to be as fucking dirty as I am," he said.

The images that brought to mind didn't repulse me in the least. It did quite the opposite. I didn't tell him that though, because it sounded a little deranged. He took the bag from my shoulder and the cookies from my hand then nodded his head toward the door. "Let's go."

I was smiling. I couldn't help it. He made me smile. This version of Saul was the one that made me happy inside. He made me forget there was another version of Saul that was very different. If he continued being like this, it was going to be hard to remember how falling for him was foolish.

It was too late about the caring for him. I cared for him before he kissed me. It hadn't been his looks that had caused it either. It had been him. It was hard to put off a bad boy vibe when you spent your days saving the people you cared about from themselves. There was more to Saul than he wanted people to know. Gran had known just how good he was and I trusted that.

He opened the passenger door of his truck and I climbed inside. It smelled surprisingly good except for the nicotine scent, although I was becoming fond of the faint linger of cigarette smoke. Probably a very bad idea but it reminded me of Saul. That and coconut. His truck smelled much like the tropical vacation commercial he should be starring in instead of driving around in this truck wearing a pair of jeans and a sweaty white tank.

I glanced down and saw a rehab pamphlet between the seats. When he was inside the truck, I picked it up. "Did Lily come home?" I asked him.

He simply nodded.

I started to put the pamphlet down, thinking it bothered him that I had seen it. He glanced at it then looked at me. "You can look at it. That's a new one she's not been to before."

It was in Washington. That was so far from here. I wondered if she always went that far or if this was something the doctor thought was a good idea.

"She swears she will be better. I'm just torn about trusting her. I don't want to make the wrong decision."

I couldn't imagine that kind of pressure. It was his mom's life and he had to decide what was best for her. That kind of responsibility shouldn't come until she was elderly and could no longer live alone. And yet he had been doing it since he was a teenager. Had he even had a chance to be a kid?

I glanced at him as he drove and wished, once again, I could help him. I also feared just how much I cared about him. The more I was around him and the more I got to know him, I let a little more of my guard down. How long would it take for me to have nothing left to protect myself? And did I care about that anymore? Would it be so wrong if I *did* fall in love with Saul? Maybe it was time I wasn't so careful… this could be my chance to truly let go and just live.

TWENTY-TWO

Rio was sitting on the massive sectional sofa with a bag of chips and the television remote in his hand when we walked into the living area. He looked up at us and then grinned. I returned his smile and Saul's hand touched my lower back. I wasn't sure if it was some sign of possession or warning to Rio. I had thought after the information about us possibly being siblings, Saul understood our relationship.

"You want something to drink?" Saul asked me.

"Water is fine," I told him, wanting any reason to stall from getting changed into my bathing suit.

"I'll take a beer," Rio said, flashing his dimpled grin at Saul now.

"You got a problem with your legs?" he shot back.

Rio stretched them out and groaned. "Yeah, they're killing me."

"Sure they are," Saul replied and left my side to walk over to the bar.

"I'm fucking serious! Do you know how many boxes of produce I had to unload the past two days? Pops is trying to kill me through manual labor. You're at the bar already. You can get me a beer," Rio told him.

"If you're serving drinks, I want a Jack," Drake called out as he walked into the room from a doorway I hadn't been through and had no idea where it led.

"His legs work fine," Rio said.

"What? Something's got to be wrong with my legs for him to get me a drink? He's at the bar already," Drake replied. "Hey, Henley," he added when he saw me.

I lifted a hand in a small wave.

His drink request forgotten, he walked over to the stairs leading up to the second level of the room and leaned on the rail. "You know you can always bring that hot little redhead that works with you at the shop when you come over. I won't complain and I'll share with Rio."

"Jesus, Drake," Saul said as he walked back my way with a bottle of water in his hand and nothing else.

I thought of the fact that Rio might just be related to Emily and knew I was going to have to deal with that very soon. "I don't want to share with you, Drake," Rio called out. "You didn't get me a beer? Seriously? What has our friendship come to?"

Saul ignored him and his hand returned to my back. "Come on, I'll show you where you can get changed."

"So I can't ask her to hook me up with the redhead?" Drake called out as Saul led me away from the room and to the door that went back to where the stairs were.

"Ignore him. That's what we do," Saul said.

"He's very..." I wasn't sure the right word to use for him.

"Fucking annoying," Saul finished for me.

I laughed. "I wasn't going to say that."

He led me up the stairs and I saw he was smiling. It wasn't a big smile, but it was something. I liked to see him smile. He seemed younger and less burdened. He didn't smile enough.

"You'll learn soon enough and that is exactly what you will be saying," Saul informed me.

"Yet he's one of your best friends and roommate," I said.

"I had to give in. He was like one of those puppies that won't go away," Saul told me as we reached the top of the stairs. He went to the first door on the right and opened it. "You can change in here. Bathroom is that way if you need it."

"Okay. Thanks."

He didn't make a move to leave and I waited, watching him. His eyes were so blue it was easy to get lost in them when his gaze was locked on you. His hand touched my chin then and he brushed my bottom lip with his thumb.

I shivered and stood very still, in hopes he was about to grant me with another of those kisses that made my knees weak. He bent his head and brushed a kiss on the corner of my mouth. "If I kiss you we won't leave this room," he whispered near my ear before dropping his hand and walking away.

I held onto the door frame for support for a moment then inhaled and gathered myself before stepping back and closing the door.

"Whew," I muttered. Every nerve in my body seemed to come to life so easily with Saul.

I looked at the bed in the center of the room and thought about what he had said. I wasn't so sure I had a problem with not leaving this room. At least my body didn't. Shaking my head in hopes of clearing it, I sat my bag down on the end of the bed and opened it up to pull out my swimsuit. I hadn't brought a cover-up, but I did have the large beach towel I could wrap around myself. There was no way I was walking through this house with nothing but my bathing suit covering me.

Quickly I changed and wrapped myself up in the towel in case Saul came back. I didn't look in the mirror for fear I wouldn't have the nerve to leave this room. I didn't look bad in a bathing suit. The turquoise somehow made my pale skin appear attractive, if that was even possible. My body was decent. I just had years of my mother in my head, telling me my flaws and how to fix them.

I folded up my clothing and put it in the bag and picked my bottle of water back up before opening the door. I didn't see Saul and I wondered if I was supposed to wait here or go back downstairs. After a moment, I decided I'd head down and wait for Saul there.

I could hear Rio and Drake talking about a volleyball game they had planned tomorrow but I didn't hear Saul. Glancing back at the stairs, I wondered if he was still up there. Standing in the foyer was dumb, so I forced myself to go into the living area. Drake would probably say something that was embarrassing or shocking, but Rio was there. I wouldn't be alone with him.

The moment I walked into the room, Drake let out a low whistle.

"Shut up," Rio told him.

"What? She's not my sister," he replied.

I glanced at Rio and he shook his head. "Ignore him."

That made me laugh. It was exactly what Saul had said.

"Guess the pool is off-limits this evening," Drake said and fell back onto the sofa. "Saul won't share. He's the selfish sort."

I walked down the three stairs and went to the opposite side of the sofa to sit down. "I saw your text," Rio told me. "Just haven't had time to respond. Work has been brutal."

"It's okay. It can wait," I replied.

"Yeah, she's a bit busy herself," Drake said with a wicked grin.

Rio glared at him then rolled his eyes.

I took a drink of my water, torn between wanting Saul to hurry up and wanting him to take a while longer so I could get my courage up about this swimming suit thing.

"I told her he's been playing the guitar again," Drake said in a low voice.

Rio glanced at him then me. "That's a good thing," he told me. "It's been awhile since he's done that."

I hoped I would get to hear him play the guitar and sing. I wasn't sure if it was something he only did alone in his room or in front of people. However, asking him would mean I had to tell him how I knew about it and I didn't know if that was an issue.

"We got a volleyball game out on the sand tomorrow. Want to join? You can be on my team," Drake said then and I turned to look at him.

"She's got plans," Saul said and my attention quickly shifted to the doorway he had just walked through. My breathing also became difficult. He only had on a pair of dark blue swim trunks and there was not one flaw on his body. It was unfair and beautiful at the same time.

Drake chuckled then and propped his feet up on the large round ottoman. "I'm sure she does," he replied.

Saul's gaze found me and I felt my entire body flush. I put the top back on my water and stood up. A crooked grin curled his lips. "Come on," he said.

We left the other two inside as we made our way out to the pool. The sun still had an hour before it set and the light on the gulf was beautiful. Standing on the pool deck, I looked out over the fading day glistening on the water. The hard things in life seemed easier when you saw things such as this.

"It's my favorite time of day to be out here," Saul said, standing behind me and placing a hand on my hip.

"I can see why," I replied softly.

Neither of us said anything more for several moments.

When Saul finally moved from behind me, I turned toward him. He gave me a wicked grin and then his eyes surveyed the towel I was clutching at my chest. "You gonna take that off?" he asked then walked over to the edge of the pool and, as if it was a choreographed move, dove smoothly into the water barely breaking the surface.

I stood there watching him glide under the surface, knowing I was going to have to take the towel off and get in too. It was either that or I could stand here like an uptight dork all evening. I did have the setting sunlight to help aid in my pale skin. When the sun was bright, I always feared my skin glowed from its lack of a golden tan.

Easing my hold on the towel, I let go of it and laid it over the edge of a lounge chair then walked to the edge of the zero-entry side of the pool and made my way down the small slant into the deeper water. I knew Saul was watching me but making eye contact seemed impossible right now. I was sure my cheeks were red and I hated that about myself. I wanted to be as cool and as tropical vacation commercial worthy as he was but that wasn't happening.

Once the water was below my breasts, I felt brave enough to meet his gaze. He had a crooked grin and I could see the twinkle of amusement in his eyes. This wasn't something I was used to seeing from Saul. The guy I knew wasn't playful at all but dark, broody, and withdrawn. The one looking at me now was different. More approachable. Less intimidating.

"Am I amusing you?" I asked.

He nodded slowly.

"And what am I doing that has you amused?" I shot back with my own playful smile. I didn't want broody Saul back just yet. I liked this version.

He gave me a full sexy as hell smirk then and I felt tingly all over. "You're shy about being in your bikini in front of me. It's fucking adorable."

I glanced down at my body under the water. My two-piece would qualify as a bikini but not by the standards of most girls I had seen at his house. When I lifted my eyes back to meet his I shrugged, acting as casual as I could about this. I didn't know what to say to his accusation since it was entirely true.

Saul moved toward me and I had to remind myself to keep breathing. His bare muscular chest looked even more amazing with water droplets running down his sun-kissed skin. He didn't stop until he was barely an inch from me. I watched as he lifted his hands from the water and cupped my face.

Knowing what was coming next, I closed my eyes just as his lips met mine. Once I had kissed Will in the rain but never had I been kissed in a pool. There was a sexiness to it that felt more intimate. The fact we had very little covering our bodies, our cold wet bodies touching, the sun setting just over our shoulders. This would be one of those kisses I remembered. Long after I left this town, this would come back to me. How it felt to have this beautiful boy touch me, how he tasted of whiskey and sunshine, and the warmth our bodies created from their nearness.

Wanting to feel his skin under my fingertips, I ran my hands up his chest. He shivered under my touch and the power that came from such a simple reaction was what I would guess a high felt like. I wanted more of that, more of him being made weak by me. This was new to me and so very different from what I had known before. Leaning closer to him, I ran my hands up to his shoulders.

His hands left my face and grabbed my waist firmly then jerked me flush against him. My breasts were pressed against his warm damp skin and this time, it was me who shivered. Our kiss changed then too. Something more desperate or needy began to take over and I had never felt this inability to control my reactions as I did now.

The moment Saul's hand slid from my waist to the fabric of my swimsuit bottoms to the sensation of his fingertips touching the bare skin of my bottom, I realized I no longer cared about my insecurities. Those had fled and had been replaced by desire.

Saul's mouth left mine and moved to the spot behind my ear and then to my neck. The hand cupping my bottom slid down to my thigh and he grabbed it to pull my leg up onto his hip. The pressure from his obvious arousal against the very thin barrier between my legs made all other thoughts fade away. My body was focused on nothing else but the sensations being with him this way were causing. I tipped my head back as he began kissing down my collarbone and the tops of my breasts.

Holding onto me, he moved us back until I felt his body hit the side of the pool and my knee press into the wall behind him. The hand Saul still had on my hip moved then and I felt the cool breeze against my nipple only a moment before his mouth pulled it into the warmth. I had to grab onto his shoulders for support and rocked my hips against him as I moaned from the pleasure coursing through me.

I hadn't come here tonight… I hadn't gotten in this pool with him, thinking this would happen. Possibly I had imagined kissing but not this. In the back of my mind, I feared what this would do to me. Deep down, I knew this would make me vulnerable, but in this moment with his body against mine and his mouth tasting me, I couldn't make myself care.

The intoxicating freedom of taking what I wanted and enjoying it was stronger than any concern for my future. Saul's mouth moved to the other breast and I buried my hands in his dark wet curls. I moved my hips against him and my head fell back further as the pressure between my legs caused my body to start clawing toward a release.

Saul released my nipple and he lifted his head up to look at me. His half-lidded eyes did nothing to hide the sky blue color of them, but his pupils were so large they were pushing the color back. His hands slid to my lower back and he began to move his body with mine. His gaze never leaving me, I felt one hand brush the skin on my side, then my stomach as he slipped it into the front of my bikini bottoms.

Breathing was no longer something I could do as I waited for his touch.

"Hate to break up the party but you got a fucking psycho ex in here that won't leave." Drake's voice rang out over the patio and with his words he might as well have tossed a bucket of ice water on our heads.

I moved first, dropping the leg I had up on his hip, and started to back away when his hands grabbed my waist. "No," he said. Then pulled me to him and buried his face in the curve of my neck and shoulder.

I stood there for only a second before I placed my hands on his arms. I wasn't sure if I had put them there to break free or not, but I didn't do anything but stand there breathing hard.

"Fuck," he said in a husky voice and then finally raised his head to look at me. I saw the same frustration and disappointment in his eyes that I felt. My body still wasn't on board with the sudden halt to the pleasure, but I was breathing again.

He brushed my cheek with the back of his hand as he stared at me. "I'll go deal with this. Wait for me," he whispered.

Did he think I would say no? Had any female ever told him no? I would wager they hadn't. I nodded.

He pressed a kiss to my temple and lingered for a moment then stepped back away from me and headed for the steps nearest to us, leading out of the pool. I watched him go and wondered if this had been fate. Had I been about to make a mistake and it was stepping in to keep me from it?

The idea depressed me. I didn't want to think being with Saul was a bad thing. I wanted to enjoy it and not think at all. If I thought too much, I was afraid of how I might see things.

"Could you fucking hurry?" Drake's voice called out. "She's batshit!"

I turned to see a white towel wrapped around Saul's waist as he walked back toward the house. I would be lying if a part of me didn't worry that he'd see Fleur and remember why he was with her. He would miss her or feel something for her. Just admitting that to myself was proof enough I was past the point of no return. When this was over, whatever it was between us, I was going to be hurt.

It was clear Fleur was hurt and he had moved on from her so quickly. To me. And I had thought nothing of it. Until now. I could easily be Fleur one day.

TWENTY-THREE

I wrapped my towel around me and stood there a moment, looking out over the gulf and wondering if I should make myself comfortable on the lounge chair or leave. It had been over ten minutes since Saul went inside and I was beginning to think he might not be coming back out. The problem with my leaving was my things were inside, specifically upstairs, and I had no vehicle. Although I could walk.

I heard the footsteps behind me and turned to see Rio walking toward me with two drinks in his hands. He was wearing red swim trunks and a Slacker Demon tee shirt. He stopped beside me and held one of them out to me.

"Take it," he said and I did. He then leaned forward to rest his elbows on the railing. "Drink it."

"Is it seltzer?" I asked him, looking down at the clear soda in my glass.

"Yep," he replied. "And some vodka. Drink the shit. You might need it."

I thought about arguing then decided he knew more about what was going on inside than I did. If he was out here to tell me that Saul was gone with Fleur then a vodka soda might help. I took a drink then shivered. It had been a while since I had alcohol.

"Thought I'd keep you company and offer to go get your things upstairs and take you home if you want me to," he said, while looking out at the waves. He then took a long drink from his glass. It was as clear as mine so I assumed we were drinking the same thing.

"Should I leave?" I asked him with an overwhelming sadness suddenly settling on me.

He glanced back at me. "Depends on what you want to do."

I didn't know what I wanted to do. "Is Saul still with Fleur?" I asked.

Rio nodded then took another drink. "Yep. She's drunk and he had to call someone to come get her. Right now she's screaming the house down about Saul's new ho," he said with a grin. "How many times you been called a ho?" he then asked me and chuckled.

I glanced back at the house. "This would be my first," I replied.

"Thought so," he replied, sounding amused.

We stood there a few minutes looking out at the water.

"You sure you wanna do this?" Rio asked me.

"Do what?" I replied, already understanding him but wanting him to clarify.

"Saul."

"You seemed okay with it before," I reminded him.

He nodded then looked back at me. "Yeah but shit like this reminds me what you are in for. Saul… he's a good friend. He's my best friend. But y'all, well, y'all don't have a future. We are just getting to know each other but what I have seen of you is that you do life much differently. Saul's life has no stability. It changes. Often."

I took a long drink and this time the burn wasn't so bad. It was needed. I understood what Rio was saying and I already knew this. He was warning me and if I was smart, I would listen. But I wasn't looking for smart. I had done that already, and my heart had still been broken. Things with Saul would never be like they were with Will.

"I don't expect Saul to be anything more than what he is. This isn't about me looking for security. It's about me not knowing or planning every step or being so careful I miss things in life. I don't want to miss Saul because I was afraid of the end."

Rio sighed heavily and straightened up. "Okay," he said then glanced back at the house just as the back door opened and Saul stepped outside. "Do me a favor," Rio added. "Don't measure Saul against anyone else. That shit ain't fair."

Rio didn't wait for me to reply. Instead, he headed back toward the house, slapping Saul on the back as he passed by. I would think about this conversation in detail later. I already knew that and there was no way I could keep from it. I could only change myself so much.

Saul looked at the drink in my hand and then at me. "Sorry," he said as he reached me.

"It happens or so I hear. I don't have an ex," I replied with a forced smile. Failing at making light of the situation.

"Vodka?" he asked.

I glanced down at my glass then back up at him. "Rio thought I might need it."

Saul frowned. "I see."

He probably didn't see, but I took a drink and didn't say anything.

"Let's go inside," he said then and nodded his head toward the house.

"Okay," I agreed and we walked back together.

Saul opened the door and I stepped inside then shivered from the cool temperature of the house against my still damp body. The living room was empty. The other two must have cleared out after Fleur's visit.

"Come on," Saul said and his hand rested on my lower back as he led me back to the stairs. I was thankful I would be getting on dry clothing, but it also felt as if this evening was about to end. As much as I didn't want it to, I also knew it was probably for the best. Saul's mood was dark again and after dealing with Fleur, I was sure he wanted to be alone.

He didn't stop at the room my clothes were in and I glanced up at him confused. His gaze met mine. "Your things are in my room," he replied and we kept going down the hallway toward a door at the very end that was closed.

He had moved my things. When had he done that?

When we reached the last door, he opened it and stepped back so I could go inside first. I moved past him and into the room. It was huge. The ceiling was vaulted, making it appear even larger. A king-size bed sat in the center of the room. There was a black leather sofa to the right and a bar stool in the far corner. Beside it was a guitar on a stand and I paused a moment and studied that. The guitar case was on the ground beside it and was open.

"This way," Saul said to me and began moving toward the door that was on the left wall. He opened the door and an equally impressive bathroom was inside, complete with a Jacuzzi tub and a shower that reminded me of a rock cave or something underneath a waterfall. My bag was sitting on the white marble countertop.

I glanced back at Saul who was standing at the door watching me. "If you need anything let me know."

I nodded but said nothing and he closed the door. The idea of taking a bath in his massive tub was tempting, but there was no way I was getting in there. I hurried and changed into my dry clothing then put the bikini I was wearing over the edge of his tub to let it dry some until I left.

Looking in the mirror, I ran a hand through my damp hair and sighed at my reflection. I wasn't going to stand here and critique myself. I walked over to the door and opened it up to find Saul sitting on the edge of the bed with a television remote in his hand. I hadn't noticed the large flat screen on the wall when we walked in since it had been behind us. He had changed too and was wearing a black tee shirt and a pair of white shorts. He turned his head to look at me and then patted the spot beside him.

I walked over and sat down. He reached out and twirled one of my strands of hair around his finger. "I like your hair wet," he said as he slowly played with the strand.

I liked his hair wet too, but I didn't say it.

"I don't want you to leave," he said as his baby blue gaze locked on mine.

"Okay," I replied hesitantly. Not exactly sure what he meant. He didn't want me to leave now, or tonight, or ever.

He smirked and dropped my hair to then run a thumb over my bottom lip. "When I'm with you, it's different," he said. "Nothing's fucked up or twisted."

I swallowed hard, having a difficult time staying focused when he began running his fingertips down my neck and along my collarbone.

"How is it that when you enter a room, nothing else matters anymore?" he asked me and my now shallow breathing was obvious.

"I don't know," I replied.

He grinned at me then and slid a finger under the strap of my dress. "I told myself I would just enjoy that, you being near and how it felt," he said in a husky tone as he slid the strap off my shoulder. "I swore I would never do more than kiss you. I would keep you safe from me," he said as he ran his palm over the top of my sundress and barely brushed my breasts underneath. His eyes dropped from mine to look at my chest.

"I lied. All the shit I swore I wouldn't do, I lied," he said and I wasn't sure who he was talking to anymore. Me or him. I also needed more oxygen than I was getting. There was no way he didn't feel my heart pounding against my chest. I could hear it.

"In the pool," he said, moving to take the other strap off my shoulder. "I would have taken your bottoms off and fucked you right there. It was like I had snapped. The rest of the world was gone and all I could see was you," he said then with one swift tug jerked my sundress down to my waist, leaving my breasts bared with nothing to cover them. "The entire time I was in here dealing with Fleur, my head was back in that pool with you, naked, straddling me."

I inhaled loudly and Saul moved over me his hands, grabbing my waist and pushing me back farther onto his bed. The sundress was gone now and he was over me. His hands flat on the bed on either side of my head. "I have never wanted something so damn sweet this bad in my life," he said to me, then his mouth came down and he bit my nipple just sharp enough to cause me to cry out before his mouth moved to my neck.

He took a small bite of my earlobe and his heavy breathing near my ear caused me to shiver. "Can I fuck you?" he whispered and I began to tremble. His tongue then traced my ear and I felt his hand slid down my stomach and inside the silk of my panties.

When his finger slid inside of me, I grabbed at his biceps and jerked against him. Never had my body been so responsive with just words. The way he said it and the things he said had me craving him, this, in a way that had to be unnatural. Just like him there was a darkness to it that called to me. I ached for it.

As he began to slid his middle finger in and out of my dampness, he moved back to my ear. "Can I?" he repeated.

I was sure if he didn't I would die from the need. I managed to nod my head as my nails sank into his thick corded arms.

Saul kissed my neck then and growled low in his throat as he moved his way down between my breasts then to my stomach. With his free hand, he reached for the back of his shirt and jerked it off then tossed it away. His perfectly sculpted chest and arms were on full display and made the yearning inside me become even more fierce.

He bent his head and pressed a kiss to my stomach. Then with both hands, he pulled off my panties and grabbed my thighs roughly, opening my legs. If I wasn't so turned on, I was sure this moment would have sent me into a panic. I had never been so exposed before yet the way Saul was looking at me made everything okay.

When he moved until his head was between my legs and the first flick of his tongue touched me, I was sure that nothing in heaven could be this good. I had never done this or had this done to me. I knew about it, of course. I read a lot of books. It was just not something I had experienced.

Saul began to lick and with each move of his tongue, I was sure I would never be the same. He was changing it all for me. One of my hands held his head there as my fingers were tangled in his curls. The other was grabbing onto the quilt beneath me for support. I cried out his name as he began to suck the sensitive nub that felt as if every nerve ending in my body was connected to that one spot.

I was so close to exploding with an orgasm when he stopped, stood up, removed something from his pocket then took off his shorts and tossed them aside. He opened the small package in his hand and rolled a condom down over his hard length then crawled back over me, moving my right leg out and opening it farther with his knee as he did so.

I stared up into his eyes, panting from my deliriously crazed desire. Maybe later I would feel guilt for the way my body was reacting to him, but I couldn't see how. This was a euphoria that I would never regret.

Saul lowered himself and when I felt the hard tip press against me, I was ready to beg him. His gaze was locked on mine. I stared up at him very close to begging him.

When he finally pushed inside me, I cried out in relief and with pleasure.

"Holy fuck," he said as he stilled once he was fully inside. He lowered his forehead to mine. "Christ, Henley, you're so fuckin tight."

He moved then and I whimpered, unable to say words. He groaned as he rocked his hips and I clawed at his back as the release I knew was coming began building again inside me. I didn't know what I was saying or if it was even words. I cried out Saul's name and possibly begged him for more. I couldn't be sure. I was lost in the experience.

"So fucking wet," he said once. He made his own noises as we began to get more frantic.

"SAUL!" His name tore from me as I finally shattered into a million beautiful pieces.

"That's it," he said on a groan. "Come for me, baby." Then he shouted as he pumped into me several times before he stilled and then moved off of me, taking my body in his arms and pulling me with him.

We lay like that, breathing hard, exhausted and sated. Nothing else mattered but what had just happened. It was one of those brief moments in life when there is nothing wrong but everything is right.

Saul's fingers trailed down my back slowly. I closed my eyes tighter and pressed into his chest. I could stay right here and be happy for the rest of my life.

He continued to gently caress my back and my body became even more relaxed. My eyes grew heavy and the warmth pulled me under. Until there was nothing but Saul and that was all I cared about.

TWENTY-FOUR

"Henley." Saul's deep voice was near my ear and I turned to snuggle closer to him.

When I heard a low chuckle, I smiled contentedly and went to slide a hand over him, but I couldn't find his body. Confused, it took me a moment and I blinked then realized it was dark. I had fallen asleep.

"It's dark." I stated the obvious. My voice was thick from sleep.

"Yeah, it's four in the morning," Saul replied.

Four in the morning? Four in the morning! I sat up quickly, almost losing my balance and falling off the edge of the bed.

"Woah," Saul said as his hands held my arms. "Easy," he added.

"Work," I said. "I have to bake."

"I know," he replied. "Let me get you home."

Oh. Okay. Yes, I could go back to Gran's and have plenty time to bake. It was fine. I started to stand up and I remembered. Several things. First of all, that I was completely naked.

I grabbed for something to cover myself with and ended up pulling the sheet up to my neck.

More laughter from Saul.

"I'm naked," I told him.

"I'm aware of that," he replied, sounding amused.

I sighed and looked around the dark room for my dress. That's when the memories of him taking the dress off and all that followed surfaced. I looked back at him and even in the darkness, I could see his smirk.

"Henley, my face was between your legs last night. Are you really worried about me seeing you naked?" he asked.

When he put it that way, it sounded ridiculous. "Yes," I told him, knowing it was dumb.

He moved then and was right back holding my dress out to me. "Here," he said.

I took it. "Thank you."

I slipped it on quickly and then stood up. He was still standing by the bed, so my body brushed against his. He didn't say anything or even touch me and I felt a slow sick knot begin to form in my stomach.

"I'll get your bag," he said then moved away.

I stood there in the dark room and watched him go. This was not what I expected him to act like after… well, after we had sex. I wasn't sure how I thought he would act, but this was not it. He was acting like he had before we had done anything.

I wasn't sure how I should act. Having sex with a guy I had only known a few weeks was not like me. Especially since the guy had just broken it off with his girlfriend. Who was I? Where had Henley gone?

Saul returned with my bag. "I'll carry it. Here's your shoes," he said and put them in front of me. Looking at him I realized that Henley had lost all common sense due to the hotness of the man in front of her.

I quickly slipped my feet into them as he began walking to the door. I followed, trying not to read too much into this. I needed to focus on getting to Gran's and baking things. I didn't need to overthink every single second of last night. I had slept with Saul. It had been incredible. I was twenty-one years old and we were single. This was completely acceptable.

I had to be honest with myself though, Saul had been with a lot of girls. This was nothing new or special to him. Whereas I had only been with Will three times before he died. That was the extent of my sexual experience. We were not the same. This was all surprising and confusing for me.

The house was quiet as we went down the stairs and then out the front door. Saul held it open for me then when we reached his truck, he opened the door for me again. Both were polite and I thanked him. However, there was no soft kiss on the lips or touch of his hand on my back. Nothing. It was all very cold and I couldn't convince myself that this was normal.

"I forgot your panties," he said as he backed up and pulled out onto the road.

"Oh," I replied. My panties weren't of great concern right now.

He didn't say anything more and a couple minutes later, we were pulling into Gran's driveway. When he cut the engine and climbed out, I was surprised. At this point, I expected him to open my door and push me out while the truck was still moving. He seemed ready to get rid of me. Was this how it worked? He got sex and now he was moving on.

I didn't wait to see if he was coming to open my door; I did it myself and when I stepped out, he was right in front of me. I stared up at him scared that I had made a mistake, sad because I was already missing him and he was right in front of me.

"Henley," he said in a low voice.

"Yes?"

He took a deep breath. "Stop looking at me like that or your baking isn't going to get done. Hillya will show up here looking for it and find me fucking your hot little ass on the counter. Do you understand?"

My face flushed and my eyes went wide but I managed a nod.

"Good. Go inside and get your stuff done. Then come back to my place," he said as he brushed a stray hair that was blowing into my face back.

"Okay," I whispered.

He groaned and stepped away from me. "Go inside."

I started to say something and he shook his head no and pointed at the house. The gleam in his eyes was a warning. One that made all my worries vanish. Smiling, I grabbed my bag and turned and headed for the house.

When I was inside and the door was closed behind me, I looked back to see his truck lights come on as he pulled out of the driveway. My cheeks hurt from grinning so big. He wanted me to come back. Which meant I needed a shower and to change. I glanced at the clock and hurried to start on my baking. While the banana loaf was in the oven, I got a quick shower. Then I put the muffins in and shaved my legs. When the granola was baking, I brushed my teeth and changed into a pair of cut off jean shorts and a red tank top.

Slipping on my sandals, I loaded the items in the car and headed to take them to work. I was only five minutes later than I normally delivered when I walked into the back door of the shop. Hillya was covered in flour, and Emily was icing some cinnamon rolls.

"Good morning," Hillya said, smiling at me.

Emily grunted. She was not good with getting up this early.

"Good morning," I replied and placed the items on the counter. "I didn't try anything new this morning. This is some of the regular stuff that sells out."

"I just appreciate you doing this on your days off. I need you to write down these recipes, so I can get someone in here to help me and you can have a real day off," Hillya said.

Thinking about this morning and having to leave Saul's bed, I decided that needed to be moved up the list of things to do. The idea of still being tucked in his bed with him made me wish I'd done it sooner.

"I'll work on that," I told her.

Hillya looked up from the bowl she was stirring. "Good!"

I said my goodbyes and headed outside. Soon, I was going to have to ask Hillya about Rebel. Just not today. Things with Saul were new. I was happy and I wanted to enjoy it. I wasn't sure how long this thing with us was going to last. Being with Saul was all I wanted to think about for now. It was as if I had a break from reality when I was with him.

TWENTY-FIVE

It was a little after seven when I pulled into Saul's driveway. I had brought another bag with a swimsuit and towel in case it was needed but left it in the back seat. Before I was halfway to the door, it opened with Saul leaning against the doorframe, crossing his arms over his chest and watching me. He had been looking for me. My chest felt warm and other things I was too afraid to label.

When I reached him, he held out a hand to me and I went willingly toward him. He kissed me then. The way I had wanted him to kiss me this morning. The kiss that said he too enjoyed last night. I went up on my tippy toes and kissed him back with all the emotions that I wouldn't speak. Not yet. Maybe never. It all depended on him and how this played out.

"I gotta get to work. Can y'all go suck face somewhere else?" Rio asked, and I pulled back to look over Saul's shoulder at Rio.

Saul didn't take his hand off my waist but stepped back and took me with him. "Mornin'," he said to Rio as we walked by him.

"Looks like a fucking good one for you," Rio replied.

"It is," Saul shot back at him.

I heard Rio laugh and then the door closed. Saul looked at me then. "You want go back to sleep?" he asked me.

I thought of getting back in his bed with him and I couldn't think of anything more I wanted to do. "Do you?" I asked him.

"Sleep?" he asked me.

I nodded.

He slipped his hand under the back of my tank top. "If I go with you back to my bed, I will fuck you again. So my question is do you want to go back to sleep?"

I had always thought using the word fuck instead of sex was crude. Until now. When Saul said it, all my female parts felt a thrill and became very alert.

"I want to go to your bed," I replied honestly.

Saul said nothing but led me up the stairs and down the hallway to his bedroom. When I heard the door click shut behind me, I turned to look at him. He reached for my waist but grabbed my shirt instead, taking it off and tossing it on the floor. My bra came next then he took a moment to look at my breasts before taking my hand and pulling me toward the bed.

He took his shirt off then his gaze went to my shorts. "Better leave those on," he said. "I'm going to let you sleep first."

"Are you going to stay?" I asked him disappointed. My body was aching now and I wasn't sure I could sleep.

"Yeah," he said and moved me to the side of the bed then pulled back the covers he had straightened while I was gone.

I sat down and took off my shoes then moved to get under the covers. Saul slid in beside me and shifted so my back was pressed against his chest. His arm sat just below my breasts and I closed my eyes, trying not to think about how incredible last night had been.

Saul's arm moved and brushed the underside of my breasts, causing me to inhale sharply. Every square inch of my body was sensitive.

"Henley," he said his voice tense.

"Yes?"

"You need sleep," he told me. "Don't wiggle."

"I'm not wiggling," I said, turning my head to look back at him. However, the movement caused my left breast to move right over his hand that had been resting too close.

He lifted his body up and pressed my back to the mattress as he came over me. "Yeah, you are," he said then lowered his mouth to mine to kiss me hard.

I moaned and arched into him, opening my legs so his body fit between them easily. His kiss became more aggressive as he pushed his erection against me. Our shorts were suddenly the enemy. I wanted them off. I wanted him inside me again.

He tore his mouth from mine. "Fuck," he growled and his hands went to my shorts. They were sliding down my legs along with my panties in seconds. Then he was shoving his down and kicking them off the bed. "You make me crazy," he said, lowering himself back over me.

It wasn't until I felt him at my entrance, sliding inside, that our eyes locked and we realized he wasn't wearing a condom. "GOD that feels incredible," he groaned frozen.

Yes, it did feel incredible but there was no protection. I wasn't on birth control and then there was his previous sexual partners to worry about. "Condom," I whispered hating to bring it up.

He inhaled sharply and then looked directly into my eyes. "I've never been with anyone unprotected. Ever."

Was he asking me to do this without a condom? As much as I wanted to be with him I wasn't sure I could do this. I said nothing but stared up into his eyes wishing I knew the right words to say.

"Henley, I would never do anything to harm you. I swear."

"I'm not on birth control," I said softly.

I could see him clench his jaw as he looked at me. "I'll pull out."

I didn't know all the details of sex but I did know that if he didn't come inside me then I wouldn't get pregnant. At least I was pretty sure that was required. I wish I had asked my mother questions about this now. Saul looked to be in physical pain as he held himself over me not moving. Waiting on me. I had to decide. I knew that making him stop and get a condom was the smart thing. His blue eyes appeared to be pleading with me. I was weak.

Unable to stop myself, I lifted my hips and he sank in deeper. His eyes closed tightly and he appeared to be in pure agony as a low and long groan came from his chest. "HOLY FUCK!" he shouted. His arms were trembling as he held himself over me.

Watching him made my pleasure increase. Lifting both legs, I wrapped them around his hips and pulled him down. He filled me completely then. Saul cursed again and he hands fisted into the sheets beside my head.

"You're so fucking wet and hot," he said between his teeth. "I've never," he was breathing fast and hard, "never been without one," he finished. "Damn nothing has ever felt this good."

He moved then and I kept my legs wrapped around him. My panting became as heavy as his. I wanted more of it. More of him.

"I'm gonna have to stop, baby. I can't stay in." He broke off with a moan of pleasure as he sank deep inside me again. "If you come on my dick, I'm not going to be able to stop," he warned me as my body began to tremble with the release that was almost within my grasp. It was there and my body was hungry for it.

"AH!" I called out, clinging to Saul as it began to claim me. The orgasm burst from me and the ecstasy took over as I held onto his shoulders and cried out his name over and over.

This one was different. I could feel the pulse of his erection as the bare skin of his cock slid inside me. The intimacy that provoked intensified everything. Just as I began to fall back to earth, Saul shouted and jerked away from me.

Startled, I opened my eyes just as he shot his release all over my stomach. "FUUUCK!" His body shook, his neck was so taunt the veins stood out, and his head was thrown back. It was the most beautiful thing I had ever seen.

When he was done, his hands fell to his sides and he drew a long deep breath as his gaze met mine. "You have no idea the strength that took," he said then moved his gaze to my stomach covered in his come.

"What?" I asked confused.

He lifted his eyes back to mine. "Not to let that go while I was inside you," he replied. "God, Henley, that was… fuck… it was," he stopped then and grinned. "Hell, I don't have words for it."

He moved back then, getting off the bed, and stood up. "I'll be right back."

I watched him go to the bathroom and come back with a hand towel. He wiped up his release from my stomach then dropped it on the floor before climbing back into bed and pulling me against him.

Like last night, he began to caress my back with his fingertips and slowly, I was drawn back to the relaxing security of being in his arms.

TWENTY-SIX

Standing outside Lily's penthouse was a much different experience than the last two times. Saul unlocked her door and went inside. "Mom!" he called out her name.

"Saul? Is that you?" she asked.

Saul looked at me before replying, "Who else has a key and calls you mom?" He motioned for me to come inside.

The penthouse smelled of garlic and parmesan cheese.

"I made spaghetti and meatballs for dinner. I hope you're hungry," Lily said as she walked into the living room from an arched doorway to the left of the kitchen. She shifted her gaze from Saul to me and a smile spread across her lips. "Henley! I didn't know you were here. Did Saul find you outside? Sometimes I think the doorbell isn't working," Lily said as she came toward us.

Saul slid an arm around my back. Lily stopped and studied that for a moment then she looked at Saul. Realization dawned on her and her eyes went wide. "Oh," she said, "You." She paused and looked at me. "You two are together," she finished.

This was not my mother and just because she was looking at me, I didn't feel as if it was my place to answer her.

"Yes," Saul replied.

Lily waved a hand in front of her then crossed her arms over her chest. "Oh, Saul. I don't know. She's Honey's granddaughter. Honey was so good to me. I loved her." She looked at Saul with an almost pleading expression. "And Honey loved her granddaughter."

I felt Saul tense, but he didn't move his hand. "I know that," was his response.

Lily fidgeted with her hands some more and then frowned at Saul this time. "She's not your type."

Of all the things I expected from Lily, this was not it. I wasn't sure if I thought she'd be happy about this, but I did not think she would be so obviously upset over it.

"It's not like that," Saul said.

Lily threw her hands up then waved them at us. "It looks like it is like that. You're touching her, she's here with you, you said you were together."

"Have I ever brought a girl here?" he asked her.

Lily shook her head. "No, you haven't. But Saul, she's not like the girls you date. Henley is a good girl. She's got a plan for her life and she has goals."

"And I can't date her because she's good?" he asked.

"I don't think I can stand it if you hurt Honey's granddaughter. And you will, Saul. You will."

Saul's hand fisted in my shirt and that was the only indication his mother's words were affecting him. I wanted to say something, but I didn't know what to say or if I should speak at all. Lily wasn't well right now and she was recovering and getting back on track. I didn't want to say something to derail her.

"I would never hurt her," Saul said.

Lily sighed then and looked at her son. "You won't mean to but you will. It's what you do."

Saul's hand tightened on my shirt again and I knew he was struggling not to say the wrong thing to his mother. Knowing she was going to keep saying things to him that upset him, I couldn't keep standing there silently.

"Honestly, Lily, you should be worried about me hurting him. I'm terrible with relationships and run when things get tough. Heck, I may be out of town by next week," I said this as **blasé** as I could, wanting to ease the tension and get Lily's focus off of Saul and his inability not to hurt me.

Lily looked at me then and her smile returned. Then she laughed. "You reminded me of Honey just now. That sounds like something she would say."

Taking this as my chance to stop all talk of our relationship and its future, I returned her smile. "And like Gran, I also enjoy Italian food. It smells great."

Lily spun around then and looked back at the kitchen. "Oh, I need to set the table for three. Do you like iced tea, Henley? If not, I can make some lemonade. I believe I have a mix in here somewhere," she said, hurrying back to the doorway leading to the kitchen

When she was out of sight, Saul relaxed and ran his hand over the part of my shirt that he had held in his fist. "Thank you," he said.

I tilted my head back to look up at him. "Don't thank me now. Remember I could run off next week with another billionaire's son who poses as a lawn boy."

Saul grinned and bent his head to kiss me gently. "Let me know when he gets to town so I can show him the way out. Only one of us per town. It's a rule."

I shrugged. "Not if he's hot. I may want to keep him."

Saul's expression changed. His smile went serious. "I'll make sure I'm the only man you want to keep."

My knees went a little weak and I wanted to make a snarky comeback to make him laugh, but in that moment, I just wanted to be back in his bedroom.

"Found the lemonade!" Lily called out.

Saul cut his eyes toward the kitchen. "Let's go get this over with," he said. "Don't take a big bite at first. Nibble. There's a good chance this taste like ass. My mom can't cook for shit."

I covered my mouth to muffle my laugh and nodded.

We walked to the kitchen together and I truly hoped the worst of the evening was over. I hated to see Saul upset or verbally attacked. Lily should have nothing but praise for her son. He had given up any plans he had in his life to make sure she stayed alive. He's sacrificed for her. I doubted she would see it that way. She was struggling to make it day to day.

Once we were in the kitchen, I assured Lily that I liked iced tea just fine and when we sat to eat, I was thankful for the warning. There was a good chance that Lily had used an entire container of salt and pepper in the sauce. Small bites were all I could manage and thankfully she didn't make dessert.

Listening to Lily talk about my gran and hearing stories of things they had done together made the meal enjoyable regardless of the food. I had no idea that my gran had gone parasailing or that she could line dance. Hearing these things made me wish that I'd spent more time with her in the summers. Not just the one week, sometimes two weeks, that I saved for my visits here. Now, I wouldn't get those times back and it was an ache I would always have.

When Lily walked us to the door, Saul hugged her and told her he loved her. She clung to him tightly and kissed his cheek. Will had been what my mom called "one of the good ones" and I'd always believed he was the best. He never broke rules, he was polite, and he was faithful. He was trustworthy and would get me to go to church any chance he could. I had always thought that a man like Will was the best kind of man. But I couldn't say that Will would have given up his plans for his mother. Had she been an addict and needed him this way, I don't think he would have been able to do this. He would have resented her for her sickness. He would have prayed for her and possibly judged her, that I was sure of… but he wouldn't have given up everything for her.

Saul stepped back and Lily moved to hug me. I returned her hug.

"Be careful," she whispered in my ear then let me go and stepped back smiling, but when her gaze met mine, I realized the smile didn't meet her eyes. She was warning me and she feared I wouldn't listen.

TWENTY-SEVEN

Leaving Saul's bed at four in the morning wasn't easy. However, work started off busy and didn't let up. Emily had woken up with a migraine and we were shorthanded. Hillya had called her other part-time employees, but no one had been able to come in on short notice.

It wasn't until one thirty that we got our first lull in the day and could take a moment. Hillya sat down on the stool behind the counter. "I should be making some food for the evening crowd, but I need to sit for a minute," she told me.

I walked over to the espresso machine to make myself a cappuccino. I had never required caffeine as much as I did today. Everything I had made this morning was gone and Hillya only had three pecan muffins and some shortbread cookies left in the bakery display. I knew she had more things in the cooler to put in the oven but neither of us went to do that.

"Want something?" I asked her, as the machine started brewing the shot of espresso.

Hillya shook her head. "Nothing you can make. Now, I could use some younger legs and a better back," she replied.

I finished making my cappuccino then went to take the vacant stool. It did feel good to get off my feet. I needed to find time to get more sleep. The past two days hadn't had much of that.

"Is your mother coming down anytime this summer to see you?" Hillya asked.

We hadn't talked much about my family, especially my mother. Knowing what I did now, it seemed weird to talk about her to Hillya. I shook my head. "No," I replied.

"I'm sure she misses you," Hillya said.

I thought about that a moment and decided I would be honest here. "She misses not having me around to control."

Hillya frowned then. "What do you mean?"

"Mom and I are very different," I told her. If she was going to open a door, I would test it to see how far I could walk into it.

"How so?"

"My mom is vain; she is very judgmental and she has an idea of what my life should look like that I don't agree with. I love her, I overlook her issues, I accept her for who she is. She just can't do the same for me," I replied.

Hillya tilted her head to the side. "You must be more like Honey," she said.

I looked at her then and decided to walk through the door. "Or like my father."

Hillya didn't give much away, but I could see her tense. She forced a smile that didn't match the uncertainty in her eyes. "Did you know him? Your father?" Hillya asked me.

"No. I never got the chance. He died when I was two years old. My mom refused to speak of him or answer my questions about him. It's something I think will always stand between us." I finished and I waited. The ball was in Hillya's court now. This wasn't how I had imagined this conversation would play out, but it was happening and I realized I was ready for it.

"How did he die?" she asked me.

"She said a motorcycle accident somewhere in Georgia, but she has never been honest with me about things and I don't know if that's true."

Hillya sat there silently for several moments and I wondered what I would do if she changed the subject. Could I do that? We were so close to it now and I wanted to know. I had wanted to know most of my life. Now, that it was opened up, I didn't think I could let her close it again.

"Perhaps she had her reasons," Hillya said finally.

All my life I had taken the responses about my father and accepted them. My mom would tell me nothing and only get angry when I asked any questions. My Gran would say she didn't know more than my mother had told her. They had both lied to me. If Hillya was who I believed her to be then I wasn't going to let her lie to me too. Gran had sent me here for a reason, and I didn't think it was because of my baking.

"Can I see the photo of Rebel?" I asked her then.

Her chin shot up and her eyes went wide as she looked at me in surprise or maybe it was shock. I waited for her to think it through and respond. I wasn't in a hurry; I had waited my whole life and I could wait a few more minutes.

"You know," she whispered.

That was my answer. The one I needed. The clarification that my father had been Hillya's son. My gran had sent me here with that letter for this reason. She hadn't told me because she was doing what my mother wanted, but she was leaving the clues there in front of me to figure it out myself.

"I didn't at first," I told her.

"Then how… who?" she asked, still searching my face for answers.

I didn't want to bring up Rio yet. "I found my mother's old letters in my gran's attic. They were written to a guy named Rebel. He was also my father, or at least reading the letters it appeared that way."

Hillya stood up from the stool and wiped her hands on her apron. "I should have told you. Honey said I could if I wanted to." She gave me a sad smile. "The letter she sent me. She said, well, would you like to read it?" Hillya asked.

I nodded. "Please," I replied.

Hillya walked over to the front door and locked it and turned the sign to closed. Then she walked to the door leading to the back. "Come with me, Henley," she said then went through it and I stood up and followed.

I had never been in Hillya's office until this moment. The door had been open at times and I had glimpsed inside from a distance, but this was my first time actually inside it. There were several photos around the room, a round rose-colored rug, a large white chair and ottoman and fresh flowers in a vase.

"Here," Hillya said, taking a letter from her desk drawer and handing it to me. I held it a moment, recognizing Gran's handwriting before opening it up.

Hillya,

If you are reading this then I am gone. The girl who brought it to you is our granddaughter, Henley. She is bright, talented, intelligent, and a human being to be proud of. Just as I hold regrets for the things I never told her, I also leave this world with regrets for not forcing my daughter to give you the opportunity to know your granddaughter. It was a disservice to you. It was wrong and something I will stand before God and answer to. Please forgive me. I made mistakes out of fear that Henley would be kept from me if I didn't follow her mother's demands.

Henley is here for the summer to complete a list of things I asked of her if I didn't survive. She's a talent in the kitchen. She makes the best gluten, dairy, and nut-free sweets you've ever eaten. And she makes these fancy bowls with her own homemade granola the kids are all about these days. Hire her. Let her update that menu of yours and get to know her. Right the wrong done to both of you.

I want her to know she comes from a line of strong women. Love my girl for me and I'll be sure to give your son a big hug when I see him.

Honey

I closed the letter and blinked to clear my vision as the first tear rolled slowly down my face followed by the next one. I wiped them away and held the letter out to Hillya. "Thank you," I said hoarsely.

"You keep it," Hillya said.

I nodded and sniffled as I tucked it into my shorts pocket.

She stepped around the desk and picked up a frame as she did. Then she walked to stand in front of me and handed it to me. "This was your father," she said.

I wiped at more tears as they spilled onto my cheeks then took the frame and stared down at it. He was older than the photos he had been in with my mom but not much older. He had facial hair in this one.

"From the day he was born that boy had me on my knees in prayer. Never a dull moment, never a moment's peace, and he if it wasn't for that charming smile of his, I think he might have killed me." She said this with fondness and love in her voice. "You have his smile. It was the first thing I noticed that day. After I read Honey's letter, I wasn't sure my heart could take it. Having you here as a reminder of all I had lost. But then you smiled and, in that moment, you looked just like him. It was the first time in twenty years I had seen his smile."

This time she was the one reaching up to wipe the tears from her face. Thinking she might be my grandmother and knowing she was changed things. I wanted to study her more, listen to her talk, I wanted time with her. Time I had lost. Time that was taken away from me by my mother's selfishness.

"I should have told you and I am sorry I didn't. I just didn't know how and I feared you may leave. I didn't know what your mother had told you about your father and I worried you might not want to be here if you knew. Every time I thought about telling you, I backed out of it. I was just getting to know you and I didn't want to lose you."

I understood that and I was glad now that I had been the one to say something. "Did he ever see me?" I asked the one question my mother refused to answer.

Hillya smiled and went over to her desk and picked up another photo and brought it back to me. She handed it to me and the emotion that slammed into my chest when I saw the image was overwhelming.

I stared down at the younger version of my father. He was holding a tiny baby wrapped in a pink blanket smiling down at her… at me. He was so young, and he looked so happy.

"They were going to be married," Hillya said. "I was so worried about him being a father at such a young age because he was still so immature and wild. He wasn't though. He was determined that he would be a good father and husband," she paused. "But things came out and your mother took you and left. She was young too and terrified. Rebel had never been easy to love and he often hurt those that loved him the most."

"Rio," I said his name without thinking. Understanding dawned on me and I spoke it aloud.

Hillya gave me a sad smile. "Why am I not surprised you already have made that connection? You've been here a month and you've connected the dots. There are people in this town who still haven't."

"It was Rio's mother then? Her being pregnant that sent my mom away?" I asked because my dots were not fully connected yet. She may think I had it all worked out but I didn't.

Hillya nodded. "Yes, Rio. Rebel left me two parts of himself on this earth when he was gone and I've missed out on both of them. Manda, Rio's mom, took off before he was born and he was seventeen when I saw him for the first time. He came in here and ordered a coffee and a cupcake. Those eyes were Rebel's and his voice. If I had closed my eyes, I would have sworn Rebel was right here with me. When he left with his things, I closed the door and went and cried for hours in my office."

I had a brother.

I stood there a moment and let it sink in. Overnight, I had a family I had missed out on knowing. It was right here in this small town all along.

"He will want to know. He'll want to meet you," I told her.

She lit up. "He would?"

I nodded.

"I would love that," she said on a sob, and I moved forward and wrapped my arms around her.

She clung to me then and cried harder. This was my grandmother and my careless, wild father had made mistakes, but he had wanted me. He had been looking at me with love in his face. He had held me.

Tears began to form in my eyes again and while I stood there with Hillya as she cried, I cried too. We had all lost something, but there was time. We had time to change what we could.

Not everyone gets this chance and not everyone understands the importance when they do. I did and although my gran had kept this from me, I understood her reasons and loved her too much to hold it against her. She had been afraid of losing me. She had also attempted to make it right at her death.

The list she had sent me had made me so angry. I hadn't wanted to think of her dying. Yet in it, she had left me so much.

Thanks, Gran.

TWENTY-EIGHT

When I arrived at home, Rio was already there. I had texted both him and Saul. Rio had responded, but I hadn't heard from Saul all day. I reached the top step and looked over at Rio who was sitting in the swing.

"Did you find more letters? I never got to read the last ones," he said.

I shook my head. "No, I didn't find more letters. But we don't need those anymore," I told him then went to unlock the door. "Let's go inside."

Rio stood and followed me in the house. I glanced at my phone one more time to see if I had missed a text or call before setting it down on the kitchen counter.

"Saul's dad showed up this morning. Drake said the limo pulled in the drive around nine. If he's not responding, that's why. He's dealing with Archer."

"Oh," I replied, wondering why his father being here would keep him from at least sending me one text.

"If you don't see or hear from him today, don't let it get to you. When his dad is here, he is different. He gets in a dark place. More moody than usual. They don't have a good relationship and if this visit concerns Lily, it will make it much worse."

I knew very little about his dad and what I did know Saul hadn't told me. That part of his world was closed to me and I wondered what else about Saul I may never get to know. Before I could dwell on it and get in my own dark place, I pushed the worries back and focused on what I needed to tell Rio. Today had been a good day. I didn't want to ruin it with my fears about Saul and the future I knew we wouldn't get.

"Do you want a drink or something?" I asked Rio.

He shook his head and plopped down on the sofa and crossed his arms over his chest. "Nope. Tell me what you know. I'm ready."

I walked over and sat down in the floral chair across from him. "Well, okay. Let me start with a few days ago. Last week to be exact. The day that Saul was missing."

"Back when we were still focused on finding out who our father was?" Rio asked with a smirk and teasing glint in his eyes. I knew he was pointing out once Saul and I decided to do whatever it was we were doing that I had been less focused on Rebel's identity.

"Yeah, well you see, I already knew who Rebel was by then. I wasn't sure when to tell you or how to tell you or if I should talk to…" I stopped and sighed. "Emily, the redhead I work with, that is also Hillya's great niece, broke a frame in Hillya's office. She came out to apologize and said that the picture of Rebel was fine, just the frame was broken. When Hillya left the kitchen, I asked who Rebel was and she said he was Hillya's son. He died in a car accident when he was twenty."

Rio was leaning forward now, his elbows propped on his knees and his brow creased in a frown. "Are you serious?" he asked.

"Yes and today Hillya and I were there alone and the topic came up about my mom and stuff so I just asked her point blank about Rebel. She confirmed that he was my father and yours." I didn't tell him about the photo of Rebel holding me or his mother being pregnant the reason my mom left town and Rebel. I wasn't sure how to explain all that or if I even should.

Rio said nothing for several moments. "Shit," he finally muttered. "You've been working for her all this time and she knew but said nothing."

I nodded. "Yeah. She wasn't sure how to."

"I've gotten coffee and cupcakes there for years," he said, shaking his head. "How could she say nothing all this time?"

"What was she supposed to say? Put yourself in her shoes. Her son got two girls pregnant around the same time. He didn't have anything to do with either, then he died young. She didn't feel like she could know us."

Rio shook his head and stared out the window. I let him process it all and remained quiet. I'd been given plenty of time to think this through and I'd spoken with Hillya. He hadn't been given the same experience.

"She wants to meet you, officially. She wants to talk to you," I told him, and he turned his head back to look at me.

"Why? What the fuck is there to say?" His tone sounded angry. I hadn't expected him to respond this way.

"You have questions and I still have some I didn't think about when we spoke. She can tell us about our father. She can tell us how he died." I stopped then added. "She said your voice is identical to his and your eyes."

He took a deep breath and stood up. "Yeah, well it's been twenty-two fucking years. Why hasn't she told me all this by now?" He started walking toward the door.

"I have those pictures I found of my mom's. You can take them and look at them when you're ready," I said, hoping he would calm down after he had some time to think this all through.

He paused and glanced back at me. "Yeah. Okay."

Relieved that he was open to at least looking at the pictures, I took out the two that my mother wasn't in and handed them to him.

He didn't look at them, but he did take them. "Thanks. I'll bring them back," he promised then continued toward the door.

When he opened it, he stopped and I thought he was going to say something more but he didn't. He walked outside and closed it behind him.

I sank back down onto the chair and let out a weary sigh. That had not gone how I expected it to. I was glad I hadn't told him about the baby picture of me and Rebel. He wasn't very fond of Hillya's silence, but I hoped he would decide to talk to her at some point.

I sat there thinking about today and about Gran. All the planning she had done when she'd set up that list. There were only two things left to do and now that I had found out the truth behind my father, it was time I faced the next task. It could be something simple like the last one had been and something truly for Gran's sake. Or it could be something that would change things for me yet again.

When I finally stood up, I went to make myself dinner. Saul still hadn't responded when I turned off Netflix hours later and headed for the bathroom to take my shower. It was after eleven and I didn't expect to hear from him tonight. I realized I had been so wrapped up in him and the way he made me feel that I'd lost sight of the facts. We weren't a couple. We didn't share everything. I hadn't told him about Hillya. He hadn't told me about his dad.

Feeling melancholy, I took extra time in the shower. Normally a shower made me feel better. Tonight, it wasn't working. The water began to run cold and I still felt the sadness that had taken over at the thought of Saul. I cared too much, too soon.

I dried my hair and wrapped a towel around my body then stepped out of the bathroom. My heart almost stopped and I let out a small scream when I saw I wasn't alone.

Saul was standing at the doorway of my bedroom looking at me.

"You shouldn't leave the door unlocked. Anyone could have walked in here."

TWENTY-NINE

"I must have forgotten to lock it after Rio left," I replied. My heart was still racing from being scared to death but seeing Saul made all that okay.

"Rio was here?" he asked with a scowl.

"Yes."

"Why the fuck was Rio here?"

He looked angry and jealous. I had texted him and he hadn't responded all day, yet he got upset because Rio was here? Seriously.

Annoyed, I clutched the corners of the bath towel tightly and scowled back at him. "Because I had some information about our father. Remember the we might be siblings' thing. Well, we are."

Saul continued to frown. "What did you find out?" he asked.

I was too tired to go over all this again tonight. I'd stayed up late, hoping to hear from him and now he was here, and I was mad. "Hillya had a son named Rebel. He is our father," I told him.

Saul moved toward me then and I wasn't sure if I was happy about that or not. "So, Rio is your brother," he repeated.

I nodded.

"Fine, but I still don't like him here," he said.

"Are you serious? What do you think we are gonna do? He's my brother!"

Saul lifted his shoulders in a shrug as if it wasn't important. "Nothing. I just don't want him here with you. I don't like any guy alone with you."

My annoyance went from slight to full-blown. "You don't get a say in that, Saul. Just like I don't get to be concerned when you don't respond to my text messages."

He stopped in front of me and took one of my wet strands of hair between his fingers. What was it with him and hair? I should step back and jerk my hair away from him, but it felt good and I had missed him. I was also exhausted and when I was tired, I got angry over stupid things. Could this be one of those times? Would I think differently about it in the morning? I had to think that through first.

"You sent one text," was his response.

"Yes, and in that text, I told you I was getting off work and going home," I reminded him.

He wrapped my hair around his finger and tugged gently. "And I came here because that was where you were."

Why couldn't he say more than a few words or half sentences? "It's midnight," I pointed out.

"You're still awake and naked."

Growling in frustration, I pulled my hair from his hand and backed up. "And I am tired and going to bed," I told him, proud of myself for standing my ground.

He looked hurt and almost confused. As if I had no reason to be upset with him. "My father showed up today. I had to deal with him and I had to take Lily to her AA meeting," he said and took another step toward me. "I didn't know you wanted me to respond. It's not something I do."

"You don't respond to text messages?" I asked him.

He was close to me again and he ran the back of his finger over my bare shoulder. "I don't tell people where I am or what I'm doing."

Great. That made me feel special. "Glad to know I am considered people," I shot back at him, unable to move away anymore because the edge of the bed was behind me.

The corners of his mouth curved up slightly. "You took that wrong."

My eyebrows shot up. "I don't see how else I was supposed to take it!"

He was grinning now. A fully amused grin. His dang teeth were perfect. "Before this thing with you, I've never conversed with a female about my plans. I just showed up when it worked for me."

"That's rude," I replied.

He ran the back of his finger across my jawline and studied my mouth. I was quickly forgetting why I was mad. He was talented at that. "I see," he said then began running the pad of his thumb over my bottom lip. "You want me to tell you where I am then?"

I managed a nod. "It would be nice."

His other hand tugged on the towel I was covered up with but I held it tightly. He lifted his gaze back to mine. "And if I do this, you won't have other guys here?"

"Even my brother?" I asked incredulously.

He nodded. "Yeah, even him. I need time to adjust to the new relative thing."

"Fine. Okay," I said with a sigh.

He slipped a hand under the towel and I jumped when he ran his fingertips over my stomach. I wasn't very angry anymore. My body had taken over and it wanted this very much.

"I'll answer your text. Every damn one of them," he said and bent down to kiss the corner of my mouth. "I'll text you even when you don't ask," he whispered then pressed a kiss to the other corner of my mouth. "I'll fucking call you if you want me to."

He slid his other hand underneath the towel and grabbed my butt then pulled me against him. "If it makes you happy. I don't want to see you upset."

My hold on the towel had weakened and this time, when he tugged on it, the only barrier I had fell to the rose-colored rug under my feet. His gaze didn't leave mine though. I stared up at him, needy and ready to be close to him again. "Am I forgiven?" he asked.

"Yes," I whispered.

He pulled his shirt off and then unbuttoned his jeans. When he pushed those down his hips, his eyes finally left mine and began slowly scanning my body. There was no part of me he hadn't seen by now, but I still felt the blush on my skin from the vulnerability.

I watched as he stepped out of his jeans and boxer briefs. Seeing his erection made the ache between my legs tingle. "Come here, Henley," he demanded in a low voice.

I went without hesitation. Placing my hands on his shoulders, I went on my tiptoes and kissed him. The truth about it all was I had missed him. Not just the sex, although it was incredible, I missed Saul. I missed being near him, hearing him talk, watching him, making him smile.

His hands grabbed my bottom and he lifted me up. I wrapped my legs around his waist, causing his hardness to press against me. I gasped into his mouth, but I didn't break the kiss. I wanted to taste him. Our tongues slid in and out, mimicking what our bodies would be doing soon.

Saul moved forward and lowered us onto the bed behind me. I kept my legs around him, not wanting to lose the friction of our bodies. He began kissing my neck as one of his hands moved to cover one of my breasts. His kissing became more demanding and then he paused at my cleavage before lowering his head and licking at one nipple and then the other.

My breathing was more of a pant at this point.

"Roll over, get on your hands and knees facing the mirror," he said as he moved away from me, causing me to unlock my legs as he left.

I did as instructed and watched in the mirror as he moved behind me. His eyes locked with mine and his hands grabbed my waist. When his erection brushed against me. I sucked in a breath and held it. Then he took it in his hand and guided it in the wetness between my legs that was more than ready for him.

He lifted his gaze once more to meet mine as he slowly entered me. I wanted to close my eyes and soak in the pleasure, but I also wanted to watch him.

"I've thought about this all day," he said with a groan. Then he rocked his hips and pulled out just enough before slipping back into me. "You are what got me through today's shit. Thinking about you and this."

He was deeper in this position and I realized that, again, he wasn't wearing a condom. It felt better. He slid in and out faster and the bare contact was unlike anything else. With each stoke, he started to move quicker and harder. His fingers dug into my hips and I moved my gaze from his to watch our bodies in the mirror.

His muscles flexing, my breasts bouncing and swinging with each thrust, it was beautiful and erotic to see us this way. My orgasm had been building but seeing us like this and watching his jaw clinch with each thrust sent me flying into pleasure. Throwing my head back, I cried out as the rapture of the moment took over.

"FUCK! That's it, baby, come on my dick." Saul's voice seemed far away as I floated on the most intense orgasm I had ever experienced.

"GAAAHHH!!!" Saul roared, and he was out of me immediately. Once his hands left my hips, I fell onto the bed as the heat from his release hit the back of my thighs. I turned my head toward the mirror to watch him.

He was on his knees, his perfectly firm body taut and slightly bent as he shot his come onto my back. "Damn," he said hoarsely. Then turned his head to meet my gaze in the mirror.

I smiled at him and a slow smile spread across his face.

In that moment, I was sure I could forgive him anything.

THIRTY

I was thirty minutes late getting today's baked items to Hillya and all I could do was apologize. There was no way I could tell her that I was late because Saul came into the kitchen this morning and we ended up having sex on the table. She was understanding but reminded me again that I needed to write down recipes so I could stop doing this on my off days. I was going to work on that today.

While I was gone, Saul had left to check on Lily and get her to a doctor's appointment and another AA meeting. He had made sure I knew his plans after he had given me an orgasm. With him gone and the house empty, I went back to sleep until noon.

It wasn't until two in the afternoon that Saul texted me. He said to meet him at his place after four and to bring a bathing suit. The images of us in the pool having sex with the setting sun had me smiling the next two hours. However, when I pulled up to Saul's house, there were two trucks I didn't recognize along with Rio's Jeep and Saul's truck.

The black bikini I was wearing under my sundress had been for Saul. It was the most revealing one I owned and I had bought it weeks ago, wanting to get out of my comfort zone. I'd never managed to do that though. The idea of wearing this in front of others made me consider going back home and changing.

There was a knock on my window that startled me. I jumped then turned to see Drake standing there grinning. My leaving would be difficult now. Deciding to suck it up, I opened the car door and climbed out.

"You were having deep thoughts," Drake teased.

"I, uh, thought I forgot something," I lied.

He didn't believe me. It was obvious by his amused expression. "Uh huh," he replied. "You forgot the redhead. She's invited to the party too. Anytime she wants."

Party. There was a party. Not what I was expecting at all.

"She doesn't like blow jobs," I told him.

He looked devastated. "Damn."

"Can't win them all."

Drake grinned at me then. "I like you. You're hot and you've got jokes. Smart mouths are sexy as hell."

I wasn't sure if I should say thank you or not.

"Get the fuck away from her," Saul said with a growl as he walked down the stairs to meet me halfway. He was scowling at Drake, and I realized he was serious.

Drake held up his hands. "My bad. Sorry, man. Didn't see you."

He wasn't helping things. Saul's expression turned threatening.

Drake finally realized it and nodded. "Not joking. Got it," he said, backing away as he reached the top step. Then he went inside the house.

Saul put his arm around my shoulders and kissed my temple. "Hey," he said, although the gruffness hadn't left his voice completely.

"Hey," I replied unsure of his mood. Did something happen today to upset him or was he truly that upset over Drake talking to me? Instead of asking, I decided to get his mind off it and change the subject. "So, there's a party?" I asked.

He glanced down at me as we walked inside the house. "Yeah."

We headed toward the living area and voices and he didn't elaborate but then he rarely ever did.

"Whose coming?" I asked, realizing I knew very few of his friends from the last party I attended with Rio.

He shrugged. "The regulars, maybe a few extras."

Man of few words.

We walked into the living room and I took in the scene. Drake was on the U-shaped sofa with a beer between his legs, yelling at some game on the television. On the other side of the sofa was a guy I hadn't met but I did remember seeing at the last party. Beside him was a blonde who was on her smart phone typing something. The guy laughed at something that happened on the television and Drake cursed.

Rio came walking inside from the balcony and he nodded his head when he saw me. We hadn't talked since yesterday and I hoped he was dealing with everything better today.

"Benji! Fix me a drink," Rio called out and I turned to see Benji behind the bar with a shaker and martini glasses.

"You want a fucking martini, pussy?" he asked.

"God no. Just a Jack and coke," he replied. "Pour up that girly shit for Genesis."

"What the fuck am I making the first book in the Bible a cocktail?" Benji asked.

Rio rolled his eyes. "Genesis is the girl here with me, dumbass."

"Jesus, who named her?" Drake asked.

Benji burst out laughing. "Maybe Jesus did!"

It took Drake a minute to realize what he meant then he started laughing.

"Gangs all here," I said to Saul.

He gave me a crooked grin. "Lucky us."

"Is Saul fucking smiling? What the hell is that?" Benji asked, and I turned my head to see him coming in our direction with a martini and a Jack and coke.

"He will do that shit all night as long as she's around," Drake called out.

Saul didn't appear amused. He moved his arm from my shoulders and put his hand on my lower back. "You want a drink?" he asked me.

I started to say no but decided perhaps a drink would help me tonight. I looked at the martini that Rio was taking from Benji. "Maybe one of those?" It sounded like a question and it kind of was.

Saul moved and led me over to the bar with him. He picked up the shaker and then poured what was in it into a glass. "What the fuck is this drink?" he asked Benji.

"Dirty martini. Add an olive," he told him.

Saul took an olive and put it in the glass before sliding it to me. "Thanks," I said as he grabbed a bottle of beer from the ice bucket.

"Don't thank me yet. It may taste like shit. I don't know what's in it," he replied.

"Vodka mostly," Benji replied.

I looked at it, wondering if maybe I should have gone with something else. How much vodka was in this? I didn't ask for fear of sounding like a dork.

"Come on," Saul said and led the way down to the balcony door.

Rio was at the pool with his date. She had just gotten out of the water and was walking toward him dripping wet to take the martini he had brought her. The back of her bathing suit did not exist I realized when she turned her back to us.

"Want to swim?" Saul asked me and I thought about my bikini. It didn't seem so bad compared to Rio's friends. At least most of my butt was covered up. It was the little bit that wasn't that had me nervous. I looked down at the drink in my hand. Liquid courage.

"After I drink this," I replied then took a sip. It was a miracle I didn't choke. I didn't know what Benji had been shaking up with the vodka because I tasted nothing but vodka. Possibly a hint of olive but that was it.

"Bad?" Saul asked, and I lifted my gaze to see him watching me.

I shook my head and he laughed.

Unable to keep from smiling, I added "Maybe a little."

He took a drink of his beer but continued smiling. I turned to look back at Rio then and saw the girl was looking at Saul. She wasn't just looking; she was checking him out. I couldn't blame her. He was hard not to look at. Especially when he was smiling.

I took a bigger drink of the martini. I was going to need it and possibly more.

Saul took my hand and led me over to the teak lounger that was wide enough for two and had a table for drinks on each side.

"Where's the music?" Drake's voice rang out.

He was walking down to the pool patio, wearing a pair of baby blue swim trunks with a beer in each hand. Behind him was Benji and a guy I hadn't seen inside. He must have just arrived.

Saul sat down on one side of the lounger then patted the spot beside him once. I put my drink on the table before sitting down. Saul rested his hand on my thigh and I reached for my drink, deciding I might just need another one after all. This wasn't so bad. Country music came over the speakers and Rio groaned loudly.

"You shouldn't have let me pick it," Drake said then dove into the water sideways.

We sat there silently and Saul traced patterns with his fingertips on my leg. It was peaceful, even with the music and other partygoers. I finished my drink and felt very relaxed.

"Do you have on sunblock," Saul asked me.

I nodded. "Always. Have you seen my skin?"

His hand slipped between my thighs. "Yes, all of it," he replied.

I smiled at him and he sat up from his reclined positon. His lips brushed mine and then he bit my bottom lip. "We need to swim or we are going to have to go inside," he told me.

"Why?" I asked.

"Because I can't fuck you out here."

"Oh," I gasped, and my body immediately reacted to his words.

He stood up then and pulled off his tank then looked down at me. "Let's get in."

I joined him and pulled the sundress over my head, realizing the vodka was to thank for my inhibition. When I dropped it on the lounger beside his shirt, he was staring at me. His gaze was appreciative but he seemed unhappy.

"Fuck," he muttered then took my hand and we walked to the water.

When we got to edge, I saw Saul glaring angrily at Drake. "Not one motherfucking word," he warned.

Drake held up his hands. "I didn't say shit."

"He's making sure you don't," Rio called out from the other side of the pool.

"Why aren't you threatening Rio?" Drake asked defensively.

"Don't," Saul said again.

Thankfully Drake let it go. Saul pulled me farther in then he let go of my hand and he went under swimming across the length of the pool. The cold water was a relief from the sun and I walked in until it was over my breasts.

"You're new," the guy that I hadn't seen before said. He had just walked over and sat on the edge of the pool.

"Yeah, I guess I am," I replied.

He nodded his head toward the other end of the pool. "How do you know Saul?" he asked me.

"We, uh, well." I wasn't sure the proper answer for this.

Saul's head came up beside me but he didn't look at me. He turned to the guy. "She's with me, Hills," he said.

The guy shrugged. "I assumed that. I just didn't know if this was a one night only thing since Fleur wasn't here."

Saul tensed beside me and his jaw clenched. The guy was making an assumption based on what normally happened here. Saul had no reason to get upset over it. Unless he thought it would upset me. I touched his arm and tried to get him to look at me.

"No, that's not what it is," he replied.

His tone made it clear he was angry. "I get it. No worries," Hills said and stood back up.

Saul turned to me then and his hands went to my waist. "I'm done out here," he said and I followed him out of the pool. He grabbed two towels and handed me one from a large teak cabinet.

I wrapped it around me and watched as he picked up our dry things. No one said anything as we headed inside. I wondered if he was always like this at parties. I didn't want to be the reason he didn't enjoy them.

When we were back in the house, I grabbed his arm to stop him. "Hey. What's wrong?" I asked.

He turned to look at me. "Nothing."

I wasn't letting him off that easily. "Yeah, there is. You were angry the entire time we were out there."

"I'm dealing with shit," he said.

"Do you want to talk about it?" I asked him. Was something going on with his mom again that he hadn't told me?

A smile that didn't match the frustrated look in his eyes crossed his face. He shook his head. "No, I don't think I do."

That stung. I was just trying to help. "Okay."

His gaze stayed on mine for a few more moments and then he reached out and took my chin between his thumb and forefinger. "I warned you I was damaged. This is a part of it I didn't realize I had an issue with."

"What does that mean?"

Saul took a step toward me and closed the space between us. "Until you, I didn't know I had a problem with jealousy. I do. I'm dealing with possessiveness and that's new to me."

"I've not done anything to make you jealous," I pointed out.

His gaze dropped down at the towel covering me up. "That bikini," he said.

"It covers up more than what the other girl out there was wearing did," I pointed out.

"I don't care about who sees her body," he replied.

But he cared who saw mine. I wanted to be mad at him. I really did. I tried to get mad at him, but I couldn't. He was being honest with me and he said he had never felt like this before. I felt it then… the falling.

And I fell a little more.

"I thought it was just going to be us," I told him.

He pulled me to him. "You wore it for me then?"

I nodded.

"I wish they would all fucking leave," he said.

"I thought you liked parties."

He pressed a kiss to the corner of my mouth. "I'm finding I don't like them at all."

"Why?"

He kissed the other corner of my mouth. "Because the void I tried to fill with shit like that isn't empty anymore."

His mouth covered mine then and I kissed him with all the words I couldn't say.

THIRTY-ONE

A week and a half after I told Rio about Hillya, he walked into the cafe. I hadn't tried to talk to him about it again. Saul thought I should wait it out and give Rio time to decide how he felt about things. Last night at Saul's, I had caught Rio looking at me as if he wanted to say something but he never did. Today he showed up at Sips and Signs so that must mean he was ready.

Hillya was putting cupcakes and lunch sandwiches in the display case and didn't see him enter. I gave the customer in front of me their bag and coffee then turned my attention to him. He was ready to talk to her or he wouldn't have come.

"Hey," I said as he walked up to the counter.

He looked over at Hillya just as she was standing up. Her gaze found him and she froze. When she'd asked me if he wanted to meet after I told him what she had told me, I had explained that he needed time. She didn't bring it up again, but I knew she was curious. I just hadn't known what to tell her.

"Hello," she said after a moment and walked toward us.

"Hi," Rio said.

"I would do the introduction but that seems pointless," I said, hoping to ease the tension.

"Yes, it does," Hillya replied, keeping her gaze on Rio.

He glanced at me then back to her. "I, uh, I have questions."

Hillya smiled and gave a small nod of her head. "I assumed you would," she said. "I want to answer all that I can for you."

Rio glanced at me again, looking unsure. He had made it this far, but he didn't seem prepared for the next step.

"Tomorrow we are closed," I reminded Hillya. It was the fourth of July and although I was sure business would be booming, Hillya said she always closed for the fourth.

She smiled brightly. "Yes, we are and I always cook a big lunch for the fourth. My sister and her children and grandchildren come over. We take the boat out and the younger ones water ski." She paused then looked from me to Rio. "I would love for the two of you to be there."

I wasn't sure what my plans might be. Saul hadn't mentioned another party at his house. The last two gatherings that the guys had, Saul had come to Gran's and stayed there with me.

"We are having something tomorrow night, but for lunch, I could come by," he said, cutting his eyes to me as if he needed some sort of agreement. I nodded.

"That is wonderful," Hillya replied, looking truly pleased.

"What time should we be there?" I asked her for Rio's sake.

"Eleven would be perfect. I can introduce you to," she paused, and I could see the uncertainty in her gaze.

"Relatives?" I asked her with a reassuring smile.

She nodded her head. "Yes, relatives."

Rio said nothing.

"We will be there at eleven," I replied. Then I turned my attention back to Rio.

He met my gaze. "Okay, yeah," he muttered then he turned and left.

When the door closed behind him, I looked back at Hillya who was watching him walk to his Jeep.

"He will come around," I said.

She sighed then turned her gaze to me. "I hope so."

I did too. I was promising something I wasn't positive about. Rio had more hurt than I did about our father. I knew his life was a much harder one than I had been dealt. Perhaps he blamed Hillya for not rescuing him. That seemed unfair. Shouldn't he hold that against his mother's parents.

Hillya walked back to the kitchen and I waited until she was gone to slip the phone from my pocket and text Rio: *You agreed to this. You better do it. She'd old and lived a very lonely life. Remember that.*

Rio didn't reply.

Before I Ieft work, I texted Saul to let him know I was leaving. For the first time in two weeks, he didn't respond. On my drive home, I decided to go to the Hendrix IV and see if he was with Lily. She had skipped the past two days' AA meetings and I knew Saul was concerned. If he didn't go with her, she would always stop going. I hated how that wore on him. He carried so much guilt over something he shouldn't have to be responsible for–his own mother.

The security guard recognized my car and waved me through without me needing to show him my card. When I turned into the parking deck, I saw him. Saul was here and he wasn't alone.

Stepping out of the main elevators, not the one that went to Lily's penthouse, Saul and a familiar blonde woman emerged. They walked out and then stopped and talked. It was obvious they were close. They stood close. Too close. They bent their heads toward the other when they spoke as if what they had to say was private.

The blonde was as stunning as I remembered her. She was wearing white shorts and a peach halter top. Her platinum blonde hair hung over one shoulder. They didn't notice me or the other guests that passed by them to get on the elevators. Whatever they were speaking of had their complete attention.

When Saul stepped closer to her, I knew this was all I could take. Backing up, I turned my car around and headed back to Gran's. The scene in my head would haunt me. I could try and explain it away, but I didn't have an excuse that seemed plausible. Saul had been standing so close to her and they had been talking like people with a connection. They knew each other, and it was obvious.

The lump in my throat grew the entire drive home. Pulling into Gran's driveway, I thought of the last time I saw the blonde woman. It had been the only time. The sweet little girl Gran had left her scarves to and babysat. Isla Evans was a married woman with a child. There was no reason she should be at a luxury condo complex, talking to a younger man with such familiarity.

Stepping out of the car, I thought of the list. I thought of Keerly. I believed Gran had sent me there for one simple purpose: to give Keerly something to enjoy. But had Gran sent me anywhere for a simple reason?

"Was that your way of warning me, Gran?" I asked her aloud.

Had Gran known this and wanted to make sure I did too? I had thought Gran put me in Saul's path on purpose. But what if she hadn't? What if Saul was just going to be there and she wanted to be sure I knew he wasn't for me?

The house was quiet when I went inside and there was still no message on my phone from Saul. I closed the door and locked it behind me. Looking out into the night, I wondered if he would come and if he did what I would say.

I didn't want to jump to conclusions, but I had to know. I would have to ask Saul. It was only fair.

Taking off my clothes, I stepped into the shower and wished it could wash away the hurt and disappointment. Gran had sent me to that house for a reason, but what was the reason? Why didn't she just leave me a list of things she wanted me to know? For example, who Isla Evans was.

The text on my phone went off as I stepped out of the shower. I dried off and picked it up to see it was from Saul. I didn't open it, but went into the bedroom to get dressed. As I pulled on the soft cotton tank top I liked to sleep in, the phone began to ring.

Seeing Saul's name, I was torn but on the third ring, I answered.

"Hello," I said.

"I'm at the door," he replied.

I stood there in my bedroom, trying to decide what to do.

"I'm sorry I didn't text you back."

His voice sounded tired. What had happened today? Would he even tell me?

"I'm going to bed," I replied.

He sighed wearily. "Please, Henley," he begged.

Closing my eyes tightly, I made the decision. I couldn't accuse him of something when I didn't know the details. It wasn't as if he had been kissing her. They had just been talking, closely, and what appeared intimately.

I walked out of my bedroom and down the hall until I saw him standing on the other side of the door. His eyes locked with mine and I stood there, wondering what if he had been with Isla … he hadn't made me any promises. He had never said we were in a relationship. We were together every day. We had sex. But did that make us exclusive.

No. But Isla was a married woman with a child. That made it adultery. If he was doing anything with her that was. I had to know before I pushed him away. Seeing him standing out there, I couldn't turn away from him. We might not be in an official relationship, but my heart didn't seem to care about the details.

I ended the call and went to open the door. Saul stepped inside and closed it behind himself. Never once breaking eye contact with me.

"You locked it," he said.

"You told me to," I reminded him.

A tiny smirk played on his lips. "Yeah, I did."

"I'm tired," I told him.

He reached for my hand and threaded his fingers through mine. "Then let's go to bed."

I looked down at our hands. His much larger and tanned one against my smaller pale one. Being with him always felt right. Or it had. Until now. Until I didn't know if all those warnings I received meant something.

Saul walked me back to the bedroom and pulled back the covers for me to climb inside. I didn't say anything as I got in bed. I watched as he undressed but left on his black boxer briefs then joined me. He pulled me to him and tucked my head under his.

"Where have you been today?" I asked.

"Lily ended up keeping me until late. She was having a hard day."

"Did she have any company?" I asked then.

"No. She never does."

"You stayed with her all day then?" I needed him to tell me. To make it all better.

"Yeah," he replied then kissed the top of my head. "Close your eyes. Get some sleep."

That was his first lie.

THIRTY-TWO

Even with the late night, my brain had been programmed to wake up at four. I lay in bed and tried to go back to sleep, but it never came. Saul looked so peaceful beside me and I didn't want to wake him. I stayed in bed, watching him sleep and going over last night's events.

He hadn't told me about Isla, but he had simply been talking to her. It may have been so innocent, he didn't think to mention it to me last night. Dealing with Lily could have been so stressful that a conversation with a woman he came off the elevator with wasn't worth remembering.

By the time six thirty rolled around, I was sure that I had overreacted. I had been to the Evans' house and I had seen Isla with her daughter. She was a happy little girl. Their house was beautiful and it looked like everything a happy home *should* look like. My gran had babysat for them, so they could go on dates and business dinners.

I didn't know why Saul had not told me where he had been when he got off the elevator with Isla, but it could easily have been a connection to Lily through Gran. My doubting him was unfair. He hadn't texted me all day, but I knew his mother could be a lot on him. He was a good son. Possibly the best son I had ever known.

Reaching up, I brushed a curl from his eyes. He was also the most beautiful male I had ever known.

"Mmm," he made a low sound in his chest then turned to nuzzle my neck. I tilted it back to give him easier access. "God, you feel good." His voice was raspy from sleep.

I slid a leg up onto his hips to get closer to him.

"Start that and you're gonna get fucked," he warned, kissing the skin beneath my ear.

"I hope so," I whispered.

With a growl, Saul flipped me onto my back and was on top of me. I stared up at him, prepared to see lust in his gaze and the dark hunger he got when we had sex. Instead, there was something more. He looked down at me with a deeper yearning. It wasn't just me that was feeling things but he was too. Either that or I wanted him to feel things so badly I was seeing more to it than there was.

"I missed you," he said, running his hand from my neck to my stomach slowly.

"I missed you too," I admitted, although it had been one day we hadn't been together. I found myself always wanting to be near him.

"I'm addicted to you, Henley," he said before he took the edges of my panties and began to pull them down my legs.

We didn't say anything more. My mind tried to tell me that his being addicted wasn't a good thing. Addiction wasn't sexy or romantic. But my body was hungry for his touch and soon it was my body that won over. Every part of me wanted to be with Saul and that want was quickly turning into something so much stronger.

I was weak when it came to him. Being weak made me vulnerable. I also realized I didn't care as long as I was with him.

The coffee was brewing and I pulled out some blueberry muffins from the fridge while Saul took a shower. I had half a loaf of banana bread that I also took out and turned on the oven to warm them up. Gran hadn't been a fan of microwaves. She was convinced they gave you cancer. She had never owned one in her home. Her reasons for not having a Keurig for her coffee had been more basic. She said the coffee didn't taste the same as when it was brewed the way it was supposed to be brewed. She also drank Maxwell House so there was that.

When I heard Saul's footsteps coming down the hall, I took out a cup and poured him some. Turning to him as he entered, I held it out. "Good morning," I said.

He grinned. "Yeah, it is," he agreed then took the coffee with his right hand and tugged my shirt toward him with his left. When he had me close enough, he kissed me softly. It was moments like this that I found last night hard to believe was something more than innocent. Sure, he hadn't told me about Isla, but then there was this.

"I like you not having to leave me at four," he said, before taking a drink from his cup.

"Me too. I'm going to work on writing down recipes this morning," I told him. "About today. What are your plans?"

"Lily needs to go to an AA meeting," he said. Which meant he would be taking her if he wanted her to get there.

"Yesterday Rio came to the shop. He talked to Hillya. She invited us to her house for lunch today to meet, people. That we were related to," I said, not sure I could call them relatives when I didn't know they existed until recently.

He said nothing for a moment and I wondered if he was going to continue to have a jealousy issue with Rio. Which was ridiculous at this point.

"You going to come to the house after?" he asked me.

I wasn't sure. He hadn't mentioned the party at his house. Rio had been the one to say something about it. "Am I invited?" I asked him.

His eyebrows drew together in a frown. "What the fuck does that mean?"

I shrugged. "You didn't tell me about the party or mention me going. I didn't know if you wanted me there."

Saul stared at me for a moment. His frown started to look more like he was annoyed. "Henley, are we not clear on things?"

I didn't know what that meant exactly, which also could mean that we were not clear on things. Saul didn't verbalize much and when he did, it wasn't detailed. He was the guyest guy I had ever met.

"I don't think I am," I replied honestly.

He sat his cup down on the counter and put both his hands on my waist. His gaze locked on mine. "I don't want to be where you aren't."

Okay, that was extremely sweet, but he was a lot of places I wasn't like yesterday at the condo with Isla. I didn't point that out though. "What are we doing?" I asked him.

"You mean this thing between us?" he asked.

I nodded. "Yes. This thing we are doing. I know we have sex and we are together at some point daily, but is this a fling and will I know when it's over or-"

Saul's mouth was on mine and I didn't get to finish that thought. He grabbed my head and his fingers threaded through my hair as he held me there. He tasted of mint and coffee. I placed my hands on his chest for support.

When he ended the kiss, he didn't pull away from me but kept his face close. Our breaths mingled as our noses touched. "I thought that was clear. You are the only thing that makes me happy."

Yes, those words made my heart feel joy and my knees slightly weak, but that wasn't exactly what I needed to know. Again, if he could be a little more clear and descriptive.

"So, that means we're exclusive?" I finally asked.

His fingers tightened in my hair as if the idea upset him. "Has someone else been talking to you?" he asked.

"No," I replied quickly. His jealousy was acting up again and we really needed to work on that. "I just wasn't sure. If we were dating or exclusive. I want to be exclusive. I mean to me we are. I don't just have sex with a fling. I'm not… I don't do that."

He inhaled deeply and his fingers loosened in my hair. "I need you," he said then. "Just you."

That was the clearest answer I was going to get from Saul.

"Okay," I replied.

He kissed the tip of my nose then released my head. "I don't share, Henley."

That was good to hear. I thought of Isla again. "Me either," I replied.

He grinned then and reached for his coffee.

It all seemed right. Nothing about us was normal because Saul was not normal. But I knew being with him was also accepting him the way he was. His world was nothing like most people. There was damage so deep I didn't think it would ever heal. I could deal with that. It was part of who he was.

Trusting him was something I had to do. We were new. In time, he would open up more. He was already starting to. I just needed to be patient until he felt safe enough to tell me everything. There was clearly something he was leaving out. I wouldn't push him and become the crazed jealous girlfriend. I would wait until he was ready to tell me everything. I had to believe in time he would.

THIRTY-THREE

It wasn't that being at a family gathering for a holiday was new to me. I had gone with many friends over the years to things like this. What was weird was knowing this was my family yet it wasn't. Rio had handled it well so far, but I could see in his eyes he felt the same as me.

These were strangers. We may share the same blood, but they were not family. Maybe one day they would feel that way but down deep, I wasn't sure if that was what I wanted. Hillya had seemed happy to have us here. Emily had introduced me to many people while Hillya spent more time with Rio.

Seeing photos of Rebel in the house, ranging from a child to a young man had been oddly emotional. Simply because there were pictures of him over the years where I could see myself. Hillya was right; I had his smile. The older he got in the photos, the more of Rio I could see in him.

A teenage boy who hadn't thought about repercussions and had been living his life not knowing what the future would hold or that his future was very limited. He'd left kids behind and for Rio, a child in a very bad situation. I was the lucky one.

I hadn't always thought that, but after hearing Rio's story and witnessing Saul's, I knew I had an easy life. A normal life even without a dad.

"It's weird, isn't it?" Rio asked and I turned to see him watching me study the photos lined along the mantle. He nodded at the pictures. "Seeing those. The second one from the left could have been me. I looked exactly like that when I was nine."

I looked back at the photos and picked up the one he mentioned. I could see Rio in his eyes. I hadn't seen photos of Rio as a child, but now I wanted to.

"You have his smile. It's almost identical," he said, walking up to stand beside me.

"I never thought much about my smile until now," I admitted. "But you're right. I can see it."

He picked up a picture of Rebel in a football uniform, standing with a football tucked under his arm and smiling at the camera. "He was a running back," he said. "I was too. I played on that same field."

"Does it fill the void? Knowing who he was?" I asked. It did for me. It wasn't the way I thought it would, but the questions were no longer there. Seeing him and the life he had made it better. Something my mother never understood.

"Yeah, it does. We all deserve to know where we come from."

"I have more pictures, albums, if y'all want to see them," Hillya said and we both turned to her. Neither of us had heard her enter and I wondered how long she had been standing there.

"I would," I replied. Seeing more of Rebel's life wasn't the same as knowing him, but it still felt like it helped make a connection. One I thought I would never have.

"Me too," Rio said.

Hillya smiled, looking relieved. "I'll go get them," she told us and left the room.

"I want to ask her why my mom left. Why your mom left. If Rebel cared about the fact he had kids," Rio said quietly.

I knew this answer or most of it anyway. I wasn't sure Rio needed to hear it though. "I'm sure in time she will be ready to share that with us. I imagine it's hard for her too. It was a choice he made and one she couldn't control."

Rio thought about that for a minute. "Yeah, I guess so," he finally replied. I was glad he wasn't going to push it right now. I wanted him to get to know Hillya and hear more about our dad before he found out the truth behind Rebel and our mothers.

It wasn't until Rio pulled his Jeep into the already crowded driveway that Saul texted. His blue Ford wasn't amongst the vehicles outside. Rio parked and looked over at me. "That from Saul?" he asked.

I nodded and opened the text message.

Saul: *Mom isn't having a good day. I will be late.*

I looked up at Rio. "Lily," I told him. "She's not doing well."

Rio sighed and shook his head. "Damn. You want to stay or want me to take you home?"

Saul had said he would be late. He hadn't said for me to go back to Gran's. "I'll stay," I told him.

"Alright, just please don't put on a bikini before he gets here," he said with a smirk, before climbing out of the truck.

He may have been smirking, but I also knew he was serious. Saul had gotten better about me swimming in front of Drake and Rio the past week, but I wasn't sure about the others. Especially if he arrived dark and broody from the stress with Lily.

I followed Rio into the house and the music was loud. That was never the case when Saul was here. Drake had been left the run of the house and it seemed he was taking full advantage.

Rio looked at me and rolled his eyes when we entered the living area. The music was even louder inside. It wasn't just being pumped through the speakers on the balcony. There was clearly a sound system built into the house as well.

"Rio! Henley!" Benji called out our names as he walked back into the living area from the kitchen. He had a tray of burgers and sausages in his hands.

"Are y'all fucking deaf?" Rio asked him.

"That's all Drake," he said with a shrug.

No one else was in the house. From here, I could clearly see the pool, and it seemed to be where everyone was at. Rio walked over and picked up a remote and instantly the music was gone.

"Need help?" he asked Benji.

Benji nodded his head toward the kitchen. "Yeah, I need to butter the corn and wrap it in foil to grill," he replied.

"I'll do that," I offered, needing something to do.

Rio shrugged. "Fine. I'll make drinks. What do you want? And don't say soda because I'll just put vodka in it."

Benji called out a thanks before heading out the door with the meat.

"I liked the cranberry and vodka Benji made last week," I told him.

He grinned. "That's what I'm talking about. I'll ruin you yet." He walked over toward the bar and I went to the kitchen smiling.

Today had been strange but also good. In all the weirdness, Rio and I had bonded more. We were both faced with the world that had been our father's. His family. His home. Memories of him. A man neither of us thought we would ever really know about. Although we hadn't grown up as siblings, there was a connection there that seemed to grow more with every step we took closer to being a part of our father's world.

In the kitchen, there was at least thirty corn cobs in a pile on the counter. I went to the fridge and found the butter then began getting them prepared. I decided to add some seasoning salt too. Rio walked in once I got started and put a glass down beside me.

"Thanks," I told him.

Using both hands, he lifted himself up to sit on the counter beside my work space. "I'm not ready to go out there yet," he said then took a drink of what looked like straight whiskey.

I understood that. I felt a little drained too from meeting all the people and talking.

"Are you going to tell your pops about today?" I asked him, knowing he hadn't mentioned it yet to his grandparents.

He shrugged. "Not sure. They knew about Hillya, my dad, his family and they didn't tell me. I haven't decided if they deserve to know."

Rio had a lot of anger to work through toward his grandparents. They loved him and he knew that but the fact they kept it from him was something he didn't understand. Unlike with me, his mother was dead. Gran had been doing what my mother wanted. If she were still alive and I was finding all this out, I wasn't so sure I wouldn't feel as Rio did. Hurt and betrayal came with the lies and hidden facts.

"It's a small town," I reminded him. "Things get around and the fact we were at Hillya's house today might make it back to them."

"I thought of that. If it does then they didn't hear it from me. Maybe then they'll understand a tenth of what their lies to me felt like."

I couldn't argue with that. He had every right to be upset. I reached for my drink and took a sip. "This is strong," I told him.

"Fuck yeah, it is. Hell, we just spent the day with our dad's family. It's not strong enough."

I laughed and sat it down. "I guess you're right."

"You know I am. Today was weird as fuck."

Glancing at him as I rolled another corn cob into the foil I asked, "But you're glad we went?"

He nodded but said nothing else.

"Ah damn," Drake said, walking into the kitchen. "What the hell?"

I turned to look at him.

"What?" Rio asked.

Drake waved a hand back and forth between the two of us. "This shit. I know y'all are fucking siblings, but Saul is crazy as hell. He don't seem to get that memo. Why are you here without him being here? Do you want him to kill us?"

Rio chuckled. "Shut up and take your drunk ass back outside."

Drake shook his head and threw his hands in the air. "Fine, don't listen to me. I may be fucking drunk but I'm gonna stay my ass outside until Saul gets here." He pointed at me and told me to stay in here.

Drake turned to leave then stopped. "Fuck, I came in here to get something, but I don't remember what it was."

"Was it for Benji?" Rio asked.

"Oh yeah! He needs a clean plate," Drake replied.

After he got a plate and left Rio, looked over at me. "He's right about the 'you staying inside' thing. Just in case Saul's in a mood when he gets here. Lily can fuck with his head."

"Okay," I replied, but I would be lying if I said it didn't bother me. Saul and his damage could be a lot to take sometimes. But then I knew I wasn't going to walk away because of it. I had let myself get too deep. I had let my caring for him evolve into more and that was enough for me to accept him completely. Damage and all.

THIRTY-FOUR

Rio took the tray of corn outside once I finished. I moved to the living room, pulled a book up on my phone, and found a spot on the sofa. I was barely on chapter three when I heard the front door close. I finished the page and then looked up just as Saul walked into the room. His gaze found mine. He didn't smile, but he didn't break our gaze as he walked down the stairs and over to me.

When he reached me, he stopped and held out his hand. I put the phone down and reached out mine. Hs fingers wrapped around my hand and he pulled me up and against his chest. He buried his head in the crook of my neck and we stood there like that silently for several moments.

I put my arms around him and held him because it seemed to be what he needed. He inhaled deeply and I wished he would tell me what all he had dealt with today. I wanted to be here for more than sex. I wanted to listen and be here for him to vent to. He needed to talk about things more. I just had no idea how to get him to do it.

"This is good," he said against my neck then lifted his head and straightened.

"Bad day?" I asked, already knowing the response I would get.

"Yeah," was all he said, just like I expected. "But you always make it better."

That was why I would stay. That was why I wouldn't give up and walk away. He had me. I had never been one that wanted to fix what was broken. I normally ran from things I didn't understand. Saul was different. I wanted to be different for him.

"Were you reading?" he asked me.

"Yes."

He kissed my forehead. "Sorry I was late."

"It's okay. This sofa is comfortable," I replied.

He grinned then and looked out the windows behind me at the party going on outside. "If you want to go out there we will. I'll even be good if you want to swim. But if you would rather go up to my room, that's an option."

Being alone with him after this day was all I wanted. "What would we do up there?" I asked playfully.

He ran his hand over my butt and slapped it once. "Watch a movie, take a shower, fuck in front of the mirror in my bathroom," he said then bent down to kiss my lips once. "I really want to bend you over my sink soaking wet from the shower and watch you come," he whispered against my lips.

"Okay," I agreed.

He smiled again. "Come on."

I picked up my phone and he took my hand to pull me toward the stairs.

"Y'all leaving?" Drake asked and Saul turned to look back at him.

"Yeah," he replied.

"At least you're in a good mood," Drake said with a drunken grin.

Saul ignored him and we headed to his room. Drake forgotten.

As soon as the door closed behind us, Saul locked it. "I fucking missed you," he said, turning back to me, his eyes already heated. My body trembled with anticipation. There were many things that I worried about with us but sex was not one of them.

"Strip," he said, his eyes traveling down my body.

"What?" I asked.

His gaze shot back up to meet mine. "Strip for me."

Okay. This was new. The idea obviously excited him. It was clear on his face. I reached for the hem of my shirt and pulled it over my head.

"Drop it," he said.

So I did. I dropped the shirt on the floor then went for the buttons on my shorts. When I pushed them down over my hips and wiggled until they fell, his eyes widened slightly. I kicked them to the side then reached up to unhook my bra.

When it fell free, I slid it off my arms and let it drop to the floor and join my shirt.

"God, I love your tits," he said as he stared at them. My body flushed with desire.

I finished by taking off my panties and then I was bare in front of him. He stood there, not touching me, only looking. When his eyes made their way back to mine, a slow wicked grin appeared on his face.

"I'm going to bathe you. Every part. Slowly," he said then stepped forward and grabbed my waist. He picked me up and walked backward toward the bed. "Then I am going to fuck you in front of the mirror." He tossed me back onto the mattress and began taking off his clothes. "But first I have to be inside you. I can't wait any longer."

He crawled on top of me and I opened my legs as he lowered himself between them. Our gazes locked as he pressed his erection against me. He inhaled sharply. "You're already wet," he said and then slowly eased into me.

I whimpered with pleasure as he took his time until he was completely inside. He looked down at me and his breathing was hard and fast. He began to slowly ease out then sink deeper until he had a rhythm. I lifted my hips to meet each thrust. I didn't close my eyes. I didn't want to look away from him.

The orgasm that hit me came so fast I hadn't felt it building. Arching my back, I cried out his name and clung to his arms. Wave after wave crashed over me. Each jolt more pleasure than the last. I said his name over and over, delirious from the most unbelievable experience in my life.

"GGGAAAAAHHHH!" Saul shouted and he pulled out of me. I wanted to watch him, but my body was weak and I couldn't manage to open my eyes just yet. He groaned again then his body came over mine, turning on his side and pulling me with him.

We lay there wrapped in each other's arms as our breathing slowed. "Henley," he whispered against the top of my head, but he said no more. He ran his fingers over my arm, causing goosebumps to cover them. Pressing my face against his chest, I fought the urge to say things that I couldn't say yet. Things I wasn't sure of and that I feared may be simply from the moment we just had. Emotion wasn't something I always trusted. It could affect reality. I kissed his chest then tilted my head back to look up at him.

There were things I was certain of though. Like I would do just about anything he asked of me. I wanted to make him smile always. And that being with Saul made me feel a way nothing or no one else ever had. I had loved Will but I realized now it had been a young love and a first love. We had never known what it was like with anyone else. I would always miss Will and love him. But feeling guilty for what I felt now with Saul was pointless. My life was moving on and it was supposed to.

Later, when we were asleep after showering and having hot sex in front of the mirror where he cursed and said naughty things that drove me to an orgasm, I would go to sleep thinking of him simply saying my name and wondering if he had wanted to say more.

THIRTY-FIVE

Over the next two days, I managed to get several of my recipes written down with the proper measurements. It took a few trial runs, but I figured them out. Hillya was excited to start testing them herself and I was looking forward to not waking up at four to bake on my days off. Emily had spent more time asking me questions about my life during our down times. Now that she knew we were related, she was curious about my mom and my past.

When I arrived at work in the mornings, it felt different. Hillya and I had a connection and it was if I had always been part of the family. They treated me that way at least. I had never had extended family before and it was nice. I realized that not having cousins had been something I missed out on as a child.

Saul had to wake up early on Wednesday to take Lily to another doctor's appointment and then to an AA meeting. I decided that today was the day I would finish Gran's list. I had put off doing the last thing simply because I feared it would be a closure I wasn't ready for just yet. But having Hillya, Emily, and Rio in my life gave me a sense of family that made finishing Gran's request easier.

I didn't want to think about summer ending and leaving here, but July had arrived and summer was halfway over. Going back to Chattanooga now seemed impossible for me but then it also meant not finishing my senior year at college and starting a life here. Saul never brought up the future and I wondered if that was just something he was prepared for- my leaving.

The last request on the list was simple, which meant it could end with a life-changing revelation. I no longer walked into these tasks on Gran's list blinded. I was ready for anything. At least I told myself I was.

I pulled my car into the driveway of a white house that had to have been built in the seventies. It had the structure that had been popular only during that decade of bad style and fashion. The slanted roof at strange angles and long skinny windows had never been attractive to me. Reaching over, I picked up the box of Southern Women cookbooks that Gran had collected. There were some over sixty years old. Whoever Betty was, she would be inheriting this collection of the south's best fried foods, pies, grits, and jello molds. Lucky her.

Carrying the box, I made my way up the drive and sat it down so I could ring the doorbell. I heard a dog begin barking and a woman talking to it like a child before the door swung open. When the smiling face met mine, I recognized Betty. She had been at the church on the day I took Gran's clothing.

She had been the one to give me the lemonade and cookies. I hadn't expected to see her again. Gran must have been close to Betty. I was glad I had taken the cookies and lemonade from her that day.

"Henley!" Betty said, beaming at me. "I have been expecting you."

That was not the response I had been anticipating.

"You have?" I asked, wondering what it was Gran had led me into this time. I should have known something that sounded simple wouldn't be.

Betty nodded and bent down to hush the barking dog again. "I'm sorry about Goldi. She gets excited about company. Won't harm a fly though but then she's not much bigger than one," she told me.

I had to agree. Goldi was a tiny white fluff ball. I wasn't sure what kind of dog she was, but she looked more like a tiny stuffed bear than anything.

Betty opened the screen door. "Come on in and you can leave those cookbooks right there by the stairs. I will get into those later. Will give me something to do other than watch television tonight," she said.

I did as I was told then followed Betty and the tiny fluff that was Goldi into the next room.

"Let me see, I have it right over here," she said, looking over at a large bookcase full of anything but books. There was every sort of porcelain figurine you could imagine. It seemed that angels and birds were her favorite. There were more of them than anything else. Scattered amongst the figurines were picture frames. Many of children, some graduation photos, a few beach pictures, and then a black and white wedding photo.

"Here it is!" Betty exclaimed and picked up a small flat box. "I pulled it out of the closet just last week, figuring you would be here soon to get it."

I wasn't here to get a box, but she held it out to me, still smiling with the perfect white teeth that could only be dentures.

"Did you do it all then?" Betty asked me.

"Uh," I replied, not sure what she was asking.

"The list," she replied then bent to pick up Goldi who had stopped with the barking but was now running circles around Betty's and my legs. She knew about the list. I hadn't known Gran told anyone about it.

"Yes. This was the last thing I needed to do," I told her.

"Did you learn anything?" she asked then kissed Goldi's head as the pup licked at her face.

"Oh, yes. I learned quite a lot," I replied.

Betty chuckled then. "I guess you did."

I looked down at the box she had given me. "What's this?" I asked since she seemed to know so much about things.

Betty shrugged. "I don't know. It's sealed and I wasn't told to open it. Just to give it to you."

"Okay, well, thank you," I said.

Betty nodded her head. "You're welcome and anytime you want, the church doors are open for you."

I wasn't going to church, but I didn't tell her that. "I need to get going," I said. "it was nice seeing you again."

Betty put Goldi down on floor again. "You drive careful and I hope it all works out," she replied. Then walked back to the door and opened it for me.

"Uh, thanks," I said, not sure what it was that she was referring to.

Goldi went back to barking as I made my way to the car. When I opened my door, I looked up to see Betty still standing there. She waved at me and I lifted my hand and waved back before getting in the car.

On the drive back, I glanced at the box several times, wondering what was inside and if I was ready for whatever Gran had left me. I was a mixture of anxiety, curiosity, and nervousness when I finally walked into the house with the box.

Putting it on the counter, I stared at it. "What is this about, Gran?" I asked aloud.

Sighing, I opened the box and there were three envelopes. The one on top said "Henley." I picked it up and broke the seal. Sliding out the handwritten letter inside, I prepared myself for whatever I was about to read. Seeing Gran's handwriting always made my chest hurt a little. Knowing she had written this for me made it more difficult. I unfolded the paper slowly and took a deep breath.

Henley,

I hope that by now you know all I wanted you to know. Things you should have known all along, and people you should have had in your life. I made a mistake keeping them from you. I did what I thought I had to do. Your mother had already proven to me that she would take you away. I couldn't lose you again.

Now I am gone and all those fears are gone with me. But I didn't leave you alone did I? Hillya is a good woman and I am thankful she's there for you. I couldn't have chosen a better grandmother for you other than me of course. She deserves some joy. She has lived many years with none. You, my girl, are a complete joy and I know she will find a reason to enjoy life again with you in it.

As for your brother, that is a regret that may stay with me even in the grave. That boy had a hard go of it for a long time. You are a gift to him more than he is to you. He has no father or mother, but he has a sister and I reckon that makes things better.

In this box are two more envelopes. One is the deed to this house. I imagine your mother wasn't happy to hear from my lawyer that my will would be revealed at a certain time. Now is that time. My lawyer, Roger, will be contacting you soon. Betty will have called him by now. He's her oldest son.

The deed to the house has been left to you along with my stocks and savings. It is up to you to sell the house or live in it. I know you have a home back in Chattanooga. I also know that you have been lost for quite some time. Trying to find your fit in this world. If you've found your way in The Shores then stay. If my small town isn't the one for you then sell my house, take the money, and go find your town.

In the other envelope is a letter to your mother and a key to my safety deposit box. What is in it is what I left for her. When you are ready, give it to her and she can do with it what she may.

You have now met the people I cared for in that town the most. Lily, Wanda, Keerly and Betty all were special to me. Don't forget them. Take time, if you can, to visit them. Lily is so broken I worry she'll always be. A friend is all she needs. Wanda loves homemade lemon cookies and to talk about the past. Keerly is special and in time I believe that you will understand why, and Betty has been my closest friend since I was a young woman.

As you go on with the rest of your journey that we call life, know you were loved by your gran and cherished. I adored you from the moment you took your first breath. I was so proud of you. I want you to have a full life. One with love, happiness, and family. But I also want you to always be there to help others. See them when they are down and do your best to pick them up.

Serving others is the best medicine this life can give you.

One last thing, if you do fall in love with him please go slowly. Be careful. Trust your gut and know not all things are easy. Damaged things can become beautiful if they're placed in the right hands. Loving someone isn't always what we need but what they need.

Love you always,
Gran

I wiped at my tears and put the letter down on the counter.

THIRTY-SIX

I wasn't ready to tell my mother about Gran's letter. I wasn't ready to tell Saul either. I needed time to think. True to Gran's list, this wasn't a twist I saw coming. Leaving here had been my plan because I hadn't known there would be another option. Mom had told me when I was done with this summer, she would be putting the house up for sale. She had also threatened poor Roger with getting a lawyer of her own and getting Gran's will.

That would have been a waste of money for her since the house wasn't something she could fight for. My mom wasn't going to be happy about the fact it was left to me along with the money Gran had saved and invested. That was a confrontation I didn't want to deal with right now. I had my life to work out first.

I put the letter back in the box and tucked the box in the closet. This was all something I would deal with, just not today. Possibly not this week.

When I walked back into the living room, the door opened and Saul walked inside.

"Door wasn't locked," he pointed out with a scowl.

"It's day time," I replied.

"You're here alone."

I shrugged. "So?"

Saul went over to the sofa and sat down. "Come here, Henley."

He liked to make demands and oddly enough I liked to obey them. I had never liked being told what to do. Even as a child I would act out when I felt I was being forced. With Saul, it was different.

He took my hand and pulled me down onto his lap. "How did the cookbook delivery go?" he asked.

"I have no other siblings if that's what you're asking."

He grinned and laid his head back on the sofa to look at me. "That's a positive."

"How is Lily?" I asked him.

"She didn't get drunk or high today and there was no cursing when I took her to the AA meeting."

"That's good," I replied.

"Definitely could have been worse," he agreed. "What's your favorite movie?" The change in subject threw me as did the number of words he had spoken. So many words was very unlike Saul.

"That's a hard question. I have a few that are all tied for first place," I told him.

"And they are?"

"*Buffy the Vampire Slayer*, *Bucket List*, and *Fried Green Tomatoes*."

He let out a burst of laughter. "That's a fucking weird top three."

I slapped his arm. "No, it's not!"

He cocked one eyebrow. "*Buffy the Vampire Slayer*?"

I shrugged. "It's a classic."

"*Fried Green Tomatoes*? How old are you again?"

I laughed this time. "Fine. I'm weird."

He slid a hand around my waist. "I'm almost scared to ask your favorite song. Is there a top three for that too?"

"Nope!" I replied.

"What is it?"

"There's a top five," I told him.

He laughed out loud again and all was right with the world. Saul laughing and smiling was becoming less rare.

"What are they then?" he asked.

I shook my head no. "Not after you laughed at me."

His hand slid up my shirt and began to caress my back. "Come on. I want to know."

"'My Church' by Maren Morris, 'He Stopped Loving Her Today' by George Jones, 'Irreplaceable' by Beyonce, 'If I Knew' by Bruno Mars, 'Rockstar' by Nickelback."

Saul pressed his lips together as if he was trying not to laugh.

"Those are great songs!" I told him. "Epic songs!"

"'He Stopped Loving Her Today' is a great song. But 'Rockstar'? Really? Come on, it's Nickelback." He was smiling and that was all that mattered. He could hate my music.

"You are judgmental," I informed him. "What's yours?"

"Movies or songs?"

"Both," I replied.

He didn't even take a moment to think about it. "*Fight Club* and 'Stairway to Heaven,'" he said.

"How old are you?" I shot back at him.

"Fucking ancient," he replied.

"Will you ever play your guitar for me?" I asked him. He never mentioned it but it was always there in his room. I knew he played it when he was alone. Drake had told me so.

"Maybe," was his one word response then his smile faded and his expression got serious. "Kiss me," he said.

I bent my head and cupped his face and did just that. Saul shifted me in his lap and I straddled him so it was easier. We kissed softly at first, but when his hands moved under my shirt and covered my breasts, it became more intense. This was a reason to stay. He was a reason to stay. I didn't think I could leave him. Not anymore. Maybe if I hadn't allowed myself to sleep with him or maybe if I hadn't made him smile. Possibly then I could have left, but I was kidding myself if I thought I could leave.

Needing to know and no longer able to give it time, I broke the kiss and looked at him.

"What happens when summer is over? When it's time for me to go?" I asked him breathlessly.

"I'm working on making sure you don't," he replied without thought.

"That I don't what?" I asked, needing to be sure I understood him correctly.

Saul leaned close to me and brushed a kiss on my cheek. "That you don't go, Henley."

His words were all I needed. There was no longer a question about my leaving. There was just a lot of sorting out of my future now. I had to close out my life back in Chattanooga. Right now, though, none of that mattered. All I cared about was that I was here with Saul.

Later that night, when Saul was asleep, I turned my head to watch him. He was so peaceful like this. His breathing had slowed and I was so tempted to touch him but didn't want to wake him. Things had changed for me and so very quickly. The first day when he had stepped out of his truck, if I had known we would lead to this, I wasn't sure I would have stayed.

I had come to The Shores terrified to live again. Saul had changed that.

"I love you," I whispered.

THIRTY-SEVEN

The rest of the week Signed Sips was insanely busy from open to close. I worked late hours to help the evening rush. Hillya had said every year the week after July 4 was the craziest around The Shores. The roads were bumper-to-bumper on main street with all the tourists in town. Getting anywhere was impossible. Walking from Gran's had become easier than driving to work.

Lily had another setback and Saul was staying with her for the most part. I wished I could do something to help, but I didn't know what I could do. He had been with me the night Lily had taken off again, except this time drugs had been involved. He believed she had been sneaking around getting it from a guy she met at AA meetings.

I missed him, but I also understood his need to take care of his mother. My heart hurt for him and the life he lived because of her. Would he ever get to live without the pressure of keeping his mom clean and alive? I tried not to get angry with Lily about what she was doing to herself and in turn to Saul, but it was so difficult.

Rio and Drake were passed trying to accept Lily's addiction and they both openly talked about their hate for her in front of me. Not in front of Saul. Rio said Drake had made the mistake once of calling Saul's mother a bitch and Saul had slammed his fist into Drake's face. Drake had woken up on the floor.

If Lily were to ever get well, what would Saul do with his life? This was something I wanted to ask him, but I was also afraid to ask. Reminding him that his entire life revolved around keeping his mom clean seemed cruel. He had accepted this role and I was sure he had thought about the long term of it.

When Saturday afternoon came and things slowed down with so many people heading back to their homes after their week of vacation, Hillya sent me home at five. I wouldn't have to work the next two days and I was thankful for the time off. It also meant I would be free when Saul was available. I missed him.

I texted him that I would be home this evening as I walked into the house. He immediately replied he would come as soon as Lily was asleep. I took my time in the shower and made myself a sandwich for dinner.

When Saul knocked on the door, it was after nine and I was on the sofa watching season two of *Downton Abbey* on Netflix. I took off my blanket and left it on the sofa when I went to open the door. Saul said nothing when he stepped inside.

He grabbed my face with both hands and kissed me hard. I much preferred this greeting to words. I held onto his arms to steady myself and kissed him back just as fiercely. He had been smoking. I could taste the nicotine mixed with the mint he had used to try to cover it up. I knew he had been trying to stop or at least cut back but dealing with his mom sent him into chain smoking.

He pulled back and inhaled deeply. "God you always smell and taste so damn good," he whispered then pressed one more kiss to my lips before dropping his hands from my face to wrap them around me and hold me against his chest.

We stood there like that for several moments. His hard chest under my cheek was warm from the summer heat. I was content just like this. If I could stay in his arms forever, I would be a happy girl.

"What the fuck are you watching?" he finally asked, and I smiled and pulled back to look up at him. He was looking at the television and frowning.

"*Downton Abbey*," I replied, doubting he knew what that was.

His expression said he did not. When he looked back down at me, he smirked. "It's British," he said.

I nodded.

"God, I've missed you," he told me.

"I've missed you too," I assured him.

He released a weary sigh then and loosened his hold on me. "Do you have any food?"

"Yes, you want me to make you a grilled cheese? I also have some chocolate chip muffins," I told him, taking his hand and walking toward the kitchen. "Or I could make some pasta."

"Grilled cheese and a muffin sound good," he replied.

I let go of his hand and went directly to the fridge to get out the real cheese I had bought last week just for him. He wasn't a fan of the dairy-free stuff I kept for myself. However, he liked my homemade gluten-free bread. I took out the loaf of bread and got busy fixing him some dinner. He didn't eat well when he was busy with Lily.

"In the morning, I am taking Lily to a rehab facility in Maine. She will stay there for a year," he said, while I was slicing the bread.

"Oh," I replied when so many other questions were running through my head. He had talked about her going to a rehab again but not that far away or for that long.

"She asked to go," he added. His expression didn't tell me much. The dark circles under his eyes, however, told me he was exhausted.

"Are you okay with this?" I asked.

He nodded his head slowly. "Yeah, I am. It's time she does something. I can't continue on like this. She's out of fucking control and I am not equipped to handle it. I'm just so damn tired of it all." As he said it, I could see the pain cross his expression.

I sat down the knife and walked around the counter. "Then why do you look like this hurts?" I asked him, reaching up to touch his face.

He closed his eyes a moment and when he opened them to look at me again, he replied, "Because she's my mom. I shouldn't feel like this. I shouldn't want her to go. I shouldn't be tired of helping her. I am all she has. But I am so goddamn tired of it. I am so fucking tired of it."

"Any one would be tired of it, Saul. You are the best son I've ever known. You have done everything you can for her, including altering your life to deal with her addiction. She wants to go because she loves you and she knows what she is doing to you."

A sad smile touched his face. "That's what she said. Or something like it," he told me.

I was glad Lily realized it. I just wish it hadn't taken her so long. I pressed a kiss to his cheek then went back around the counter to make his grilled cheese. He watched but remained silent. I didn't ask more questions, but I did want to know when he would be back.

It wasn't until I was grilling the sandwich on the stove that he spoke again. "I should be back on Tuesday. Latest Wednesday," he said.

I put two muffins on a plate and slid them over to him. "I'll pour you some real milk," I told him with a smile.

"Real milk as in whole milk from a cow?" he asked, as I took the half gallon I had bought for him out of the fridge.

I showed it to him. "Yep."

For the first time since he arrived, a grin broke out on his beautiful face. "Damn, I feel special."

I poured him a glass. "You should," I said teasingly and handed it to him.

He took a long drink before setting it back down. I finished his sandwich while he ate the muffins. When I placed the grilled cheese in front of him, he was watching me.

"What?" I asked him, smiling at his serious expression.

"Nothing. I was just thinking," he replied, picking up the grilled cheese. "Thank you," he said before taking a bite.

"You're welcome," I told him then picked up a muffin and walked around to sit on the bar stool beside him.

Saul was changing. He was talking to me more. Trusting me. I realized it and I also knew he still needed time. Keeping things to himself was the way he had dealt with life. I couldn't change it overnight. But he was doing it for me, for us...

THIRTY-EIGHT

During my days off, Saul was gone to Maine. I tried some new recipe ideas and when they worked, I was sure to write them down for Hillya. Emily came over Sunday evening and we had a Grey's Anatomy season three marathon while eating cupcakes and popcorn.

Saul called me twice and texted me updates, but he never mentioned what day he would be home. I didn't ask him because I knew he was dealing with having to leave his mom there. Although he was relieved she had decided to do this, he had so much guilt about not being able to help her himself.

Monday night I was going through the kitchen and organizing Gran's kitchen cabinets to work for me since I intended to stay. That was something else I had decided in Saul's absence. I was going to tell him when he returned. Gran was right about me needing to start over in a new place. To find my town and build a life. I couldn't imagine doing that anywhere but here. In this house, where I had so many wonderful memories and in this town, where I had found family and where I had found Saul.

The knock on the door had me jumping up and rushing to open it, thinking it was Saul and he was home. However, when I turned the corner, it was Rio I saw on the other side of the door. Slowing my pace, I walked the rest of the way and unlocked the dead bolt then opened it.

Surprised that he was here, the only thing I said was "Hey." It wasn't that I didn't see Rio often; it was just that he normally texted before he came over.

"I need to talk to you," he said, walking past me and into the house. I didn't miss the tone of his voice. It was strained and upset. I couldn't tell if he was angry or something else.

I closed the door and turned to look at him. "What is it?" I asked, my mind already running through all that it could be.

He ran a hand through his short hair and locked his gaze on me. "Do you remember when I told you to be careful with Saul?" he asked. "I warned you and you, you didn't listen to me. I know him. I've known him since we were sixteen."

"What is this about, Rio?" I asked, feeling panic building inside me. Of all the things I thought he had barged inside upset about, Saul and I hadn't been one of them.

"Saul is a loyal friend. He's a fucking saint of a son. God knows I would have walked out on his mom years ago if I were him. But he's not perfect, Henley. He's so fucked up from the shit he's lived through." Rio sighed loudly and stared at me hard. "Are you in love with him?"

I was. I had accepted it and even embraced it. I hadn't told Saul yet, at least when he was awake. Telling Rio before I told Saul seemed unfair, but then the way Rio was acting right now I wasn't sure I could lie about it.

I finally nodded my head yes.

"Dammit!" he growled. "I was afraid of this and I fucking let it happen. He was different with you," he said, pointing at me and then beginning to pace back and forth in front of me. "I thought, I thought because he was with you all the time and he was so damn possessive of you, I thought it was over. If I had known it wasn't then I would have told you sooner." He stopped pacing and looked at me again. "I wouldn't have lied to you and let you get hurt. Know that. You're… well, you're my sister. And I've not known you long but what I do know I'm proud of the fact I'm related to you. If you'd known my mom, you'd get it. She was… she wasn't something to be proud of. But you, well, you are. It doesn't matter that Saul is my best friend. I would have told you. I wouldn't have just warned you to be careful."

"Rio, what are you talking about!" I interrupted his anxiety ridden ranting. He had my stomach in knots and he wasn't getting to the point. He was making it worse with all his talk about protecting me.

Rio took a deep breath. "There's this woman. She's older, married… and well, Saul and her. He sees her. He has never brought her around but I've seen him with her sneaking around. So has Drake. It's been going on for three years, I guess. I've ignored it and pretended like I didn't know. There were always other girls. Fleur was the latest until you came along. I hadn't seen Saul with the woman in a while and I thought he'd stopped that shit. Hell, she's even got a kid," Rio stopped and looked at me.

I wasn't sure I was breathing. My chest hurt and my knees were weak. I needed to sit down. "How do you know it's still going on?" I asked, but my voice was barely a whisper. Images of Saul and Isla at the Hendrix were playing over in my head. That gut instinct that told me something wasn't casual about that meeting. I ignored it. I wanted to believe it wasn't anything.

"When I came home from work, Saul's duffle was at the foot of the steps and there was an empty beer, his beer, on the counter in the kitchen. Drake hates Saul's beer. I assumed he'd come in and then come over here. I didn't think anything more until I was on my way to get some takeout and drove past this street. His truck wasn't here either but your car was and your lights were on inside."

Rio sighed and shook his head. "I wondered where he was but I didn't think about it too hard. It wasn't until I pulled into the Crab Shack and saw his truck pulling out of the Hendrix parking lot and not headed toward your house or ours that… I got suspicious. I just knew. I followed him. He went to some fancy ass neighborhood and pulled into the driveway of one of the houses. When the door opened, it was her. Whoever the fuck she is. He went inside and she closed the door. I… I didn't know what to do. I just knew I had to come tell you now. Before he came back here. You need to know the truth. He may fucking hate me for the rest of his life, but I can't overlook this shit because his life has been hard. He has demons. A lot of them but hell so do I. My mom was fucked up too and I don't go around having affairs with married women."

I walked over to the nearest chair and sank down into it. My hands trembled as I laid then flat on my knees. Deep down had I known? Had I truly ignored this and let myself continue falling in love with him? Had Gran known about this? Was that what she sent me to that house for? How could she not have known if she kept Keerly? Why wouldn't she just have told me? If she had known I was going to meet Saul and fall for him, why wouldn't she have done more than send me to that house? How was I supposed to figure that out on my own? She couldn't have known. Gran wouldn't have been okay with it. I knew her and this would not have been okay with her. She would have called him out on it. I know that.

No, Gran hadn't sent me there because of Isla and Saul. This was something she had missed. This small town had more secrets that even Gran had known.

"Isla Evans," I said aloud and lifted my head to see Rio sitting on the sofa. His elbows on his knees and his concerned gaze on me. "Her name is Isla Evans. Her daughter's name is Keerly."

"You knew about it?" he asked me.

I shook my head. "No, of course not. They were on my list of things to do. I had to take Keerly my Gran's scarves. Gran used to babysit her on occasion. They go to Gran's church. She was such a nice lady. When I saw her with Saul, I told myself it was innocent. How could it not be?" I asked and a sob rose in my throat.

"Damn him," Rio cursed and stood up to walk over to put his hand on my back. "I am so sorry, Henley. I should have told you sooner. I just didn't think it was still going on and I didn't see a reason to throw Saul's past in his face. I have enough shit in my past I want to leave there. I was respecting it. I didn't know this."

I sniffled and wiped at my tears. "It's not your fault. You did tell me to be careful. You weren't the only one. I chose to love him or maybe I couldn't stop myself from loving him."

"Do you want me to stay here with you in case he comes over?" Rio asked gently.

I shook my head. "This isn't between you and Saul. He's your best friend. I won't be the reason that ends. I think, I think I'll call Hillya. Go stay there for the night. Just to give myself some time before I face him."

"Henley, this is going to come between us and you can't stop that. I can't look at that motherfucker after this. He had a chance to change things and he didn't do it. I can't forgive him. Not for this. Not this time." Rio's voice was hard and the anger was back.

"Please don't do this. You don't have to tell him you told me anything. Act like you don't know. Just continue like you were. I will handle the rest. This is between Saul and me."

Rio shook his head. "No. I'm sorry, but I can't."

"Rio, I've been your sister for a little over a month. He's been your best friend for six or seven years," I argued.

"It's not just that we are related. You were good for him. You were better than he deserved. He was happy with you. He fucking smiled. Saul doesn't smile. He is rarely happy. You changed it for him. He had a chance at something more. Then he does this shit? It's like he's punishing himself for something. He won't let himself be happy. He's as messed up as his mother."

I thought about that. Was he refusing to be happy? Had he gone to Isla to ruin us because he didn't feel like he deserved it? I stood up and looked at Rio. "Maybe that's it. Maybe he is punishing himself. I don't know and I will never know. I thought I could be the one to fix him but instead he broke me."

THIRTY-NINE

When I had called Hillya to ask if I could stay with her tonight, she hadn't even asked me why. The raspy sound of my voice from the crying probably kept her from asking. She opened her door before I could knock and her worried gaze studied me then she stood back and waved her hand. "Come inside. Make yourself comfortable in here and I'll make a pot of tea," she told me.

"Thank you," I said.

"Of course. I'm always here and I'm glad you called me," she replied. Then she hugged me. "I didn't get to be there for your other heartbreaks in life but I am here for this one. Whatever it is."

I sniffled then and tears stung my eyes as the lump returned to my throat. All I could do was nod. She held me a moment more then took my shoulders and looked at me. "Cry. Get it out. Don't hold in pain."

Tears spilled onto my cheeks and she gave me a sad smile. "With each tear more of the sorrow leaves us. Now, go sit down in the burgundy recliner. There is a box of tissues beside it. I'll get some tea on and break out the fresh honey I bought from Barney May yesterday," she said and patted my arm before heading toward her kitchen.

I sank down onto the recliner and folded my knees under me. Hillya's house smelled much like Gran's. She spent hours baking like I did. The familiar scent of vanilla and cinnamon was comforting. I reached for a tissue and blew my nose. My phone began to ring then and I pulled it from my pocket and saw Saul's name on the screen. Pressing the side button, I waited until the phone turned off then put it down.

I didn't want to see his phone calls or texts. Not tonight. I wasn't ready. I needed time first to face him. I was shattered. I had no other way to describe it. In such a small amount of time I had met him, let myself fall for him, and then been destroyed by him. Was it because I was so naïve? I had such little experience with relationships. Had I taken what we had too seriously and cared too deeply?

Hillya entered the living room with a floral tea pot and matching cups. "It's mint. The only decaf I have in the house," she said, setting it down on the coffee table. I watched as she poured the tea into both cups then added honey to both. I took mine when she handed it to me, although I wasn't sure I could swallow past the lump in my throat.

"Thank you," I told her.

She took her cup and settled down in the chair across from me. "I'm old and it's been a long time since I was in love, but I know heartbreak when I see it. The boy. The Hendrix one. He's hurt you," she said.

I nodded.

"It takes boys many many years to grow into men. They are reckless and build up a world of regrets often before they level out and mature. My Jim was about thirty-three when he finally got it together. Then he passed away when he was forty-four. Massive heart attack took him out so young," she said then took a sip of her tea.

I had never asked about her husband, my grandfather. She wasn't married and she never mentioned it, so I figured I had better leave it alone. I hadn't known she had been a widow and for so many years.

"How old was Rebel when your husband passed away?" I asked then.

"Ten years old. I often wondered had John lived would he have been the strong hand Rebel needed. Maybe he would be alive today." She lifted her shoulders in a small shrug. "Life doesn't prepare you for what is to come. It just happens and we are stuck with finding a way to live through it or giving in and letting it take us down."

I took a drink of my tea. The lump was there but talking about Hillya's past and my father helped get my mind off of the pain that I feared would remain in my chest for a long time.

"Gran left me her house," I told Hillya. I hadn't told anyone, but I wanted to tell her. I guess in a way I hoped she'd have some wisdom on what I should do now. I had thought I knew but could I stay here in this small town after this?

Hillya smiled. "Was that on the list?" she asked.

"Yeah, it was the last thing. I had to take cookbooks to a lady named Betty. She had a box for me too. Gran had a letter in the box and the deed to the house."

"Honey and Betty were friends as long as I knew them," Hillya said. "I'm not surprised she left the last part with her. Especially since Betty's son Roger is Honey's estate lawyer, at least I would assume that."

"He is," I replied.

Hillya took another drink of her tea then tilted her head to the side as she looked at me. "So, what are you going to do?" she asked.

"I don't know. I did. I thought I did. But now," I trailed off and stared down into my cup.

"Well, that isn't something you have to decide overnight. Nor should you. Decision like this take time. You take your time. Wait it out. See what happens."

Take my time. Wait it out. I wasn't sure I had the strength to do that. The idea of leaving Hillya, Rio and even Emily behind made me sad. I was just getting to know them. However, staying seemed almost impossible.

"Tomorrow things won't be clearer. That my child is a crock of shit. People think things will look brighter the next day and that's simply because they got some sleep. Life doesn't clear up over a good night's rest. Time is what clears it up. My dad used to tell me 'This too shall pass, Hillya.' And as a teen, it would make me so mad. Things would be hard at the moment and seemed like the world was over. It wasn't until I was a mother myself and I realized how quickly it all does pass. Too quickly."

I wanted to believe that this pain would pass but I also knew if I stayed in this town, I would be reminded every day of Saul. I had finished Gran's list. Staying all summer had been my plan because I had thought this town would clear things up for me. Give me direction.

Instead I was going to leave more lost than when I arrived.

FORTY

Saul was sitting on Gran's front porch when I pulled into the driveway right beside his blue truck at six the next morning. He stood up when he saw me and started down the stairs. Just seeing him was hard. It hurt so bad that breathing became difficult. I had missed him and now I would miss him even more. Taking a deep breath, I opened my car door and stepped out. Sleep had never come for me last night and Hillya was right, nothing looked clearer or brighter this morning.

I closed the car door and looked at him. He stopped then. His eyes had darker circles than the last time I saw him. His hair looked as if he had run his hands through it a dozen times. I wondered for a moment if he had been here all night.

"Where were you?" he asked, his voice deeper than usual.

"Hillya's," I replied. "I didn't expect you to come here last night."

His brows drew together. "I called and texted you several times."

This was so hard. Even after all I knew, I loved him. I couldn't forgive him, but I couldn't stop loving him either. "I turned off my phone."

"Why?"

He was angry with me. It was clear on his face. He was here ready to accuse me of something. Did he honestly think I was lying to him? The irony of it all struck me and my exhaustion from his betrayal didn't mix well. My temper flared for the first time since I had been told about him and Isla.

"Oh, I don't know Saul. Maybe because you went to your married girlfriend's house first before you came here? That might have been a reason for me not to want to talk to you."

His eyes narrowed and he took a step toward me. "What?" he finally asked.

He wasn't going to admit it. Instead he was looking at me as if I was making this up. The way a guy looks at a girl he thinks is crazy. Anger coursed through me. Anger that he had hurt me, that he had made me love him, that he had lied to me. Anger that he would have an affair with a married woman. A mother with a child!

"You heard me," I shouted. "I know where you went last night and that's not the first time I've seen you with Isla. I saw you before at the Hendrix, but I convinced myself that it was innocent. Even after I asked what you did that day and you lied to me. You never said a word about seeing Isla. Then you don't tell me you're coming home. You go straight to her house to see her. Jesus, Saul! Do you not have any morals? She is married. She has a child! I understand that you have had a hard life. I get it. I have seen what you go through. That doesn't give you an excuse for sleeping with a married woman. Forget that you lied to me and told me we were exclusive. Forget that you cheated on me. We haven't been together that long. We weren't serious enough. Whatever but she is married!" I stopped, needing to breathe. I had been yelling. All the pain inside had finally burst free and I blurted it all out. It didn't make me feel better just as my tears hadn't taken away any of the sorrow. Maybe in time but not yet.

Saul's expression was now blank. There was no reaction. No anger, no remorse, no anything. We stood there, me glaring at him and breathing hard. Him cold and calm. I was sure my heart had broken enough, but in those seconds, I could have sworn it splintered into a million pieces.

"Is that all?" he asked, breaking the silence.

I couldn't speak. I just stood there wishing he would say something to make this better. Something that made sense. I wished… I wished… he cared just a fraction of how much I did.

I stood there even after he walked past me.

I stood there after he got into his truck and I heard the door close.

I stood there when the engine started up and the shells in the driveway sounded like gravel as his tires backed out onto the road.

I stood there until I no longer heard the engine.

Then I walked up the stairs, unlocked the door, walked inside and crumpled to the floor as sobs shook my body.

It was like this that Rio found me. I didn't look up at him when he said my name. When he bent down and wrapped his arms around me, I didn't hear what he said. My sobbing subsided and a numbness began to ease over me. It seemed like a dream when Rio stood me up and walked me back to the bedroom. Once I was lying down, he covered me up and walked out, closing my bedroom door behind him.

The week passed and I managed to pull myself together. Rio had moved into the guest bedroom at some point while I was at work the next day. Hillya had told me to stay home, but I needed to work. Staying home meant thinking. I didn't want to think. Thinking always led to Saul. It was easier to stay busy.

I didn't ask Rio about what had happened between him and Saul. I couldn't say his name and I didn't want to hear it spoken. I knew though from things he had said that after he found me that he and Saul had a falling out. That was what I didn't want to happen, but I didn't have a way to fix it. I hadn't set this ball in motion. Saul had.

When Sunday came, I didn't want to take the day off, but Hillya insisted. My distraction came however in the form of my mother. I was brushing my teeth, trying to think of something to do to fill my day when Rio called down the hall. "Uh, Henley, you got company."

I spit the toothpaste out of my mouth and hadn't even rinsed it yet when I heard her footsteps followed by, "Why the hell have you not been answering my calls?"

I dried my mouth and turned to look at her. "Hello, Mother."

"Don't start with me. You've ignored me about this will and forced me to come to this… this place. We have to discuss what we are going to do with the house and you have some guy here with you? Already? Seriously, Henley what has gotten into you?" My mother's loud, annoyed tone was not for this specific occasion. She spoke this way to me most of the time.

I walked past her and toward the kitchen. "Good to see you too," I replied.

Rio was eating a bowl of cereal and sitting at the bar when I walked in the room. His eyes went wide when he saw me. I hadn't heard her come in so there was no telling what she said to him.

"Do not walk away from me. I had to take off work to drive down here," my mother said as she followed me into the kitchen. Her high heels clicking against the hardwoods.

"You didn't have to do anything, Mom. You chose to," I replied and reached for a coffee cup. I had just brushed my teeth, but I needed more caffeine to deal with her and some whiskey would help.

"We have to make a decision about the house and my daughter wouldn't answer my calls. I had no choice," she informed me.

I looked at her. "We don't have a decision to make. The will states the house is mine. Not ours. Mine. Me. It's mine."

She glared at me. "And you know what to do with it?" She pointed at Rio. "You move here to do some ridiculous list for my mother and end up shacking up with some guy you just met. That's not maturity, Henley. It's foolishness."

I took a drink of my coffee before responding. "I'm not shacking up with him. That would be disgusting since he's my brother and all. Remember Rebel, my dad, well, this would be his son." I looked at Rio. "Rio meet Lyra Warren, my mother. Mother this is Rio March. I'm sure you remember his mother, Manda March. Since y'all once loved the same guy."

My mother's face paled. Finally she was at a loss for words. I took advantage of it. "Gran's list wasn't ridiculous stuff she wanted me to take to people at her death. No, it was much more than that. Gran led me on a path and along the way I found Hillya, you know my other grandmother, and Rio here."

My mother looked at Rio then back at me. "You spoke to Hillya?" she asked.

"Daily. I work for her," I replied then took another sip of my coffee. I couldn't remember a time in my life I had spoken to my mother like this. But then before now, before this summer, I hadn't known all the lies she had fed me my entire life.

"Can we talk about this in private?" she asked with her teeth clenched.

"Nope. Rio can hear whatever you have to say and as you can see he is eating," I told her.

My mother shot him an annoyed glare then crossed her arms over her chest. "So you find out these things and you are now planning on what? Staying here in The Shores? Working at a coffee shop for Hillya? You have one year left of college, remember? Or did you decide to settle down here and give up your dreams of owning your own boutique?"

This was something that had needed to be said a long time ago but I hadn't wanted to upset my mother or let her down. I put my coffee on the counter and then looked at her. It was time I told her the truth too.

"Those were your dreams, Mom. That's your boutique. That was what you wanted. Not me. I never wanted it. You just told me I did. I don't enjoy fashion. I'm not good at it. But I am good at something else and you always acted like it was a hobby and I believed it was too. Until I came here and realized I could have a future doing what I loved. I can still finish college and in fact I intend to. I want my business degree. I just don't want it so that I can own a boutique."

My mother looked at me as if I had just spoken another language that she didn't understand. "What hobby do you think you can have a career at, Henley? I've built that boutique and the brand. It's ready to expand and even franchise. We planned this. We worked for it."

I shook my head. "No. You planned it. Not me. And baking, Mom. I love creating new things. I love taking recipes and making them dairy-free and gluten-free. I enjoy the challenge to make it good. To make something people want."

She laughed then. A hard, cold laugh. "You are joking, right? That college degree you have worked for, you think you can use to bake cookies? Henley, that is insane. You can't make a living doing something like that."

"Hillya does," I replied.

"Hillya bakes regular things most people eat and she makes coffee drinks. That is not the same thing," my mother shot back, looking pleased with herself.

"This past month I began making gluten, dairy, and nut-free things for Hillya's shop. Every morning, they sell out. Every day, someone new comes in because they heard we have the things I bake. Hillya said that fifty percent of last month's revenue was from the things I baked and the coffee drinks I created for allergy-sensitive people."

My mother sniffed and shook her head as if she didn't believe me. She was running out of argument and I could see it on her face. She was difficult and headstrong. She was also vain and selfish, but she was mine. She was the only mother I would ever have and I loved her despite her flaws. I loved her despite the fact she lied to me.

However, I could love her and choose my own path. I was done letting her decide for me because I didn't want to upset her. The fact was my mother was always upset about something. It was just how she was. I had just given her something new to be upset about.

"Your plan is to live in this house, work for Hillya and then what? Take over her place one day? That's what you want?" she asked, some of her steam was gone.

I shrugged. "Right now I don't have a plan. I don't know that I am staying here. All I know is that I don't have to make a decision overnight. I have time."

Mother reached up and tucked a dark strand of her hair behind her ear. She fidgeted when she was upset or anxious. My changing things on her had done both. She liked knowing what the future held. It was the reason for her constant state of aggravation. Since she wasn't a fortune teller.

"I have a boutique to run. I can't stay here and talk sense into you. Since Will died, you've been changing. This shouldn't surprise me. But I will give you time. You'll come to your senses. I think your gran passing has put more of a strain on you than I realized. I'll just go back home and when you are ready to join me, I'm there."

I would never be ready to join her back there again. That much I did know.

"Drive safe," I told her. "And Mom, I love you."

She took a deep breath and stepped forward to give me a brief hug before moving back. "I love you too, of course," she replied. My mother was so different than her parents, I often wondered how she came from them.

She glanced at Rio again who was now eating his muffin. "I hope your grandparents are well," she said. "I am sorry about your mother." Her words were stiff, but she was trying. This was the best one could expect from Lyra Warren.

Rio nodded. "They're just fine," he replied. "Thank you."

Mom started for the door and I wondered if I should ask her to stay the night but decided against it. The longer she stayed, the more she would want to try and convince me to come back to Chattanooga. I didn't need to deal with that right now. I didn't have the strength.

She paused at the door and looked back, but she didn't look at me. She looked at Rio. "You look like him and your voice. It sounds just like him," she said.

Rio turned to look at her.

"Rebel that is. Your uh, father," she added. Then she turned around and opened the door.

"Bye, Mom," I called out.

She lifted her perfectly manicured hand and waved at me. "Bye, Henley."

When the door closed behind her, Rio let out a low whistle. "Jesus Christ, lord and savior, that woman is scary as hell."

I leaned against the counter and picked my coffee back up. "You have no idea," I replied then took a drink and watched from the window as she drove away.

FORTY-ONE

When the door to Signed Sips opened and Drake walked in, my stomach immediately knotted up. Seeing someone connected to Saul, other than Rio, was not easy. I had managed to get through the week after my face-off with my mother. I was still crying nightly in the shower mostly so that Rio wouldn't hear me. I missed Saul and I hated that I did.

"Hey," I said to him, wishing someone other than me was out front to wait on him.

"Henley," he said with a crooked grin. "Just the girl I wanted to see."

That did not make me feel better. "Oh, okay," I replied, trying to smile but failing miserably at it.

"Don't look so damn thrilled," he teased.

"I'll try not to," I replied, wishing he'd say what he had to say and leave.

"Look, this isn't my place and Rio told me to stay out of it but hell, I'm the one living with this shit. Rio put his fist in Saul's face then packed up and left. Now it's me and Saul and I'm telling you, I don't think I can take much more."

Rio had hit Saul? I assumed they had words, but I didn't think he had hit him.

"Henley, he is a fucking psycho right now. Whatever you did, you wrecked the guy. I can't even breathe hard in the house. He loses his shit over everything. Do you know how many things he's broken? If I have to sweep up anymore glass, I am going to fucking scream. Unless you want another roommate, I need you to talk to Saul. Work this out, whatever it is."

I shook my head. "I can't," I whispered.

Drake sighed. "Why? You love him, don't you? Y'all were all over each other then BAM it's done. I mean what the hell could have happened that was so bad?"

He didn't know and I couldn't tell him. It was all back. The deep ache that made daily living hard. All the progress I had made was gone. Hearing Saul's name and knowing he's not okay either should have felt better but it didn't.

"Please, Drake. Just go," I pleaded. "I can't talk about this."

He studied me with a confused frown, but he finally nodded his head. "Fine. I'll go. But whatever happened know he's falling apart. Day by day."

I turned and ran to the back then. I couldn't hear anymore. Pushing the kitchen door opened, I rushed inside just in time for the first sob to break free from my chest. Grabbing the side of the sink, I held on as it all exploded again. The top that I had managed to loosely hold it down with was gone.

"Henley," Hillya called out and then she was there beside me. I turned toward her and she held me as I clung to her and cried. She didn't ask me why. She just held me.

I heard Emily return from the store and ask what was wrong. "Go work the front," Hillya told her. "She'll be okay."

I used all my strength to pull myself together and wiped my face with the back of my hand. Hillya handed me a clean paper towel and I took it and dried up then blew my nose.

"Go home," she told me. "I mean it. You need time, Henley."

I simply nodded.

She squeezed my arm. "Can you drive or do I need to call Rio?" she asked.

I shook my head. "I'm fine. I promise."

She let my arm go. She didn't promise it will all be better soon and I was glad. I didn't think I could hear that right now.

I didn't go back to work the next day either. Hillya called and told me she didn't want to see me back there for the rest of the week. She said I was welcome at her house any time but not to return to the shop. I knew she was concerned but staying home was not going to be a distraction.

Gran had a box of photos sitting in her room beside an album that looked unused. I had noticed it when I first arrived and the thought of Gran buying the album and how she had never gotten the chance to use it. She wouldn't be returning to finish that job. Going into her room, I picked up the box and the album and went to the living room to work on it. The photos weren't old. They were pictures from her life over recent years. I could tell by the one on top of her and Betty posing behind a table at what looked like a yard sale.

I found myself enjoying the images from her life and seeing how happy she had been here. Even after Granddad's death, she had continued to live and find purpose. I slid another photo of her at what appeared to be the same yard sale into the album and realized it was something the church had held.

The pictures were mostly of church events and there was one with her and Wanda sitting in a garden with glasses of iced tea. She must have been visiting Wanda that day. I saw Lily's face in the next picture and my chest constricted. It hurt to look at a reminder. Any reminder. I started to put the box away and stopped when I noticed something odd. Lily's stomach.

I reached for the photo and picked it up. This wasn't Lily as a young woman but how she looked now, except her stomach was large and round. Lily was very pregnant. She was sitting in her penthouse, smiling at the camera with her feet propped up on the white sofa that sat in her living area. I stared at it confused.

I turned the photo over because Gran often dated her pictures when she had them printed. There was a note on the back instead of a date. "For Keerly," it said simply. Keerly?

I turned the picture back over and looked at it again, searching for something to make sense of that. Then I checked in the box for another photo. Something else of Lily or possibly Keerly. Understanding was starting to click... and what I thought this meant... but if that were true... then oh my god. My heart began to race as I dug in the box, looking through the pictures. Then I saw it.

I grabbed the photo and stood up as I looked down at the image in my hand. Covering my mouth on a cry, I shook my head as realization was dumped on me like a bucket of ice water. This could not be it. If it was then... oh God.

I turned the photo over slowly, afraid of the words but hopeful at the same time.

"For Keerly – April 15, 2018" were written clearly and I stood there putting it together. Every moment. Every single detail. It seemed impossible, but here it was.

The picture was Lily in a hospital bed, looking exhausted and sweaty. In her arms is a baby wrapped in a pink and white blanket. A little girl born three years ago. To Lily.

"Oh my god," I whispered aloud.

"Gran, why didn't you explain this to me?" I asked the empty room.

Sitting back down, I went through every picture in the box. There were six more with "For Keerly" on the back of them. I sat them all aside. Three were of Lily in different stages of pregnancy. One was of Isla and her husband holding the baby while Lily sat there in the hospital bed smiling up at them. Then the last one was of Saul holding the pink bundle in his arms. His younger face smiling at the camera.

FORTY-TWO

Rio sat on the sofa with the photos laid out on the coffee table in front of him. The same disbelief I had experienced mixed with so many other emotions. Guilt being the main one. At least for me.

"Holy shit," he said, lifting his head to look at me. "Why didn't he tell us? Or me? Back then he didn't tell me. Why?"

I shrugged. "I don't know. I mean Lily is, what in her late forties? She was old when she had Keerly. I just… I just don't understand why he didn't tell me. When I yelled at him and accused him of having an affair with a married woman. Why didn't he explain? Why did he keep so much from me?" I hadn't thought the pain could be worse, but I had found that mixed with guilt and shame it was, indeed, much worse.

"Saul has always been closed-off. It's just this, he has a sister. He never told me. Not even when I went to the house and confronted him."

"Was that before or after you punched him in the face?" I asked.

Rio winced. "Uh, before, and how did you hear about that?"

"Drake," I replied.

He sighed and dropped his head into his hands. "This is my fucking fault. I assumed for years that woman was an affair. I never would have guessed the truth. An affair was all that made sense. I didn't give him a chance to defend himself."

I sat down in the chair across from him. "He could have told me. Sure, I yelled at him, but I didn't punch him. I stood there waiting and he just left."

Neither of us spoke for several minutes. My gaze was locked on the teenage Saul holding the baby girl in the photo. What had happened there? Why didn't he tell me?

"I owe him an apology," I said. "But this doesn't really change anything. I love Saul and if the roles had been reversed, I wouldn't have walked away. I would have explained. I would have begged him to listen to me."

Rio turned his head and looked at me. Understanding in his eyes.

"He doesn't love me. If he did, he wouldn't have let me go without a fight," I said for myself more than anything. I needed to hear it and accept it.

"Saul is different, Henley. You know that. He doesn't react like normal people." Rio tried to sound encouraging but he failed at it.

"That may be true but if he loved me, he wouldn't have been able to walk away."

I waited for Rio to argue and when he didn't, I had to accept the truth.

Rio didn't leave that night to go see Saul. I knew he wanted to make things right with him, but he refused to leave me. I don't know what he thought I'd do if left alone. I went to bed and stared at the ceiling for hours before sleep finally came, and when it did, the dreams were all of Saul. His clear blue eyes, dark curly hair, and his smile. I knew it would forever haunt me.

The sound of a lawn mower woke me and at first I thought it was a dream. One created from my memory. However, the sound got louder, and when I opened my eyes, the sunlight streaming into the room made it very clear I was not dreaming. Sitting up, I swung my legs off the bed. My feet hit the soft rug and I walked over to the window to look outside.

Saul was cutting the grass. I acted on instinct. If I sat here and thought it through, I was afraid I wouldn't do what needed to be done. What Saul deserved. My fear of what looking into his eyes would do to me shouldn't keep me from apologizing.

I slipped on the cut-off shorts that I had left on my floor last night and slipped on flip flops then hurried outside. My heart was pounding from nerves as I walked down the steps. I had lain in bed last night, thinking about what I would say to him when I saw him. All of the well thought-out speeches left me though when I turned the corner and he stopped as his eyes met mine. The cowboy hat on his head shaded his eyes and I couldn't see his expression to know how well my apology was going to be accepted.

He cut the engine off the lawnmower, but he didn't move.

"Did I wake you?" he asked.

I nodded.

"Want me to come back later?"

I shook my head.

"The grass was getting high and I doubted you were gonna cut it," he said.

"I'm sorry!" I blurted out. Nothing like the big speeches I had orchestrated in my head.

He said nothing and I wondered if I had time to fix this and try to do this more eloquently.

"I accused you because it was all that made sense. You never told me. You didn't even tell me then. You just left. And that's fine. You would rather walk away from me. I just wanted you to know I was sorry I accused you. You deserved better. From both me and Rio. You didn't have to come cut the grass. I know you do it for Gran, but this isn't her house anymore. It belongs to me."

I was not going to cry. I was not going to cry. I was not going to cry. At least not in front of him.

He didn't respond and I realized he wasn't planning on it. I turned and went back to the stairs. With each step I took away from him, my chest hurt. My eyes stung and I wanted nothing more than to feel as he did. Nothing.

I stepped inside the house and listened for the lawn mower to start back up or perhaps his truck. Neither happened.

When the door behind me opened, I turned around to see Saul standing there in his sweaty white tank, faded jeans and the cowboy hat he had been wearing in his hand.

"I didn't cut the grass the last time for your gran and I'm not doing it for her this time," he said.

I waited. He was talking. I was afraid if I started talking, he would stop. Possibly leave.

"I did it for you then and I'm doing it for you now."

"Why?" I asked, my heart pounding so hard I was sure he could hear it.

A half-smile touched his lips. "Because I love you. Pretty damn sure I've been in love with you since the first week."

"You just left me," I said, as my voice cracked from the well of emotion building inside me.

"Yeah, I did. I've never been in love. I've never been that vulnerable. Until that moment, I have never been so fucking terrified. I realized you could destroy me in a way I was unfamiliar with. I didn't want anyone to have that power. So I left. I thought it would go away. This," he paused and let out a hard laugh. "This overpowering need I have for you. To be near you, to touch you, to see you." He took a step toward me. "It didn't. Not for a moment. I've been lost. I can't do this life without you and I was just fucking fine before you came, Henley. I didn't feel much at all. But I do now. I feel too goddamn much."

"You love me," I said it, wanting him to say it again. To be sure.

"More than I thought was possible," he replied.

I closed the distance between us and threw myself into his arms, wrapping my arms around his neck. His arms came around me tightly.

"This better fucking mean you love me too," he said as he buried his face in my hair.

I nodded my head against his chest and a sob escaped with a laugh.

"Say it," he said. "I need to hear it."

I lifted my head from his chest and looked up into his eyes. The ones I had been dreaming about in my sleep. "I love you, Saul Hendrix."

He closed his eyes for a minute. "That's good," he said then his lips met mine.

Loving Saul would always have its bumps. I didn't expect it to be easy, but I knew living without him was something I never wanted to do. With him, I was complete.

"Come back to my house. I'll finish the yard later," he said.

"Okay," I agreed and then fear hit me that this could be a dream. It would make more sense if it were just a dream. I held tightly onto Saul's arms afraid at any moment my eyes would open.

"What if I'm dreaming?" I asked softly, as if talking too loud would wake me up.

"You're not," he said and kissed my forehead.

"If it's a dream then you would say that. I would want you to and so you would."

He chuckled. "If it's a dream then it's about to have a naughty turn because I'm about to lock you in my bedroom with me and not let you out for days."

I looked around the room to make sure it looked normal. "Everything looks normal," I whispered.

"Henley, you're not dreaming," he assured me.

I gazed back up at him. "How can you be so sure?"

He leaned down and kissed me softly. It was sweet and wonderful and-

"OH!" I yelped, jerking away from him. "You just bit my lip!"

He grinned wickedly. "And you felt it. Which means you're awake."

I pressed my lips together to keep from smiling. "You could have just pinched me," I told him.

"If I have an excuse to put my mouth on any part of your body, I'm going to take it. Every damn time," he replied.

A laugh bubbled out of me as I stared up into his baby blue eyes.

Our story wasn't over. It was just beginning.

EPILOGUE

In the spring of 2018, Lily went on a binge and was gone for two weeks. When Saul found her, she was in a run-down trailer in Mississippi. She was high, soiled, and worse than he had ever seen her. Six weeks later, while at a doctor's appointment, she was told she was pregnant. She didn't know who the father was because there had been too many men in and out of the place she had been staying and she had been messed up on drugs the entire time.

Lily had planned to have an abortion, but Gran talked her out of it. She told Lily about a young couple at her church that had recently been told they'd never have children of their own. Lily was a high-risk pregnancy with her past drug use and her age. There were many things that could have been wrong with the baby.

My gran stayed with her during her pregnancy. She intervened with the Evans and helped set up the adoption process. Gran kept her clean and sober. She made sure she took her vitamins and ate properly. When Keerly was born that following October, she was a healthy baby girl. Lily held her then handed her to parents who would give her a happy life and love her.

The Evans had agreed with Gran's suggestion that Saul get to be a part of Keerly's life. He had no other siblings and he had asked if he would ever get to see the baby again. Gran fixed it so that he could see her often.

The night Saul returned from taking his mother to Maine, he stopped by the Evans to let them know about Lily. Keerly often made Aunt Lily art that they would take to her at the penthouse. He gave them her address and told them they could mail her things whenever they wanted.

I stepped out of my car and had to shade my eyes from the bright sun. Although it was two weeks into fall, south Alabama hadn't gotten the memo and it was hot. Reaching into the back seat I picked up the plate of lemon cookies that I had Hillya make this morning.

Saul and I had a lot of details to work out, but we had time. It didn't have to be fixed overnight. I was finishing my last year of college online and Saul was considering an offer from his father to be the head of Hendrix Condominiums. With Lily in Maine, he was ready to figure out his future.

Stepping up to the door of the nursing home, I opened it and headed into the cool air-conditioned building.

"Hello Henley," one of the nurses called out and waved at me.

I waved back. "Helllo!"

Then I made my way to room fourteen.

You can connect with Abbi online in several different ways.
She uses social media to procrastinate.

Facebook
Twitter
Instagram
Snapchat: @abbiglines

Made in the USA
Middletown, DE
12 November 2021

52244823R00165